R.

STORM WARNING

"I saw you with Lord Thorverton last night," the exquisite Lady Hazelmore told Meribe. "I felt it was my Christian duty to come and warn you." Lady Hazelmore smiled, but Meribe saw neither good humor nor kindness.

"There is no need to warn anyone," Meribe replied rather sharply. "Thorverton is well aware of the rumors connected with my name."

"No, no, my dear, I was not thinking of that. Knowing how much you have suffered," Lady Hazelmore said, "I came here to warn you that if you are so foolish as to fall in love with Lord Thorverton, you will also know the pain of unrequited love."

"Why is that?" Meribe asked.

"Because he will never love anyone but me," Lady Hazelmore said with supreme smugness.

Meribe had resisted all temptations to fall in love ever again—but there were some challenges devilishly difficult to resist. . . .

CHARLOTTE LOUISE DOLAN attended Eastern Illinois University and earn⸏⸏⸏⸏⸏ man from Middlebury⸏⸏⸏ throughout the United Sta⸏⸏ Germany, and the Soviet⸏⸏ three children and curren⸏⸏ Falls, Idaho, with her hu⸏⸏

THE BLACK WIDOW

by

Charlotte Louise Dolan

A SIGNET BOOK

SIGNET
Published by the Penguin Group
Penguin Books USA Inc., 375 Hudson Street,
New York, New York 10014, U.S.A.
Penguin Books Ltd, 27 Wrights Lane,
London W8 5TZ, England
Penguin Books Australia Ltd, Ringwood,
Victoria, Australia
Penguin Books Canada Ltd, 10 Alcorn Avenue,
Toronto, Ontario, Canada M4V 3B2
Penguin Books (N.Z.) Ltd, 182-190 Wairau Road,
Auckland 10, New Zealand

Penguin Books Ltd, Registered Offices:
Harmondsworth, Middlesex, England

First published by Signet, an imprint of New American Library,
a division of Penguin Books USA Inc.

First Printing, October, 1992
10 9 8 7 6 5 4 3 2 1

This book is dedicated to my father,
Weldon Nicholas Baker,
who always believed I could do
whatever I set out to do.

1

May 1809

There are some moments in life so perfect that one would like to hold on to them forever. This was definitely one of those times, Demetrius Baineton, Lord Thorverton, decided. Inside the cool dimness of his own stable, he was surrounded by the familiar smell of the hay and horses; and the occasional murmurs of grooms and stable lads as they went about their business did nothing to disturb the peaceful serenity of the morning.

But even more crucial to his feeling of total satisfaction and complete contentment was his recognition of the fact that he was exactly where he wanted to be, doing exactly what he wanted to do.

"I do not think I will ever become so jaded that such a sight does not thrill me," he commented, keeping his voice low to avoid spooking the mare in the stall before him. She was nudging her newborn foal, urging it to its feet. The beautifully formed little filly wobbled and staggered, but soon managed to coordinate its gangling limbs well enough to find its breakfast.

"All in all, we have been unbelievably lucky," Lawrence Mallory replied. "Dolly here is the last one, which means we did not lose a single mare or foal this spring."

Demetrius glanced at his cousin, who did not seem terribly pleased with their good fortune. "Why the long face? You look as morose as a man who has just watched his horse come in last at Newmarket."

"It has been my experience that luck has a way of balancing out. After so many months with things going exactly the way we would wish, I cannot help but feel disaster is lurking just around the corner."

Demetrius chuckled. "Forget such superstitious nonsense and come up to the house. Watching that little filly gulp down her first meal has made me realize we missed breakfast completely.''

"I shall be along in a minute, after I speak to Tompson about Daisy's sore hock.''

There was a clatter of hooves outside, and Demetrius emerged into the bright sunlight in time to welcome Andrew and Anthony, the thirteen-year-old twins from the neighboring estate. As usual, their little cousin Jenny was riding on Anthony's lap.

"Has Dolly had her foal yet?" Andrew asked, swinging down from his horse.

"Not more than ten minutes ago,'' Demetrius replied. "A filly, and as pretty as a picture. Did Anne not come with you?''

With supreme confidence that he would catch her, Jenny threw herself down into Andrew's uplifted arms. After two years of observing the child's total lack of fear, Demetrius should have been accustomed to such hair-raising sights, but his heart still skipped a beat.

"Bronson is bringing her in the phaeton,'' Anthony explained, dismounting in a more normal fashion. "She is increasing again. It is such a bother. Now she won't be allowed to have any fun all summer.''

"I don't know why she could not simply have had twins the first time around,'' Andrew complained. "She usually does things more efficiently than this.''

Smiling broadly, Demetrius held out his arms, and with a gurgle of laughter Jenny came to him, hugging him and "talking" a mile a minute. She was quite a little chatterbox, and always spoke with great earnestness, but so far no one could understand a single word she said, which luckily did not seem to bother her in the slightest.

The twins vanished into the stables, and standing there with the baby in his arms, Demetrius felt an intense longing—a deep regret that he was not married with a child of his own. But it was only a momentary sadness, which he easily dispelled by simply remembering his former betrothed. If Diana had not jilted him, he would not be standing here enjoying the beauties of spring in Devon;

he would be in London suffering through the frenzy of the Season.

Moreover, any child they might have had would undoubtedly have been raised by the servants. Very few parents followed such revolutionary practices as Bronson and Anne did, of taking care of their children themselves. Most men paid more attention to the training of their horses than they did to the education of their children, and most women spent more time with their hairdressers than with their own babies.

If only, Demetrius thought, watching the phaeton approach, he could meet a woman like Anne—a woman who was fearless, capable, self-confident, intelligent, and knowledgeable about any and all subjects. There was nothing Anne could not do, and do to perfection, and in a contest of any kind, whether physical or mental, it would take an extraordinary man to beat her. And yet such masculine traits did not detract in the slightest from her womanliness.

Bronson and the twins adored her and openly basked in her warmth and approval. Actually, the entire household at Wylington Manor revolved around her, as if she were the sun and they were planets orbiting in her sphere.

Diana had also wanted—no, demanded—to be the center of attention, but it had not been the same. Thinking about it, Demetrius realized she had always taken from him; she had never given anything back. If he had married her, she would eventually have sucked him dry, until he was only an empty husk . . . rather like her father.

No, since there were no other women who could begin to equal Anne, it was better that he stay single, Demetrius decided, not for the first time. His brother, Collier, would doubtless marry in due course and provide for the succession, and if not, then there were any number of cousins who would be more than happy to move into Thorverton Hall.

"Why so pensive this morning?" Bronson, Lord Leatham, asked, helping his wife out of the phaeton. "Has my daughter been talking your ears off?"

Going to meet his guests, Demetrius replied only half-jokingly, "Your daughter is a delight as always. If I look thoughtful, it is merely because I have been considering how best to effect your demise, Leatham, so that I can marry your widow. Good morning, Anne, you are looking in remarkably good health.''

"So I have tried to convince my husband, but Bronson persists in treating me as if I were made of delicate porcelain, merely because I am in an 'interesting condition.' I have told him repeatedly that in the Mohawk tribes the women continue their normal activities right up until the day their babies are born, but still he will not let me ride.'' She gave her husband a darkling look.

Being a prudent man, Leatham ignored the open invitation to quarrel, instead retrieving a small packet of papers from the phaeton. ''Our groom picked up your mail along with ours when he went into Tavistock this morning.''

"Thank you. I was about to go up to the house and have a bite to eat. Will you join me, or would you rather be introduced to the new foal?''

Food being Anne's choice, she and Demetrius left Bronson with the children and strolled up to the house, where the cook produced a veritable feast, including a bowl of clotted cream with berries for Anne, whose partiality for the same was well-known in the neighborhood.

His pleasant mood vanished, however, when Demetrius glanced through his mail and found along with the London newspapers a letter from his mother. Only the presence of a lady prevented him from uttering a curse, but he could not keep his face from revealing some of his annoyance.

"Bad news?'' Anne asked politely.

"A letter from my mother,'' he replied, breaking the seal. ''Doubtless full of recriminations and accusations— pointing out to me that I am an unnatural son who will drive her to her deathbed by breaking her heart, since I willfully choose to hide myself away in Devon rather than escort her around London, et cetera, et cetera, et cetera.'' He glanced at the tangle of swirls and loops that covered the sheet of paper. ''She does seem more upset than usual this time, since her handwriting has gone from barely adequate to completely illegible. I wonder at her purpose in sending me a letter I cannot begin to read.''

"Would you like me to see if I can decipher it?" Anne offered politely. "When I was a governess, I acquired considerable skill with such things."

"I am not at all sure I want you to," Demetrius replied with a wry smile. "Lawrence warned me not half an hour ago that we are due for some bad luck, and I have a feeling that I would be happier were I to throw this letter in the fire unread." As strong as the temptation was to do just that, he nevertheless handed the missive to Anne, who studied it for a while before speaking.

"It would be easier if she had not crossed and recrossed her lines, and then too, in so many places her tears have caused the ink to run."

"I doubt she was actually crying. I have long suspected that she keeps a dish of water on her writing desk so that she may sprinkle her letters with the appropriate number of drops to indicate the level of despair and heartbreak I have caused her."

"There is something here about unnatural . . . yes, you were quite right, the next word appears to be 'son.' She seems to require your presence in London . . . something about death . . .''

"My unfilial actions over the years have repeatedly brought her to her deathbed, which is amazing, considering she is as healthy as a horse," he interjected.

"No, it appears to be Collier's early demise that she is worried about."

Demetrius sat up straighter. "Collier? What has that idiot brother of mine done? Has he challenged someone to a duel or some such fool thing? Or is he merely pestering her again to buy him his colors and let him go off to fight Napoleon?"

"It is hard to say. The crucial words have been quite washed away. Luckily she has a tendency to repeat herself . . . ah-hah! I have it. Collier has fallen in love with a widow . . . no, with the Black Widow."

"The Black Widow? Not the Scarlet Hussy?"

"Apparently there is more danger than just to his heart . . . your mother seems to be saying that young men who dangle after the Black Widow have a shortened life expectancy. Surely I cannot have read that right.''

Demetrius had an ominous feeling that the misfortune he had joked about earlier was about to overtake him.

''No, that seems to be what she is saying—that Collier has fallen in love with a widow whose charms have a tendency to be fatal.''

''I suspect my mother is exaggerating the situation.'' Demetrius shoved back his chair and stalked over to the window. ''It is doubtless all a plot to get me to London, where the crisis will naturally have quite resolved itself, but since I am there anyway, would it not be delightful if I were to meet the daughter of one of her friends? Such a sweet girl, so good-natured, so accomplished. Bah! I know my mother, and I am not falling for her stratagems, no matter how many letters she dispatches, nor how many tears she sprinkles on them.''

Behind him Anne said nothing, nor did she need to. He knew very well that he would have to go to London. Nothing else would have sufficed to get him there, but danger—real or imaginary—to his little brother must always make him run to the rescue.

''I would appreciate it if you would stop grinning. I see nothing amusing about being forced to go haring off to London when there is so much work to be done around here.'' Demetrius scowled at his cousin.

''I am sorry, but I cannot help but be happy that misfortune, when it did strike, struck you and not—''

''Not yourself. Thank you so much. I do appreciate your concern.''

''I was going to say, and not the horses,'' Lawrence said. ''Speaking of which, you are not to worry about them. I can handle the stud in your absence, as I proved three years ago.''

''Well, at least this time I shall not be gone very long. Odds are my mother has merely taken a queer start and is imagining danger where there is none. After all, most young men on the town for the first time fall in love with some unsuitable female—an opera dancer or a dashing widow—but that does not mean they marry such persons.

I am sure I can persuade Collier to be reasonable, or if worse comes to worst, I can drag him back here bodily, although I do not think my mother would like that any too well. She prefers to keep him dancing attendance on her, something I was always too disobliging to do."

"I feel I should tell you that Tompson has his nose bent out of shape since he heard that you intend to take one of the lads instead of him. He feels his seniority should give him the right to accompany you."

"As head groom, he is needed more here. I am also leaving Fredericks behind, and he is equally miffed. The two of them can doubtless console each other."

"You are not even taking your valet? How eccentric do you wish to be thought?"

"Eccentricity has nothing to do with the matter. If I take him along, my mother will do her best to coerce me into attending any number of balls and dances and ridottos and rout parties and musical evenings and Venetian breakfasts and whatever else the hostesses have come up with by now. This way, I shall have an excuse to cut my visit short. And to strengthen my case, I am also taking along only enough clean shirts for one week."

Lawrence smiled. "Be as devious as you wish, but I will wager ten guineas that you will be sending for Fredericks and the rest of your wardrobe before that week is up."

Demetrius did not arrive at his mother's residence in Grosvenor Square until late on the afternoon of the third day after he received her letter. Technically the house had belonged to him since his father's death, but his mother always acted as if she still owned it. Given his distaste for London, he had never made any effort to assert his rights in the matter.

Having sent his horses and groom around to the stables, he banged on the front door more vigorously than was perhaps necessary, but then, he had been in a foul mood for every minute of those three days.

He was just lifting his hand to the knocker again when the door was opened by his mother's starched-up butler, who ignored his scowl and welcomed him quite formally to London.

Stalking past the man into the entrance hall, Demetrius did not bother to disguise his mood. ''It is not a good day, McDougal. I have not had a good day since my mother sent for me. Fetch me a bottle of brandy and then tell her I am in my study. The sooner this farce is played out, the sooner I can return to Devon.''

''Your mother is out, m'lord.''

''Out?'' Demetrius paused in the doorway of his study.

''She always goes for a drive in the park at five, m'lord.''

''I see. The situation with my brother is desperate, yet she has not let it interrupt her social activities. I was a fool to have come here. You may tell her that if she wishes to speak with me, she may visit me at Thorverton Hall.''

Turning on his heel, he retraced his steps, but escape was not to be that easy. By scurrying in a most undignified manner, the butler managed to reach the front door before him and blocked his exit.

Looking embarrassed by his own temerity, McDougal spoke up, his voice quavering with unbutlerish emotion. ''Begging your pardon, m'lord, but I fear your brother has indeed gotten himself into mortal danger. We have all been praying you would arrive in time to save him. He appears to be so infatuated with the Black Widow, Lady Thorverton is afraid that if she allows him even to suspect she has sent for you, he will take offense at her interference and be goaded into doing something rash.''

''Something rash? Surely he cannot be seriously contemplating matrimony at his age?''

''That is precisely what is worrying us all, m'lord. Even Lady Thorverton is convinced that young Master Collier intends to offer for that woman as soon as he is twenty-one, which will be in another six and a half weeks. They do say that the odds in the clubs are now three to two that your brother will not survive the Season.''

Demetrius could not believe how overly dramatic everyone was acting. What had this widow done—poisoned several husbands? If so, why had she not been brought to justice? "So how am I to persuade him to give up this woman without letting him suspect that I am opposed to the match?"

"Lady Thorverton is hoping that you will pretend you have come up to London for some business reasons."

"That is all well and good, but has she figured out what I am to do after that?"

The butler looked completely miserable. "She has not made me privy to all her plans."

"Which means she does not have any plans." Biting back an oath, Demetrius turned away from the door. "I do not suppose my brother is in?"

The butler cleared his throat, then said, "I regret to inform you that young Master Collier no longer resides under this roof. He has taken rooms at the Albany."

Demetrius began to suspect that he had at last discovered the real reason his mother had summoned him to London—not, as she was trying to pretend, to save his brother from the clutches of a scheming widow, but rather to coerce Collier into residing once again under the parental roof, where she could more easily control his every activity.

Demetrius had no difficulty tracking down his brother, who was with two friends in his rooms at the Albany. Unfortunately, the guilty expression on Collier's face did not bode well for the quick accomplishment of the task assigned to Demetrius.

"What are you doing in London?" Collier blurted out.

"Mind your manners," Demetrius answered, more than a little put out by his brother's obvious discomposure. How deeply was the boy involved with this Black Widow?

"Oh, of course. Uh, these are my friends, Ernest Saville and Charles Neuce."

"Your brother and I have already met," Neuce immediately told Collier.

Demetrius cast his mind back, but could dredge up no recollection of the other man, who was watching him with all the eager expectancy of a young, untrained foxhound.

"I bought a hunter from you four years ago," Neuce prompted. "A chestnut gelding, name of Hey Go Mad."

"Ah, yes, I remember." Demetrius did not bother to mention that while he could recall the horse quite clearly, he still had no memory of the man who had bought it.

"Quite the best hunter I ever owned, in fact. Shame I lost him to Nethercott on a wager."

Shifting his weight from foot to foot, Collier repeated his question. "So, uh, what are you doing in London? Thought you never came here during the Season."

"I have come to see a man about a horse," Demetrius said vaguely, wishing he could have discussed strategy with his mother before this confrontation. Actually, it was doubtful if she had any useful ideas on the subject. What he should have done was have a long talk with Anne before he left Devon. If she could not have come up with a foolproof plan to separate Collier from the Black Widow, doubtless the twins would have. Two more ingenious boys he had never met . . . nor ever wanted to meet.

"How fortunate!" Neuce exclaimed. "I have my eye on a team of matched grays that is being auctioned off at Tatt's. Would you perhaps have time to accompany me tomorrow? I would appreciate the advice of an expert."

"Since I raise hunters, I am not an expert on carriage horses," Demetrius pointed out. Then, seeing the look of relief on his brother's face, he changed his mind. If Collier did not want him hanging around, then Demetrius was determined to stay as close to his brother as sticking plaster. "But I shall be happy to go along and check them out for you. I can at least see if they are sound and not broken in wind."

"Capital! I say, why don't you come with us this evening? We are dining at White's and then dropping by the Cholmondseys' ball. I am sure they would have extended an invitation to you, had they known you were in town."

Deliberately ignoring the horrified expression on his brother's face, Demetrius readily agreed to change into evening dress and meet the other three at White's at seven.

* * *

Demetrius stared in amused disbelief at the Cholmondseys' ballroom, which was decked out to resemble
the grounds of an Italian villa—or perhaps a Spanish
grandee's estate? It was difficult to determine exactly what
had been intended, but the labor involved in dragging in
garden statues and large marble urns had to have been
immense, not to mention the cost of the hundreds of
flowers that competed with the guests for elbow room.

The last three years might well have been three days,
so few changes could he see in the people around him.
To be sure, there was a new row of eager young things
seated beside their chaperones. But the look of desperation on their faces so precisely duplicated the expressions
worn by the girls being presented three years ago that,
with very little effort, one could convince oneself that
they were the identical young ladies.

Looking around, he gradually began to recognize a
few people he had been acquainted with before, although
he could not put names to all the faces. There was, of
course, the usual assortment of perennial bachelors and
bored husbands, eager mamas and ancient beldams, dan-
dies and Corinthians, high sticklers and dashing young
matrons.

Unfortunately, no matter how he studied the other
guests, Demetrius could not determine which of the
women was the one called the Black Widow. For a moment he thought he might be wasting his time—that she
might not even be in attendance this evening. But then
he remembered the look of dismay on his brother's face.
No, Collier's inamorata was sure to be here already, or
she would be before the evening was over.

His job would be immensely easier if he had some idea
what she looked like. Perhaps if he circulated through
the room, he might overhear a conversation that would
give him an indication as to whom he was looking for.

Heading in the general direction of the refreshment
table, he listened carefully to what people were saying,
but none of the gossip he heard mentioned the fatal
widow.

In the corner, halfway hidden behind the statue of a
wood nymph, he spotted the former Miss Everard, one

of Diana's bosom bows, batting her eyelashes at Lord Huxmere, whose wife was dancing with Major Thomas. Although Demetrius could not remember the name of the man Miss Everard had married, he was reasonably sure it was the man presently flirting with Lord Buckner's second wife. Which meant Miss Everard was not a widow, and so she could be eliminated.

Demetrius could not completely hold back a smile when he approached Lionell Rudd, who was sitting with the chaperones. Three years ago Rudd had aspired to be the leader of fashion. This evening he had definitely achieved the dubious distinction of being the most foolish-looking fop at the ball.

Underendowed by nature, the skinny little man was wearing a coat that had been padded to give him a most impressive set of shoulders, then nipped in so sharply at the waist, it was a wonder the man could breathe. To add to his magnificence, the colors he was sporting would have made a peacock blush, plus he had at least twenty fobs and seals dangling from his waistcoat.

As silly as Rudd looked, the dandy was apparently not lacking in mettle—he was conversing with Hester Prestwich, whose sharp tongue had left scars on many an inoffensive young man. Her looks were not to be despised, and they had even gained her a number of suitors during her first Season, which had been—Demetrius counted back—about six years ago, when he himself had been an unlicked cub like Collier, set loose in London for the first time and determined to make a fool of himself.

If memory served him right, she had even been betrothed for a short period of time, but a few weeks later a retraction had appeared in the *Morning Post.* No one had been terribly surprised, since any man who married her could expect to live under the cat's paw.

Demetrius's attention moved on to the girl sitting beside Miss Prestwich. There was enough resemblance to make it likely that she was a younger sister.

Her hair was a rich chestnut and was piled on top of her head, exposing a very graceful neck. She had not the classic beauty of her older sister—her nose was definitely not regal, and her upper lip was a bit too short, while her lower lip was too full. Actually, her lips looked quite kissable.

Overall, her features were softer, more rounded, and definitely more appealing than those of Miss Hester Prestwich. Idly he wondered what the younger sister's given name was.

Unexpectedly the girl glanced up and caught him staring right at her. Her eyes were dark and appeared overlarge for her face, like those of a newborn foal. For a long moment he was able to look deep into her eyes. He saw such sadness there—such a look of injured innocence—that it was disconcerting, and he felt almost relieved when she again lowered her eyes to her hands, which were busily engaged in twisting up a handkerchief to its obvious detriment.

"Young man, I will thank you to go about your business," the hatched-faced woman sitting next to the two girls snapped out at him. "My niece is not a raree show, to be gawked at so rudely."

Recognizing Miss Prestwich's aunt, also a Miss Prestwich, since she had never married, Demetrius bowed and murmured all the correct apologies, but the old harridan was not to be appeased. She seemed determined to blame Demetrius for all the shortcomings of the male of the species—failings that in her mind appeared to be innumerable.

Giving up the obviously futile task of coaxing her out of her bad temper, he moved on and resumed his quest, feeling a moment of pity for the youngest Miss Prestwich, trapped as she was between a sharp-tongued sister and a man-hating aunt. It was small wonder none of the young bucks were crowding around, eager to sign her dance card.

Finally reaching his ostensible goal, he helped himself to a glass of champagne, then turned to survey the crowd once again. Belatedly it occurred to him that all he actually needed to do was pay attention to his brother and notice which of the ladies *he* paid attention to. With luck, Collier would betray himself.

Demetrius should have remembered that luck was what he no longer had. By the time the evening was half over,

Collier had done nothing more reprehensible than dance with a few young ladies, none of them twice. Demetrius was about to give it up as a lost cause and go home when he spotted his mother's brother, Humphrey Swinton, signaling him frantically from the other side of the room.

With great resolution and determination, Demetrius once again began to squeeze his way through the press of people, but this time he moved as quickly as the crowd allowed.

Before he could indicate his desire to speak privately with him, his uncle caught him by the arm and dragged him behind a pillar. "Demetrius, my boy, thank the dear Lord I have found you. Your mother insisted I come here this evening to help you rescue your brother, but it is too late—he is already asking that wretched woman to dance a second time. Either Collier is dicked in the nob or he has grown tired of this life. I cannot help thinking he should be locked up."

Demetrius peered around the column and spotted his brother not fifteen feet away, bowing in front of . . . No, that was clearly impossible!

Ducking back behind the pillar, he questioned his uncle further, thinking there had to be some mistake. "You cannot mean to tell me that Miss Hester Prestwich is the Black Widow?"

"No, no, of course not. It is her younger sister, Miss Meribe Prestwich, whose charms are so fatal."

2

Among all the women Demetrius had suspected that evening, the youngest Miss Prestwich had definitely not been included.

"They are doing it on a dare, you should realize."

A man's high-pitched voice spoke right behind him, and Demetrius turned to see Lionell Rudd, who was smiling with malicious glee.

"The young bucks think they are proving their courage by dancing with her. Your brother is pushing his luck even further than most by asking for a second dance. It does raise a question about his intelligence, would you not say, Thorverton?"

Restraining his impulse to toss the dandy out the nearest window, Demetrius moved a few feet away until he had a clear view of his brother, who was still standing in front of Miss Meribe Prestwich. He was saying something, but whatever it was, she did not appear to be pleased. Her eyes still downcast, she was shaking her head repeatedly.

"Got to stop your brother before he ends up cold in his grave like her other suitors," Uncle Humphrey said in a loud whisper.

While Demetrius watched, Miss Hester Prestwich said something sharply to her sister, who gave a start, then stood up and with obvious reluctance allowed Collier to lead her out to join a set that was forming.

Having seen enough, Demetrius took his uncle's arm and began to urge him toward the door. Behind them Rudd snickered nastily.

"Are you not going to make a push to rescue your brother?" Uncle Humphrey protested. "Are you intend-

ing to leave him in that woman's clutches? Have you no
sense of duty? You are the head of the family, after all.''

''My brother can go to the devil with my blessing,''
Demetrius retorted, continuing out of the room and down
the stairs. ''And while he is starting on his journey, you
and I are going to have a long talk.''

''I am not sure I wish to get involved,'' his uncle said.
''It is bound to upset my digestion.''

Pausing briefly to retrieve their hats and Uncle Humphrey's cane, they soon emerged into the cool night air,
which was a welcome relief. It was hard to believe that
the same people who complained about the smell of
horses and the ''stink'' of the stables could spend hours
in stuffy, overheated rooms that reeked of hot wax, stale
sweat, and musky perfumes.

''Did you bring your carriage?'' Demetrius asked.

''No, I came with Mannlius, and he is going to think
it dashed queer of me to take off this way without a word
to him.''

Shrugging, Demetrius began to walk in the direction
of Grosvenor Square. His uncle hesitated, then hurried
to catch up. ''You cannot expect me to converse while
galloping along like this.''

Obediently Demetrius shortened his stride to match his
uncle's slower pace. ''Begin,'' he said curtly.

''The question is, precisely what *is* the beginning?''
his uncle tried to hedge, but a sharp look from Demetrius
made him clear his throat and start over.

''Well, I suppose it began three years ago when Miss
Meribe became betrothed to Collingwood. He was quite
a catch for a young lady of seventeen in her first Season.
Son of an earl, and all.''

''You are referring to Lord Wittingham's heir?''

''Not any longer. Less than a week before the wedding, he was thrown from his horse and broke his neck.
Fortunately, he has three younger brothers, so there is
no problem with the succession.''

''I am not concerned about the succession, I am interested in Miss Meribe Prestwich.''

''Well, after that disaster, she retired to the country,
of course. I believe they have an estate in Norfolk or

Suffolk or some such place. Well, what else could the poor girl do? She could hardly be expected to finish out the Season. Wouldn't have been proper, don't you know. Although,'' his uncle continued reflectively, ''I am not sure how long one is expected to mourn for one's betrothed. Undoubtedly not as long as for a husband, of course. But you can ask your mother; I am sure she would know.''

''You are wandering off the subject, uncle.''

''Hmmm? Oh, yes. Well, the next Season, she got betrothed to Lord Thurwell. Only a baron, and not nearly as well-funded as Collingwood, but still and all, a decent catch.''

''What happened to him?'' Demetrius prompted.

''Got run down in the street by a dray three days after the betrothal was announced in the *Morning Post*. The driver claimed it was an accident—insisted Thurwell just stepped out in front of him. Most people disagreed.''

''Did they think there was foul play? Was there any investigation?''

''Foul play? No, no, nothing like that. Most people thought that she was under an evil spell, and Thurwell was merely an innocent victim of that curse, don't you know. And time has proved them right. Miss Prestwich removed herself from London again, and I, for one, never thought to see her turn up here again last Season. Well, stands to reason, don't it? A girl has two suitors die on her—who's going to want to risk his neck getting betrothed to her?''

Apparently someone, Demetrius thought. Prompting his uncle, who had paused overly long in his recital, he asked, ''Who?''

''Arleton and Fellerman, that's who. Not at all up to the level of Collingwood and Thurwell, but then, the girl probably counted herself lucky that she still had any suitors at all. Didn't even manage to get an announcement in the *Morning Post* last year, though. Right from the first week of the Season, the betting was heavy in the clubs as to which of them would make the first offer, but only four weeks into the Season, Arleton was killed by a highwayman on Hounslow Heath.''

"A highwayman? In this day and age?"

"Probably about the last one left in England, which just goes to show how unlucky it is to associate with Miss Meribe Prestwich. When they fished poor Fellerman out of the Thames, even the last diehards were willing to admit that she is afflicted with a fatal curse—fatal for her suitors, that is. It was after Fellerman's funeral that everyone started calling her the Black Widow."

They walked in silence for a few moments while Demetrius thought about the story his uncle had related. "But I fail to understand—why the Black Widow? It would seem she has never actually been married, much less widowed, and her hair is a glorious chestnut rather than black."

"It was Mannlius who rather cleverly came up with that sobriquet. Related it all to me. Explained how they've got a spider over there in the colonies called the black widow. Not only deadly poisonous, but the female eats the male after they . . . well, you know . . . after he does what he is supposed to do . . . well, when she's done with him as her bridegroom, so to speak, she turns him into dinner, as it were."

"That is the most disgusting thing I have ever heard."

"Well, can't be helped—rather hard to persuade spiders to behave in a more civilized manner. No way to communicate with them, don't you know. Best just to step on them."

"I was referring to your friend Lord Mannlius. He should be ashamed to have added fuel to the gossip. Why, this is all nothing more or less than a witch hunt. I am amazed that people could be so superstitious—present company included."

Uncle Humphrey hurried to justify himself. "Well, you will have to admit, it is somewhat peculiar that the girl—"

"I shall admit nothing of the kind. Rather it is typical of the blind cruelty displayed by ignorant mobs when they engage in such sports as bearbaiting."

"Oh, come now," his uncle blustered, "you are exaggerating. No one is being cruel—they are just being cautious."

Remembering the look of sadness in the poor girl's eyes, Demetrius said, "I disagree. They are acting like the most superstitious of savages and are managing to ignore all the progress civilization has made in the last thousand years."

"But . . . but really, Demetrius, how can you expect a man with the slightest common sense to risk his life? No, no, it is clearly your duty to rescue your brother from the Black Widow."

The rage that had been building up in Demetrius now spilled over. Catching his uncle by the front of his waistcoat, Demetrius pulled him up until their faces were mere inches apart. "Do not ever—*ever*—let me hear you call her by that disgusting nickname again. Her name is Miss Meribe Prestwich, and I shall thank you to use it."

Uncle Humphrey's mouth gaped open and he stared at Demetrius in amazement. "But what about Collier?" he finally blurted out.

Obviously it would take something more than rational arguments to persuade his uncle to abandon the superstitious nonsense he was spouting. Feeling frustrated beyond measure, Demetrius released him. "I shall take care of Collier tomorrow."

"Thank the dear Lord, the boy has a chance of surviving."

"Not really," Demetrius answered, his voice grim. "I intend to have his head on a platter."

Riding home in the carriage, Meribe counted the number of days left until her twenty-first birthday. Five weeks and four days. Only thirty-nine days until she would be free to return to Norfolk. And never again, under any circumstances whatsoever, would she return to London.

She loathed everything about the Season—every evening party, where the young men dared each other to dance with her, every ride in the park, where people pointed her out and whispered behind their hands about her, every morning call, where the conversation ceased the minute she walked into the room.

"Did you see that gown Lady Fosterwell was wearing?" Hester asked. "Someone should tell her that her

carroty hair is not best set off by mulberry silk. Of course
she will insist that her hair is actually blond. And Mary
Douglas was wearing azure blue again. Her folly, I fear,
is all the result of a certain young man telling her several
years ago that blue brought out the beauty of her eyes.
She has worn that color exclusively ever since, even
though the young man who complimented her offered for
Helen Chesterfield and is now the proud papa of two
children. But then, Mary was always such a fool, even
when she was two years ahead of me at Mme. Millicent's
School in Bath. She is never going to catch a husband,
and I wonder why she has not yet put on her caps.''

When her chattering did not elicit a response from
either Meribe or Aunt Phillipa, Hester altered her tactics. "I was surprised to see that Thorverton has come
to town. He seemed quite taken with you, sister dear—
staring at you as if you were . . . how did Aunt Phillipa
phrase it? . . . as if you were in a raree show.''

Knowing full well that her sister was baiting her, Meribe bit her tongue and remained silent.

Aunt Phillipa was not so reticent, however. "That
wretched man! You are not to have anything to do with
him, Meribe. I have discovered he is nephew to that horrible Humphrey Swinton, and I shall not allow either of
you to associate with any member of that family. I still
shudder at the memory of how Swinton treated me thirty-
two years ago when I was a young thing like you.''

"Just what did he do that was so terrible, Aunt?'' Hester asked, but as usual when the subject of Humphrey
Swinton came up, Aunt Phillipa refused to divulge the
circumstances.

"My lips are sealed,'' she said as dramatically as ever
Mrs. Siddons declaimed her role on the stage at Covent
Garden. "I have vowed to carry that secret to my grave.
But as for you, Meribe, you are not to do anything to
encourage Thorverton, do you hear me?''

"Yes, Aunt Phillipa, I hear you,'' Meribe replied, remembering the kind eyes of the gentleman in question—
kind eyes that unfortunately were filled with pity. Pity.
Somehow that hurt worse than any of the whisperings and
wagers and being stared at. She would have given any-

thing to leave London before her birthday, but to her lasting regret, she had no say in the matter.

"Do not worry, Aunt," Hester said gleefully. "I will wager Lady Thorverton sent for him after she heard that her precious son Collier danced with Meribe twice at the Bridgefords' ball last Friday. Doubtless we shall never see either of those two young men again." At least she hoped not, Hester thought, clenching her fists in her lap.

Thorverton had been in London six years ago, and seeing him again tonight had brought back too many memories. Luckily no one in the *ton* had ever suspected that Peter had jilted her—that he had waited until the marriage settlements were ready to sign before he had informed her that he was going to marry his childhood sweetheart instead—an insignificant little nobody back in Dorset.

Apparently fearing a scene if he informed her in the privacy of her own home, he had taken her aside at a dance and in a low voice had told her he had sent a retraction to the paper the next day. Unfortunately for him, she had not been so devastated that she had been unable to turn the tables on him.

He had obviously expected her to beg and plead with him, but instead in a scathing voice, which was not moderated in the slightest, she had denounced his character without ever mentioning the fickleness of his affections.

Enough people had heard quite clearly when she called him a hardened gamester and a libertine, that when his retraction had appeared in the paper, he was the one who was the object of the titters and the whispers, and no one had suspected that her heart was broken.

But as bad as he had hurt her, her father's subsequent betrayal had been even harder to bear. She had thought that he loved her, but after his death she had discovered she meant nothing to him. His love and affection had been as much an illusion as had Peter's.

The carriage came to a stop in front of their house, and Hester rubbed her forehead, futilely trying to ease the headache that had come over her as soon as she'd seen Lord Thorverton staring at her.

She hoped that he would soon go back to Devon. See-

ing him brought back too many unpleasant memories. In
the years since she had been jilted, she had acquired a
reputation as a hard-hearted, sharp-tongued female, but
she did not care. Nothing mattered as much as concealing from everyone how deeply she had been hurt by the
two men she had loved.

"You wanted to discuss something with me?" Collier
asked, his tremulous smile betraying a slight nervous-
ness.

At least Collier had come promptly in response to the
note Demetrius had sent around to the Albany, but that
was not sufficient to put Demetrius in charity with his
brother. "Sit down. Have some breakfast. The grilled
kidneys are quite good."

With alacrity Collier dropped down into a chair, but
declined to partake of any of the food spread out on the
sideboard. With a bow, the footman left the two of them
alone, closing the doors behind him.

Staring at his brother, Demetrius continued to eat, and
the longer the silence stretched out between them, the
more uncomfortable his brother became. First Collier
began to fidget in his chair; then, abruptly getting to his
feet, he filled a plate for himself.

"Decided to have a bite after all," Collier explained,
returning to the table. He did not, however, actually eat
very much, but at least pushing his food around on his
plate gave him something to do with his hands.

When Collier had reached the proper stage of jumpi-
ness, Demetrius began his attack, having decided that
any attempt at subterfuge would be a waste of time.

"On Thursday last I received a frantic letter from our
mother," he said calmly. "She informed me that you
were courting death by courting Miss Meribe Prestwich."

Collier let out his breath, then smiled naturally for the
first time since he had entered the room. "Oh, is that
why you have come to London? I thought Mama had sent
for you to make me give up my rooms at the Albany."

"Which reminds me, how can you afford to rent your
own place?"

"Lady Luck smiled at me. Won two hundred pounds playing faro three weeks ago. You needn't tell Mama, however, because she will get it into her noggin that I am a hardened gamester, and I am no such thing."

"And what of Miss Prestwich? Are your intentions serious?"

"I should say not," Collier replied indignantly, "and I think it is a cursed nuisance that m'mother has dragged you away from your horses for such a silly reason. Despite what everyone is saying in the clubs, dancing with her is not all that dangerous. So far this year, no one has died, although Lambreth did take a bad tumble down the stairs directly after he stood up with the Black Widow, but all he broke was his arm. Got a thick skull, Lambreth does."

His temper inflamed by hearing that repulsive nickname, Demetrius was hard put to resist the impulse to knock some sense into his *brother's* thick skull. But with a herculean effort he managed to keep his tone of voice mild. "So you have been asking Miss Prestwich to dance in order to . . . how shall we phrase it? To prove your manhood?"

Collier shifted uneasily in his seat. "Well, you have to understand how it is, Demetrius. Everyone must dance with her at least once or be called a coward."

"So you think it is a mark of bravery to persecute a poor defenseless female?" Unable to remain still any longer, Demetrius rose to his feet and scowled down at his brother. "You think a real man goes around blithely causing misery to a young lady? Tell me again—how do you justify such odious, dishonorable conduct? Explain it to me, because I must admit it seems to me to be the most low-down, cowardly kind of behavior imaginable, and I am ashamed that my own brother has taken part in such a despicable affair."

His head hanging low, Collier did not immediately reply. "It's all m'mother's fault," he said finally. "I never wanted to be stuck here in London in the first place. There is nothing to do here but gamble or flirt with silly chits who have little on their minds but clothes and dancing. I wanted to go to Spain and fight against Boney, but you know Mama has refused to buy me my colors. If she has her way, she will forever keep me on leading strings, as if I were still in short coats—you can't know what it's like, Demetrius!''

''Indeed? At this point, I cannot blame her. You sound exactly like a petulant little boy whining because he cannot always have his own way. You say you want to prove you are a man, and yet at the first sign of trouble you hide behind your mother's skirts. 'It's all m'mother's fault,' '' he mimicked. ''And you think Wellesley needs 'men' like you in Spain. Bah!''

Demetrius turned his back on his brother and stalked out of the room, pausing in the doorway only long enough to add, ''And I warn you, if you ever again refer to Miss Prestwich as the Black Widow, I shall thrash you to within an inch of your life.''

''You have just made a green daisy, sister dear.'' Hester pointed out the mistake with the usual note of glee in her voice.

Meribe looked down at the embroidery in her lap. Oh, blast, her mind had been wandering again, and she had finished the leaves and continued on without remembering to change colors of floss. Now she would have to unpick the whole flower, which she despised doing . . . but which she was well experienced at.

Given her propensity for daydreaming, she should stick to hemming sheets, but Aunt Phillipa insisted that Meribe could become as proficient with all types of needlework as she herself was if Meribe would only put her mind to it. Which was the problem, of course. Meribe had trouble putting her mind to all the tasks Aunt Phillipa assigned her.

The only thing she really enjoyed was growing plants, but her aunt refused to let her have a garden spot of her own. Grubbing around in the dirt was not, in her aunt's opinion, a ladylike pastime.

''Yes, what is it, Smucker?'' Aunt Phillipa looked up from the book of improving sermons she was reading aloud.

"There is a gentleman here to see Miss Meribe," the butler replied. "A Lord Thorverton."

"Why are you bothering us, Smucker?" Hester replied before Aunt Phillipa had a chance to answer. "You know we no longer allow gentlemen callers into the house."

"He said it was most important," Smucker explained.

"No," Aunt Phillipa said flatly, and the butler left the room without further argument.

"He probably wishes to gape at you again, Meribe," Hester said gleefully. "I vow I do not know how you endure being stared at everywhere you go. If 'twere me, I would have the hysterics, but then, you never had the least sensibility."

"That is enough, Hester," Aunt Phillipa finally intervened. "Now, where was I?"

Neither of the two girls answered. In that one respect Meribe knew she and her sister resembled each other— neither of them actually heard a word of the improving sermons their aunt delighted in reading aloud.

"Beg pardon," the butler interrupted again. "But my lord insists that it is a matter of the gravest concern."

"Grave?" Hester said with a titter. "Oh, Meribe, my love, do you suppose you have dispatched another poor young man to his heavenly reward? Oh, Aunt, do let him come in, or I vow I shall myself expire of suspense."

"I do not think—" Aunt Phillipa began, but before she could flatly refuse, Hester made another effort to persuade her.

"Only consider, dear aunt, that if he has indeed come to tell us his baby brother has met with an unfortunate accident, how it will appear to others if we turn the grieving man away from our door."

As irritated as Hester was making her by talking such nonsense, Meribe was still thankful when the butler was finally given instructions to admit Lord Thorverton.

Would the viscount be as handsome by daylight as he had appeared by candlelight? A ridiculous question when she thought about it, but no matter how she tried, Meribe could not help wondering about the answer.

"Good afternoon, ladies." Lord Thorverton bowed

formally, but Aunt Phillipa did not offer him a seat. He was about half a head taller than Smucker, who was only an inch or so taller than herself, Meribe thought. And he was quite handsome enough for any man.

"I wish to extend my apologies to you ladies, and particularly to Miss Meribe Prestwich, for any discomfort my brother may have caused you by his actions. I have spoken to him, and in the future he will not bother you in any way."

It was very prettily said, but it was quite obvious that his words had not softened Aunt Phillipa's heart in the slightest. She continued to look at him with an expression of extreme loathing.

"Thank you," Meribe said softly. "I accept your apology on behalf of your brother."

He smiled at her, then caught her completely off-guard by continuing, "It would give me great pleasure if you would drive out with me this afternoon, Miss Prestwich."

Hester tittered, and Aunt Phillipa turned to look at Meribe, who hurried to decline. "No, thank you, my lord."

He looked as if he were going to press her to agree, so she repeated more firmly, "I do not wish to drive out with you."

"Tomorrow, perhaps?"

She shook her head. "I prefer to stay at home."

Aunt Phillipa signaled the butler, and Smucker said smoothly, "If you will come this way, my lord."

Thorverton paused, but then followed the butler out.

"Do you suppose he came here on a wager?" Hester asked.

"No, I do not," Meribe said, then wished she had held her tongue. Every time she responded to her sister's deliberate baiting, it only encouraged Hester to continue.

"How many pounds do you think he has won by such great daring? Do you suppose it was one hundred pounds? Or perhaps even more?"

Doing her best to ignore her sister, Meribe looked down at her embroidery. Whatever had induced her to attempt a fire screen? She had already been working on it for an eternity, and between unsnarling tangles and unpicking green flowers, she was not even a quarter of the way done. If there had been a fire in the grate, she would have thrown the wretched thing into the flames.

Demetrius looked around the room to see if he had forgotten anything, then buckled the straps on his portmanteau. As he had hoped, he had managed to clear up this mess quickly, and he would be back in Devon before the week was up.

Leaving his bag where it was, he ambled over to the window and looked out. The two days he had been here had only confirmed him in his dislike of London. He would be overjoyed to get back to his beloved horses. But he continued to stand staring out at the street.

His mind was not on the street vendors peddling their wares from house to house. He kept seeing a pair of large dark eyes with long silky lashes. Beautiful eyes . . . but also the saddest eyes he had ever seen. So much pain in them.

"Oh, blast it all," he said, leaning his forehead against the cool pane of glass. He could not persuade himself that his responsibility to that poor girl was ended simply because she had accepted his apology.

Knowing very well what course of action he should take, unpalatable though it might be, he did not allow himself any further vacillation. He rang for a footman and gave orders for a message to be sent to Devon requesting his valet to join him in London.

Meribe checked her list to be sure she had gotten everything—five ells of yellow ribbon for Hester's orange sarcenet, a packet of pins, two ells of lace for herself, and blue floss to match the sample Aunt Phillipa had sent along. Yes, all the purchases were taken care of, which meant they had nothing left to do but stop at the lending library and exchange books.

Looking around for Jane, the abigail she shared with Hester, Meribe found her view blocked by a pair of broad shoulders and kind brown eyes.

"Good afternoon, Miss Prestwich." Lord Thorverton

tipped his hat to her. "May I offer you my escort while you do your errands?"

Now—now, when it was too late—Jane appeared, carrying the parcel of books to be exchanged. The maid's eyes got big at the sight of Meribe conversing with a man, and the expression of awe on Jane's face made it overly clear she thought Lord Thorverton to be quite a man.

"I am done with my shopping," Meribe said faintly.

"Except for the books," Jane blurted out. "Don't be forgetting, miss, that we still have to go to Hookham's. Hester will be that displeased if you don't fetch her home some new novels." Although ostensibly speaking to Meribe, Jane's fatuous smile was directed at Lord Thorverton.

"Hookham's?" he said with what Meribe could only describe as a wicked twinkle in his eye. "Why, that is precisely where I was headed myself." He offered his arm to Meribe as if it were the most natural thing to do.

A single glance around sufficed to show her that they were already the center of attention. He could not know what an imbroglio he was getting himself mixed up in. Without doubt by evening his name would be on everyone's lips, and wagers would be laid in the clubs as to the length—or shortness—of his life expectancy.

Clearly it behooved her to explain to him the dangers inherent in associating with her, but she could not do it here—not with all the eager listening ears.

With great trepidation she laid her hand on his arm and allowed him to escort her out of the shop. Behind them there was a scurry of movement accompanied by whispers, and knowing exactly what it all signified, Meribe felt her face grow hot.

"Lord Thorverton," she said earnestly, "you must have been rather isolated in Devon, for it appears that you are unaware of my reputation."

"Not at all," he said calmly. "That is precisely why I have sought you out."

Feeling betrayed that he had turned out to be no better than any of the other "gentlemen," she tried to pull her hand free, but he caught it with his other hand and held it in place.

"No," he said, "you need not be angry with me. I have made no wagers—accepted no dares. My purpose is merely to help you. It seems to me that what you need most is a friend, preferably one who is not swayed by superstitious nonsense."

Eyes downcast, she said, "Suppose it is not nonsense? Suppose I am truly . . . cursed."

"Do you believe that? Do you honestly think you are in any way responsible for what happened to those young men?"

She could not answer, and finally he touched her chin, and using no pressure at all, raised her head so that he could look into her eyes. "Do you believe there is even a grain of truth behind the gossip?" he repeated.

"Does it matter what I believe?" she asked. "Reality or illusion, the effect is the same. Dozens of young men have 'shown their bravery' by dancing with me. What do you think is the likelihood that at least one of those men will catch a chill or fall off his horse or get himself shot in a duel? And whom do you think everyone will blame if that happens?" Again she tried to retrieve her hand, and still he held it fast. "I can only be grateful that I never had occasion to meet the prime minister, so that at least his assassination has not been laid at my door."

"But suppose there were only one man courting you—do you not think people would forget about all those others if they were supplanted, so to speak?"

She looked up at him in horror. "Surely you are not suggesting . . . ?"

He smiled, but this time his smile was quite terrifying to behold. "But I am, Miss Prestwich. I intend to defy all this superstitious nonsense, and I also intend to remain quite hale and hearty in the process."

"But . . . but . . ."

"But what? Either you agree that it is nonsense, in which case I have nothing more to fear than gossip, or you are saying, in effect, that you did cause those unfortunate accidents. So which is it going to be? Are you afraid of the illusion or the reality?"

She thought about what he was proposing, then said, "I do not believe there is a real curse. But on the other hand, I cannot ignore the little voice in the back of my head that keeps saying, 'What if there is a curse? What if all these other people are right? What if every man who comes near me is endangering his life?' Unfortunately, no matter how I consider the evidence, I cannot answer those questions with absolute, unequivocal certainty. Therefore, after careful consideration of your suggestion, I find I cannot allow you to risk your life this way, Lord Thorverton. My answer has to be no, I do not wish you to pretend to court me."

With that she resolutely jerked her hand free and hurried down the street, not even looking back to see if Jane was keeping up with her.

3

"Good evening, Miss Prestwich." Lord Thorverton bowed politely. "May I have the honor of this dance?"

The corners of his mouth turned up slightly, and for Meribe it was the last straw. The man was so aggravating—he had been following her around town for days, popping up where she least expected it. He refused to take no for an answer, but no matter what he tried, she was not going to cooperate with his efforts to prove there was no curse.

"I am sorry, Lord Thorverton, but I do not feel like dancing this evening." Her smile was as patently false as she could make it.

"That is quite all right, Miss Prestwich. I shall be happy to sit out the dance with you." Without waiting for permission, he took the chair recently vacated by Hester.

"Nice weather we have been having lately," he commented.

Staring straight ahead, she tried to act as if he were not there, but he refused to take offense and leave.

To add to her problems, Aunt Phillipa, who was sitting on her left, began to grumble. "I have told you not to associate with Swinton's nephew, and yet you persist in encouraging him. You, young man"—she leaned around Meribe and spoke directly to Lord Thorverton—"go away and stop annoying my niece!"

Although Aunt Phillipa's voice was little more than a loud whisper, several women sitting near them tittered behind their fans, and Meribe wanted to sink through the floor.

Her direct order being ignored, Aunt Phillipa began to

animadvert on the perversity of all men. Then, to make matters worse, the music ended, and Hester returned with Lionell Rudd and found seats on the other side of Lord Thorverton. The two of them immediately began to comment with acerbity on the other dancers.

As if that were not bad enough, a young man approached, obviously intending to ask her to dance. Feeling like a trapped fox harassed by a pack of hounds, Meribe turned to Lord Thorverton and wordlessly beseeched him to do something.

Responding to Meribe's silent plea, Demetrius scowled at the man heading toward her. The young man faltered, then abruptly veered off in a different direction. There were advantages to advancing age, Demetrius decided. His eight-and-twenty years, while not rendering him ancient, did make it easier for him to intimidate the young bucks of nineteen and twenty who had become accustomed to having their sport at Miss Prestwich's expense.

Unfortunately, nothing gave him an advantage where the aunt was concerned. It amazed him, in fact, that with such a dragon for a chaperone Miss Meribe had twice succeeded in becoming betrothed. The eldest Miss Prestwich had not ceased glaring at him since he had first sat down beside her niece, and he had obviously been meant to overhear her *sotto voce* comments about men. She would have been amusing, except that she was obviously upsetting Miss Meribe.

Compared to her elder niece, however, Aunt Phillipa was the very model of congeniality. Rudd and Hester seemed to vie with each other as to which of them could be the more sweetly malicious.

It belatedly occurred to him that rescuing a damsel in distress was all very good in novels, where the hero simply carries the heroine back to his castle. But in real life one had to contend with the girl's relatives.

Surely Miss Meribe must be getting just as fed up with her aunt and her sister as he was? Perhaps, now that she had made use of his assistance once, she would be a trifle more amenable? "It is rather stuffy in here. Would you like to take a bit of fresh air? I believe there are several balconies available.''

"No, I would not," Miss Meribe replied, once again spurning his attempts to help her.

No sooner had she rejected his offer, however, than another young man approached. This time when she turned to Demetrius for assistance, he merely smiled at her.

The young man bowed, then shot a quick glance over to where a group of his friends was watching. "May I have this dance?" he asked with a smirk.

"I am sorry," she said softly, "but I have promised to take a turn around the room with Lord Thorverton."

Not expecting to be rebuffed, the young man hesitated, clearly uncertain what to do next, but Demetrius did not delay in rising to his feet and offering Miss Meribe his arm.

As soon as they were far enough away that her aunt would not be able to hear them, Miss Meribe said, "You should be ashamed of yourself for taking advantage of my situation to achieve your own ends."

"I would apologize," he replied, "except that I have reached the limits of my tolerance for your aunt's baleful glances and your sister's spiteful tongue."

"I will admit my aunt and my sister can be a bit tiresome. Have they vexed you out of reason?"

"Why do you ask such a thing? Merely because a lesser man would have strangled your aunt by now? And doubtless ripped your sister's tongue out by the roots?"

She smiled briefly, then said, "They are not always so bad. My aunt has never had any fondness for men, but in your case, since you are closely related to Humphrey Swinton, she is particularly displeased with you. Whatever your uncle did years ago, it was bad enough to turn her against your whole family."

"And your sister? Is she always this acid-tongued? Or has she been displaying her wit strictly for my entertainment?"

"I believe Mr. Rudd is a bad influence on her," Meribe explained. "He encourages her to cast poisonous darts in all directions. While I would never describe her as sweet, at home in Norfolk she does not make such a deliberate effort to find unkind things to say about our neighbors.''

As they strolled along, Demetrius gradually became aware that a path was magically clearing in front of them and that all conversation ceased with their approach. Not wishing to be overheard by one and all, he deemed it wiser to lead his companion out onto one of the afore-mentioned balconies overlooking the garden.

Another couple had had the same idea, but as soon as they recognized whom they were sharing the cool night air with, the woman uttered a little squeal of dismay and the man hustled her back into the ballroom.

By the light coming through the French doors, Demetrius could see Meribe's face reasonably well. At first he thought she had not noticed anything amiss about the other couple's behavior, but then he saw that her hands were clenching the railing tightly, and he knew the incident had indeed upset her.

Since she apparently wished to pretend nothing was wrong, he did not mention what had just happened, but instead began to talk about an innocuous subject. ''I think what I miss most about Devon is my horses.''

''Did you not bring them to London with you?''

He smiled. ''I brought my team and one riding horse, but I could not very well bring them all. I raise and train hunters, you see. The Thorverton stud is quite well-known in hunting circles, by which I must conclude that you do not hunt.''

''I am afraid it is even worse than that. I do not ride at all.''

For a moment he was at a loss for words. Not ride? Even his former betrothed, Diana Fairgrove—now Lady Hazelmore—who despised horses, could ride, albeit not with any degree of style, and not on a horse that showed even a modicum of spirit.

''My aunt ranks horses only slightly below men in her esteem,'' Meribe explained. ''They are all too big and too full of energy. They are also clumsy, which means they are constantly breaking things, added to which they eat too much and have a fatal tendency toward gambling and strong drink—''

"Gambling, drunken horses?"

Meribe laughed. "No, no, that is her opinion of men. But horses, she contends, have much the same failings, plus they have been known to bite, kick, and throw off their riders. Aunt Phillipa therefore holds that skills such as riding and driving are completely unladylike and not to be acquired."

"And do you share your aunt's opinion, or would you like to learn to ride?"

"My opinion matters little. My aunt is the one who decides what I shall do and not do."

"Then, given her dislike of men, I am surprised she has brought you to London for the Season."

"Oh, that is beyond her control. In his will, my father put in a stipulation that I must have a Season every year until I am one-and-twenty. My birthday is less than four weeks away, at which time I shall gladly return to Norfolk and never again show my face in this fair city." She paused, then continued in a rush, "But you must not think I am hinting that you should stay here and bear me company until my birthday. On the contrary, I am persuaded it will be better for all concerned if you return to your horses."

"Not at all," Demetrius heard himself saying. "I shall be happy to stand your friend until you are free to return to your own home." Now, why was he persisting in playing the hero, when his noble sacrifices were obviously not welcomed by their intended recipient?

After a short pause, she said, "I thank you for the offer, Lord Thorverton, but as I have told you over and over, I cannot be responsible for the danger you will be putting yourself into if you persist in your efforts on my behalf. I have managed this far alone, and am sure I can make it through these last few weeks. After all, what harm is a little gossip?"

There was a gasp behind them, and they turned to see another couple standing in the doorway, clearly surprised to discover the balcony was already occupied. They were so flustered, in fact, that it was equally obvious that they had recognized Meribe. With looks of horror, they backed away as hurriedly as if she were a poisonous snake coiled to strike.

"Gossip is anything but harmless," Demetrius said, his voice sharp with anger. "Sometimes I feel it is the worst curse of all. What fools these gentlefolk of the *ton* are!"

"Do not let them upset you, then. They are not worth fretting over."

"I am not fretting, Miss Prestwich. Nor am I willing to let them have a clear field. All it takes is a little boldness—a little resolution."

"I feel I should warn you that I am not terribly brave."

"Not wishing to boast," he said with a smile that was again quite infectious, "but I have an ample supply of courage and will be more than pleased to share it with you."

Looking into his eyes, Meribe could almost feel his strength pouring into her, and without conscious volition, she straightened her back. Let the people stare at her, she decided. She was not going to cringe any longer, no matter how they whispered. And if some of the young men pestered her again, she would send them to the rightabout herself.

"No troubles are so bad," Lord Thorverton continued in a low voice, "that they cannot be lightened by sharing them with a friend. Will you not accept my friendship, Miss Prestwich?"

Almost she said yes, but then that little voice in the back of her head nagged at her: But suppose I am in truth cursed? Suppose he is struck down like the others?

So instead of accepting his offer, she equivocated. "I shall think about what you have said. And now I believe we should return to my aunt. I am becoming a trifle chilled."

For a moment he looked as though he was prepared to continue arguing his case, but then he led her back inside without further delay. As usual, people moved away from them, but to Meribe's surprise, when they were halfway around the room, one lady deliberately planted herself in their path. She was dressed in a red gown with a shockingly low décolletage, and either she had painted her face or she was suffering from a high fever.

"Demetrius, my dear, I am so happy to see you in London again," she positively cooed. "But I am afraid I have never met your companion. Pray introduce us."

Meribe could feel the tension radiating from Lord Thorverton, and when she looked up at him, she was shocked by the strong emotion she could see in his face. Before she could identify what he was feeling—whether joy or anger—his features altered, and she might as well have been looking at a statue carved of marble.

In a wooden voice he performed the introductions. "Lady Hazelmore, may I present Miss Meribe Prestwich; Miss Prestwich, Lady Hazelmore."

Then, before the woman could say anything further, he bowed, made their excuses, and hustled Meribe back to where her aunt and sister were sitting.

Once there, he did not offer any explanation for his strange behavior, which had bordered on rudeness, nor did he say what connection he had with the lady who had made free with his given name and who had called him "my dear."

But Meribe could not help noticing that throughout the rest of the evening, no matter how they talked about this and that, his eyes kept straying toward Lady Hazelmore, who for her part was not making the slightest effort to disguise her interest in Demetrius.

Black Jack Brannigan walked into the Spotted Dog and sat down at the bar. O'Roark immediately set a bottle of gin in front of him, then unobtrusively slid a screw of paper toward him. Black Jack palmed it; then, glancing around to be sure he was not observed, he stuck it into his pocket. Tossing a few copper coins on the counter, he walked out the back, taking his bottle with him.

Climbing the rickety stairs to his room above the tavern, he smiled in anticipation. Another job, it would seem. The gentry mort who was hiring him thought his identity was well-concealed, but the last time Black Jack had taken care of a little problem for his anonymous employer, he had also managed to ferret out the man's identity. There was no telling when such knowledge might be needed, and Black Jack was by nature suspicious of people who desired to use him without giving any security in return. He had therefore provided his own protection against a betrayal.

Once in his room, he took a swig from his bottle, then retrieved the note from his pocket. Untwisting it, he stared in frustration at the letters written on it. Then he pounded on the wall and bellowed, "Peg!"

A few minutes later, his neighbor and occasional mistress appeared, already dressed for an evening on the streets. "Read me this," he said, thrusting the paper at her.

"It'll cost you a penny," she said, but he raised his fist and she immediately reconsidered. Walking over to the table, she peered at the note in the light of the single candle. "It don't make much sense. It just says 'Lord Thor-ver-ton,' and underneath is writ 'fifty guineas.' Coo-ee, that's a lot of money."

She looked at him with speculation in her eyes, but he made no effort to explain. The fewer people who knew about this business, the better. Taking back the piece of paper, he sent Peg on her way with a scowl that promised she'd be sorry if she ever mentioned a word of his business to anyone else.

Meribe paced back and forth in the sitting room. Aunt Phillipa and Hester had gone to Madame Parfleur's to order some new dresses, leaving her behind, and all because she was afraid that if she went out, Lord Thorverton would once again "chance" to meet her. Why, she was becoming little more than a prisoner in her own house. Things had clearly gone too far.

But what could she do? That wretched man persisted in playing the hero. Hadn't anyone ever told him that heroes were quite often killed while performing their acts of bravery? Why could she not make him understand that it was not worth risking his life just so that she would not have to endure being stared at and whispered about?

Her thoughts were interrupted by a knock at the door, which was opened a moment later by Smucker. "Beg pardon, Miss Meribe, but there is a lady here to see you."

Meribe looked at him in astonishment. None of her friends had paid a single call since she had been dubbed the Black Widow. The few visitors they'd had this Season had come to see either Aunt Phillipa or Hester.

"Are you sure she wishes to see me, Smucker?"

"Quite sure, miss."

"Very well, I shall see her." Perhaps it was a friend from back home—someone only visiting in London for a few days. Or perhaps . . . No, she could not think of any other possibilities.

A few minutes later the butler ushered Lady Hazelmore into the room, and it was all Meribe could do to hide her astonishment—and her curiosity. Whatever had compelled this woman to approach her?

Lady Hazelmore's greetings were not only profuse but also couched in such terms that anyone hearing her might easily mistake the two of them for bosom bows. Then Meribe waited with impatience while the other woman rattled on, expressing her views on the weather (unseasonably hot) and the dance the night before (a terrible crush) and the new dress she had ordered (a delightful confection in silver and pink).

Finally, after about ten minutes of idle chitchat, Lady Hazelmore came to the point. "I noticed you were with Lord Thorverton last night."

Somehow Meribe was not at all surprised that his name had come up—in fact, she had been expecting it ever since Lady Hazelmore had entered the room. "Yes," she said briefly. She had never before taken anyone in instant dislike, but she now had a strong premonition that this woman was not here to offer her friendship—that Lady Hazelmore had some ulterior motive for her visit.

"I felt it was my Christian duty to come and warn you." Lady Hazelmore smiled, but Meribe could see neither good humor nor kindness in the smile.

"There is no need to warn anyone," Meribe said rather sharply. "Lord Thorverton is well aware of the rumors connected with my name."

"No, no, my dear, I was not thinking of *that*. Know-

ing how you have suffered from your terrible afflic-
tion . . .''

Meribe felt herself stiffen, and she began to hate the
other woman for her casual remarks, whose cruelty was
scarcely concealed by the smiles that accompanied them.

''. . . and knowing what scandalous gossip has already
been spread far and wide about your, uh, misfortunes,
shall we say?'' She smiled sweetly, revealing matching
dimples. ''I felt it was no less than my duty to come here
and warn you, lest you suffer even more on my account.
I should feel forever guilty if I caused you even a second
of additional pain. You see . . . Demetrius and I . . .
How shall I say this?''

Meribe suspected that Lady Hazelmore knew exactly
how she was going to say whatever spiteful words she
had come prepared to spill out. More than likely she had
practiced each little hesitation, each falsely sweet smile,
in front of the mirror.

''I have known Demetrius since I was quite young. We
were, in fact, childhood sweethearts, and everyone knew
that someday we would marry.''

She paused, watching Meribe out of the corner of her
eye to see what effect her words were having, but Meribe
managed—she hoped—to keep her smile bland. ''How
nice,'' she murmured, not wishing to let this woman
know exactly how much pain her words were causing.

''Three years ago, we became formally betrothed, and
dear Demetrius swore that he would love me forever.
Indeed, I thought at the time that I loved him also.'' She
dabbed at her eyes with her handkerchief, but Meribe
could see no sign of tears.

''But alas, I was young and did not know my own
heart. I certainly did not plan to fall in love with Hazelmore, but he was so persistent, and I could not resist his
entreaties. A week before I was to have wedded dearest
Demetrius, I eloped with Hazelmore to the Continent.''

Meribe stared in astonishment. ''You *jilted* Lord
Thorverton?''

''Oh, you must not think badly of me,'' Lady Hazelmore cried out, affecting deep distress. ''I was quite
young and so much in love, I could see no other way out.

I did not wish to break Demetrius's heart, but how could I marry him when my own heart was given to another?''

"You could have simply asked him to release you from the betrothal," Meribe said.

"I was not brave enough to face him," Lady Hazelmore said, again dabbing at her eyes. "I could not bear to see his grief. I was so young, barely eighteen, and since I had ceased to love him, somehow it seemed as if he must also have stopped loving me. If I had known I was breaking his heart—alas, I do not know what I would have done, for Hazelmore threatened to kill himself if I wedded another. As it was, we were forced to flee to France, lest Demetrius challenge my dearest Hazelmore to a duel. He is a deadly shot, you know—Demetrius, that is. But Hazelmore is more adept with a clever rhyme.''

How ridiculously dramatic this foolish woman is, Meribe thought. It amazed her that anyone could be so silly and yet take herself so seriously.

"It was only later that I realized I had broken dear Demetrius's heart, but by then there was nothing I could do to ease his pain. I returned from France to discover that he had withdrawn from society completely, shutting himself away in Devon, finding what consolation he could with his horses.''

"I fail to see how this concerns me," Meribe said flatly. "I am not at all interested in old gossip.''

Looking a trifle sulky that her efforts were not achieving the proper effect, Lady Hazelmore continued. "When I heard Thorverton was again in London, I was properly astonished. I thought—I hoped, I even dared to dream—that perhaps his heart was mended. But when I saw him last night, I could not doubt that he still loves me. What am I to do, Miss Prestwich?''

"Well, you and your husband could leave London for a while," Meribe said. Her matter-of-fact answer did not at all please her visitor.

"Leave London? But it is the height of the Season! Surely you are not suggesting I forgo all the festivities?''

"It would seem to be the proper thing to do if you

truly wish to avoid causing Lord Thorverton any unnecessary pain.''

Lady Hazelmore pouted, which she did most becomingly. ''I cannot believe that dear Demetrius would want me to suffer also. Loving me the way he does, I am sure he would want me to be happy.''

Meribe shrugged. ''It would appear that one or the other of you must suffer, then.''

Standing up, Lady Hazelmore said rather crossly, ''I came here out of the goodness of my heart to warn you that if you are so foolish as to fall in love with Lord Thorverton, you will also know the pain of unrequited love.''

''Why is that?'' Meribe asked, deliberately playing the part of a naive little fool.

''Because he will never love anyone but me!'' the beauty cried out, displaying for the first time an honest emotion unaccompanied by any practiced expressions.

Watching her visitor stalk out of the room, Meribe did not know whether to laugh or to cry. It was hard to believe that Lord Thorverton could ever have loved such a silly, posturing nincompoop as Lady Hazelmore. On the other hand, it was common knowledge that love made fools of men . . . and women.

It was quite likely that she herself was the biggest fool. Without admitting it to herself, she had been hoping that Lord Thorverton would fall in love with her—that the pretense would become reality and that he would court her in earnest.

How ridiculous. Even if he had recovered from his broken heart—and the expression on his face yesterday evening when he had first seen Lady Hazelmore suggested that he had not—then why on earth would he fall in love with her?

Walking across the room to the fireplace, she stared at herself in the mirror above the mantel. There was nothing in particular wrong with her looks, but on the other hand, there were dozens of other girls equally pretty or even prettier. Moreover, she was getting rather long in the tooth—why, she was almost one-and-twenty!

Returning to her seat by the window, she picked up

her needlework and stared at it in disgust. It was really time to admit that she was never going to become proficient at embroidery . . . or tatting . . . or watercolors . . . or playing the piano . . . or speaking French and Italian. Aunt Phillipa insisted that she had the ability to learn if she would only set her mind to it, but that was the problem: she just could not bring herself to care about any of those things.

Maybe when they returned to Norfolk—since she would then be of age—she could insist that she have a garden plot of her own. Maybe once she put on her caps and admitted to the world that she was a spinster, then it would not matter so much if she grubbed about in the dirt? Maybe she would only be thought eccentric, which was surely allowable for an old maid, was it not?

Maybe she could even stand up to Aunt Phillipa and *demand* that she be allowed to make her own decisions. And maybe pigs could fly.

She knew herself well enough to admit that she would never be able to win an argument with her aunt, or her sister either. Which was another reason Lord Thorverton was not likely to fall in love with her. A man of his courage and strong convictions would want a woman who was brave, who was resolute, who could stand up to people and stare them out of countenance. He would definitely not want to marry a girl with no backbone at all.

Angry with herself, she stabbed the needle into the cloth so hard, one of the cross threads broke, creating a small hole. She looked at it in dismay, well aware that her aunt would be most annoyed with her.

Then, with resolution she had not known she had, she removed the piece from its frame, carried it down to the kitchen, and threw it into the fire. She felt more satisfaction watching it burn than she had ever felt while she was working on it.

Demetrius looked up from his desk to see his mother enter the library without knocking, a militant expression on her face.

"I want a word with you. How *dare* you refuse to come up and take tea with my guests! When McDougal told me you said you were too *busy,* I was so mortified I almost *died.*"

"I regret if I caused you any embarrassment, but I have already told you repeatedly that I am not interested in meeting the daughters of any of your friends."

"And yet you are apparently eager to *throw* yourself at that brazen hussy, that Black Widow!"

"Be careful what you say. I will not allow you or anyone else to use that disgusting nickname, Mother."

"I shall call that wretched female anything I like!"

Demetrius stared at her coldly, wondering what he had done to deserve such a mother, whose idea of Christian charity consisted of giving ten pounds to the poor of the parish once a year during the yuletide season. "Understand this, Mother: If you ever again refer to Miss Prestwich in such a way, I shall no longer allow you the use of this house."

"You would not dare do such a thing! Why, what would people say?"

"Do you know, Mother, I have never especially cared what 'people' say. Please believe me—I am quite serious about this. Do not think to test my patience, for on this subject I have none."

"You are an unnatural son to speak so to your own mother. And I am sure you are encouraging your little brother to disregard my wishes also."

"Collier is no longer little. He is almost one-and-twenty and quite capable of being disobedient on his own."

"Oh," she moaned, clutching her handkerchief to her breast, "you are going to be the death of me. It is a good thing your dear papa is not alive to hear you speak to me in such a manner!"

With that parting shot, she left the room before Demetrius could remind her that "dear papa" had been every bit as insubordinate as his elder son.

4

Being in Tattersall's was not quite as good as being in his own stables back in Devon, Demetrius admitted to himself, but it was the next best thing. Not only were there horses here, but also men who knew horses, which made it a welcome change from the ballrooms of London.

"Now, why would you be so interested in watching a pretty little filly like this be put through her paces?"

Recognizing the voice behind him, Demetrius was smiling even before he turned around. "Hennessey, well met! What brings you across the Irish Sea? Are you buying or selling?"

"Now, that's a daft question—if it was another horse I'd be needing, it's Dublin where I'd be finding meself. Not that there's anything wrong with an English horse if an Irish one is not available."

The redheaded Irishman delighted in playing the role of unlettered country bumpkin, especially when buying or selling horses, but Demetrius knew that despite outward appearances, Thomas Hennessey was not only the owner of a large Irish estate with a flourishing thoroughbred stud, but he had also been educated at Oxford and was married to the daughter of an English earl.

"Which means you will not be bidding against me today?"

"Certainly not if you're looking to buy this sweet little thing. She's not up to my weight, and certainly not up to yours, which makes me wonder if there is some truth to the rumors that are trotting around London. I've heard you're planning to be hitched in tandem with a certain young lady, although I'd not have credited it. Still and all, if you're buying a lady's mount . . . ." He let his voice trail off suggestively.

"Miss Prestwich does not ride," Demetrius replied, deliberately ignoring the obviously more intriguing question of what his intentions were concerning the lady in question. He had no doubt that Hennessey could hold his tongue if need be, but on the other hand, Tattersall's was not the place to hold a private discussion.

"Doesn't ride? Now you have really piqued my curiosity."

"Tell me, are you superstitious as well as curious?"

"As an Irishman born and bred, I would be denying my heritage were I not to believe in the little people—elves and fairies and leprechauns and the like. But if you are asking do I believe a certain young lady is afflicted with a fatal curse, then I must admit I would find it easier to believe that horses had wings."

"I plan to exercise my horse early tomorrow in Hyde Park," Demetrius said in an undertone.

Hennessey nodded his agreement to the proposed meeting, and Demetrius continued smoothly, "Actually, I did not come here to purchase a horse. My brother asked me to meet him, but I confess, he did not say whether he wishes to avail himself of my expert advice about horses or about women."

As it turned out, it was neither horses nor women, but gambling debts. "You've done what?"

"You needn't shout. It is only one hundred and fifty pounds," Collier said, his eyes not quite meeting Demetrius's.

"Only? People have been thrown into debtors' prison for owing less than that amount. Whatever possessed you to gamble with money you did not have?"

"Don't lecture me, big brother. I have already berated myself thoroughly for being so gullible. I freely admit it was a stupid thing to do, although at the time it seemed as if it would be a sure thing."

"A sure thing? Saints preserve us," Demetrius muttered.

"I will pay you back when I get next quarter's allowance."

"And in the meantime, I am not to consider you a 'hardened gamester,' as you put it so nicely the other day?"

Collier's expression became somewhat sulky. "Just tell me whether you will lend me the money or not, because if you refuse to oblige me in this, I shall have to look elsewhere."

"Oh, I will be happy to lend you the money, but only under one condition."

"What condition?"

"That you give up your rooms at the Albany and move back home."

The sulky expression was gone now, replaced by open anger. "Blast it all, Demetrius, I am not a child to be ordered about so. I am a man, and it is entirely my own decision where I live."

Demetrius shrugged. "I could point out that running up debts that one does not have the means to pay off is not the mark of an adult, but I do not wish to prolong this discussion unduly. I have told you what your options are, so tell me your decision—do you wish me to lend you the money or not?"

Collier was obviously torn between the desire to reject Demetrius's money and the strings attached to it, and the knowledge that he would doubtless have difficulty finding a friend his own age who had one hundred and fifty pounds to spare this close to the end of the quarter.

"Very well, I shall move back home," he said finally, and Demetrius wrote out a bank draft on the spot.

After Collier departed, Demetrius proved himself just as foolish as his brother by outbidding Fabersham for the filly that would be perfect for Miss Meribe Prestwich . . . if she could ride, which she could not.

London was obviously having an adverse affect on him, he admitted while arranging for his new horse to be delivered to his stable. Perhaps it was time to give up playing knight-errant and return to Devon before he did something even more rash.

* * *

Although the day was overcast, the park was crowded, and shortly after they entered Hyde Park, Meribe was asking herself why she had ever thought her situation might have changed since the last time she had walked along Rotten Row. Had she been secretly hoping that Lord Thorverton's efforts might already have convinced people that she was not all that dangerous?

If so, it had clearly been wishful thinking, because the stares were still quite rude and the people moved out of her path just as rapidly as they had done when she had come here in the beginning of April. After that first expedition, she had decided that nothing would induce her to repeat the experience.

So why had she given in to Hester's importunities? With Jane, their abigail, feeling too poorly to walk in the park today, Hester could just as easily have stayed home for once, rather than persuading Meribe to accompany her.

"Look over there—Lord Thorverton is just driving through the gate," Hester now said in a sharp voice. "Although I must say I am not surprised to see him. He manages to turn up wherever we go. I begin to suspect that you are secretly sending him notes informing him in advance of all our plans."

"Hester! That is a terrible accusation to make. I would never dream of behaving in such a brazen manner. How can you even suggest such a thing?"

"Well, perhaps you have not, but the only other explanation is that he has set one of his servants to spy on us. Well, this time his deviousness is not going to benefit him in the slightest." Hester grabbed Meribe's arm and began to hustle her along the path away from the approaching carriage.

"Release my arm," Meribe hissed, pulling back. "You are only making us conspicuous by charging along at such a reckless pace."

"I? It is not me everyone is staring at. And if you do not wish to be gawked at, you should have stayed home today. I could have brought one of the other maids in your place."

Which was not at all what Hester had asserted earlier

when she had insisted that she would be utterly cast down if Meribe refused this one tiny favor. But at least her sister now moderated her pace somewhat, for which Meribe was thankful. "Oh, Hester, must we always quarrel?"

"As long as you keep seeing that man, we must."

"What do you have against Lord Thorverton?"

"I strongly suspect he is playing you for a fool. Everyone knows that Diana Fairgrove broke his heart when she eloped with Lord Hazelmore. You delude yourself if you think Lord Thorverton will marry an insignificant little nobody like you after he has been betrothed to such a beauty. After all, if it were not for the fact that all your suitors have met untimely ends, you would be quite overlooked by society."

Meribe dug in her heels and stopped so abruptly she managed to pull her arm free from her sister's grasp. "You go too far this time," she said in a choked voice.

Turning around, she began to walk as quickly as possible in the opposite direction, her only intention being to put as much distance between herself and her sister as possible. The tears in her eyes made it difficult to see where she was going, so it must have been fate that led her directly past Lord Thorverton's carriage, which was stalled behind another phaeton and two landaus.

"Good afternoon, Miss Prestwich," he said politely, his familiar voice halting her headlong flight. "Would you care to join me for a turn around the park?"

About to make her usual excuses, Meribe abruptly changed her mind. The opportunity to spend a little time with a person who did not fuss and crab at her—with someone who seemed actually to enjoy her company—was too tempting to refuse.

Amid murmurs and gasps from the passersby, she allowed his groom, who had sprung down from the back of the phaeton, to assist her into the carriage. Then he stepped back out of the way, and Lord Thorverton flicked the reins, and the carriage moved forward, albeit slowly, since the crush of vehicles was too great to permit sustained progress.

"Something has upset you," he said in a low voice.

Surreptitiously wiping a tear from the corner of her eye with the tip of her glove, Meribe was grateful that he was looking at his horses and not at her. She did not want him to gain the erroneous impression that she was by nature a watering pot.

"It was nothing, really. My sister sometimes . . ." She could not think of a tactful way to say that Hester's barbed comments sometimes cut to the quick, but Lord Thorverton nodded anyway, understanding what she meant without needing her to finish the sentence. It was one of the things that made him such an easy person to converse with.

"Do you know," he said, a smile tugging at the corners of his mouth, "it is not always easy being the elder brother or sister. I imagine my younger brother sometimes finds me every bit as aggravating as you do your sister."

Now, that was plainly a taradiddle. Lord Thorverton was so easygoing, so kindhearted, so . . . so amiable that he could never say anything unkind to anyone, especially not to his own brother. Although—she sneaked a peek at him—she had to admit that when he became angry about an injustice, he could look truly formidable.

Luckily he had never become angry at her, and she could only pray that circumstances would never force her to feel the brunt of his wrath.

Glancing at the carriage approaching them, Meribe was caught totally off-guard by the sight of Lady Hazelmore, who waved gaily at them, or rather, she was waving and smiling at Lord Thorverton while ignoring Meribe as if they had never been introduced—as if she had never come to the Prestwich residence and poured her heart out to Meribe.

Perhaps it was the deliberate slight that made Meribe ask the question that had been nagging at her for days, ever since she had heard the tale of the broken betrothal . . . or perhaps it was pure jealousy that Lord Thorverton had just now politely tipped his hat to the other woman. Whatever her motive, as soon as the other carriage was safely past them, Meribe heard herself blurt out the question she had never intended to ask.

"Was your heart truly broken?"

Lord Thorverton looked down at her, his expression enigmatic. "My heart?"

Even though she would have preferred to jump down out of the carriage and run away, she said with the best display of boldness that she could muster, "Lady Hazelmore paid me a visit a few days ago and told me the whole story of your betrothal and her subsequent elopement."

"She did what?" Clearly Lord Thorverton was as astonished as she herself had been. "Why on earth would she do something like that?"

"I am sure I could not say what her true motives were," Meribe answered, unaccountably feeling a little miffed that he had not immediately asserted that his heart was still completely intact. "In any case, she told me she felt it was her duty to warn me that you are merely trifling with my affections—that you will never actually marry me."

"You did not tell her about our plan, did you?" he asked, intentionally—or so it seemed to her—ignoring the much more interesting question of whether or not his heart had been broken.

"As a matter of fact, I did not tell her anything. Unlike some people, I am quite able to control my tongue," Meribe said rather crossly, deliberately overlooking the fact that her tongue had been running away with her ever since she joined Lord Thorverton in his carriage.

"I am relieved to hear that," he said. "I should hate to think my exertions on your behalf were all for naught."

It was common knowledge back in Norfolk that Meribe's disposition was quite even. She had never been given to displays of temper like her older sister. Right now, however, Meribe realized that a few well-chosen oaths would go a long way toward relieving her aggravation—aggravation caused both directly and indirectly by the man seated beside her.

Instead, remembering her aunt's frequent admonitions to behave in a ladylike manner at all times, Meribe contented herself with saying, "We were not discussing your efforts to disprove the curse. The question that I asked—

and which you have not yet answered—is whether or not your heart was broken.''

And secondarily, she said to herself, some of us were wondering what your intentions are. But she knew the answer to that. He had made it clear from the beginning that he was merely being gallant—that he was not smitten by her charms, which Hester had just insisted were nonexistent.

He grinned, then actually chuckled. ''Without wishing to say anything derogatory about someone I have been acquainted with since childhood, not a day has gone by since then that I have not been grateful to a merciful providence for my narrow escape.''

There was no way she could doubt that he was telling the truth—there was too much boyish glee in his smile to think he was merely attempting to conceal a broken heart. She could not keep a similar smile from her own face, and the rest of the drive around the park was spent discussing quite amiably the news he had received from Devon about his stud.

It must have been an evil fairy that had inspired Lady Letitia to invite Lady Thorverton to take a turn around the park in her carriage. Although Dorothea could be a pleasant-enough companion in the normal course of events, she was really a most disagreeable woman when things did not fall out according to her wishes. And it had become immediately—but unfortunately not immediately enough—obvious to Lady Letitia that her companion was most definitely having an off day.

Instead of showing proper appreciation for the honor of sitting beside Lady Letitia, Dorothea was casting fulminating looks at her son, whose carriage was but a short distance ahead of them.

''Control yourself, Dorothea, if you please. You look as if you are ready to throw yourself in front of your son's phaeton, which is a bit too dramatic even for you. Are you so set on having your son remain a bachelor?''

''Do not be ridiculous—I should like nothing better than to have him marry and set up his nursery, but that wretched boy refuses point-blank to meet the daughters of any of my friends.''

"I rather think he has already got his heart set on a particular young lady.''

"Fustian! That wretched girl is nothing more than a scheming hussy seeking to entrap my son, and he is only encouraging her because he knows it will upset me. His father was just such a one—obstinate, stubborn, pig-headed. And Demetrius takes after him—he positively delights in running counter to my wishes. I am sure if I welcomed that chit with open arms, he would drop her in an instant.''

Dorothea had always been prideful, even as a young girl, and Lady Letitia found it no more attractive now than she had years earlier. It was surprising that Demetrius and Collier had turned out so nicely. They obviously had a lot of their father in them. He had been such a sweet man, but no match really for his wife.

"I suppose you have had a hand in this,'' Lady Thorverton now muttered. "I know very well that you delight in matchmaking.''

"I? Really, Dorothea, it was not I who sent a letter to Devon demanding that Lord Thorverton come posthaste to London.''

"Well, now that he has accomplished the task I gave him, I am amazed that he has not rushed back to his precious horses.''

What amazed Lady Letitia was how quickly certain people could give her a headache. Thank goodness neither Demetrius nor Collier had inherited their mother's self-centeredness and conceit.

After having been abandoned in public by her sister, Hester was quite relieved when Lionell Rudd minced over to where she was standing and invited her to walk along with him a bit.

"It is not fair,'' she said, taking his arm.

"What is not fair, my love?'' Lionell asked.

"Over there—my sister,'' was all Hester said before she turned her head away, unable to bear the sight of Meribe smiling and talking with Lord Thorverton. Only a few more weeks and it would not matter, but for now he absolutely must not court Meribe—not when everything could still be lost.

"He does give the impression of being totally infatuated with her, I must admit," Lionell said with a smirk.

"You may find it amusing, but I do not."

"Tsk, tsk, do I detect a note of jealousy in your voice? Pray moderate your tones, my sweet, else you will encourage all and sundry to be amused at your expense."

Lowering her voice, she persisted in trying to elicit his opinion. "I want to know what you think. Are Thorverton's intentions serious? Or is he merely trifling with her? It is most important that I know."

"Who can predict what any man will do? All I can tell you is that the odds in the clubs are now two to one that Thorverton will expire before the month of May is out, and seven to one that he will not live to see July, so I would say the consensus is that he is seriously courting your sister."

"It is just not fair," Hester repeated, feeling physically ill at the mere thought of her sister being betrothed once again.

"Might I suggest your new periwinkle-blue waistcoat?" Fredericks said, his expression carefully bland.

"I was unaware that I had a new waistcoat," Demetrius replied with a frown.

"A present from your mother," his valet answered a bit too promptly.

For a moment Demetrius was torn between anger and amusement. "Need I point out that I have not allowed my mother to pick out my clothes since I ceased wearing short coats?"

"Do you wish me to dispose of the offending garment, then, m'lord?"

"That depends on how offensive it is," Demetrius replied, unable to keep a straight face any longer.

"Oh, it is actually quite stunning." With a flourish, Fredericks produced the aforementioned waistcoat from behind his back.

He was right. At the first sight of the waistcoat, Demetrius was too stunned to speak for a few minutes. The garment may have been blue, but very little of the fabric was showing, so encrusted was it with gold and silver embroidery, seed pearls, and . . .

"Diamonds, Fredericks? Have my mother's wits gone begging? Does she really expect me to wear that . . . that . . . ?" Words failed him again.

"Actually, this is only the first of many. The boy who delivered it informed me that your mother has ordered an entire wardrobe for you from Nugee."

"Ecod, you make my blood run cold!"

"I took the liberty of using your name to cancel the remainder of the items," the valet said smoothly. "I trust that meets with your approval?"

"Can you doubt it? You have definitely earned yourself a raise," Demetrius said, still staring in awe at the waist-coat.

There was a knock at the door, and Fredericks opened it to admit the butler.

"Beg pardon, m'lord, but Lady Thorverton requests that you join her in the drawing room."

"Who does she have with her this time?"

"Why, no one," McDougal answered. "I believe she is expecting company for dinner, but for the moment she wishes to speak with you alone."

"Then tell her I shall be down when I am finished dressing."

It was about ten minutes before Demetrius joined his mother, who eyed him through her quizzing glass with distaste.

"That coat was obviously made by that wretched little man—I shall not dignify him by calling him a tailor—in Tavistock. Well, you will be pleased to know that I have taken steps to procure a wardrobe for you that is more suited to London."

Demetrius was far from pleased, and he was tempted to tell her that her plans had already suffered a major setback, but he held his tongue. He was not really in the mood to listen to the recriminations and accusations that were bound to ensue when she discovered for herself that her orders had been canceled.

"Was there anything else you wished to discuss with me besides the unsuitability of my attire?"

"Yes, I have invited several friends over for dinner this evening. They have all expressed an eagerness to meet you."

"I am sorry to disappoint them, madam, but I have already made my plans for this evening." He hadn't actually decided how he would spend the evening, but under no circumstances was he going to let his mother know that. She was too determined to play the matchmaker.

"Then you must simply cancel them. It lacks but an hour until our guests arrive, and you will quite throw off the numbers if you refuse to oblige me in this small matter."

Demetrius shrugged. "I am afraid that is not possible. You should have consulted me earlier."

"And would you have agreed if I had?"

"Certainly not," he said bluntly, "but that would have given you time to arrange for someone in my stead."

"I cannot understand why you delight in embarrassing me this way in front of my friends."

"You wrong me, madam. I have always done my best to avoid any contact with your friends."

"Oh, oh, how can you speak this way to your own mother?" Clutching her hands to her breast, she collapsed against the back of the settee. "What have I done to deserve such ungrateful sons? If your father could only see how you flout my every wish, he would turn over in his grave. That I should have nursed two such vipers to my bosom! It is all that wretched woman's fault—she has turned you against me!"

"If by 'that wretched woman' you are referring to Miss Prestwich, you might consider inviting her to dine with us. I should be quite agreeable to a dinner party here that included her."

Instantly his mother abandoned her die-away airs. Jumping to her feet, she closed the distance between them and glared up at him. "The Prestwichs may still be acceptable to some people, although they are never invited where there are marriageable sons, but be that as it may, never, *never* shall I invite any member of that family into *my* house!"

Accustomed as he was to his mother's dramatic utterances, Demetrius stood his ground without flinching. "I was unaware that you were acquainted with Miss Meribe Prestwich."

"I have never been introduced to her, nor do I ever intend to acknowledge her in any way. She is niece to that hateful Miss Phillipa Prestwich, which is enough to condemn her in my eyes. If you only knew what that horrid woman did to my dear brother, you would cast aside your inamorata."

She was not precisely his beloved, but Demetrius had no intention of revealing to his mother the exact nature of his relationship with the youngest Miss Prestwich. But on the other hand, his curiosity was definitely aroused. "So what did the aunt do that was so terrible?"

"I do not actually know the details," his mother replied, "but whatever she did, it was terrible enough that dear Humphrey's life was ruined."

"Ruined? In what way? He has never complained to me, and he appears to be quite happy with his current situation."

"That is all that you know! Why, that beastly woman is the reason he has remained a bachelor to this day."

"You do not think it has been merely my uncle's fondness for self-indulgence that has kept him from stepping into the parson's mousetrap?"

"Now you insult my poor mistreated brother! Oh, I knew you would not understand. You have not an ounce of sensibility."

And his mother, he decided, had not a particle of sense. "So far you have given me nothing to understand—you have made only the vaguest of accusations."

"Which should be enough if you were only a loving, obedient son. In any case, I cannot tell you what I do not know. If you wish to discover all the sordid particulars, you must apply to your uncle."

"I intend to do just that," Demetrius replied.

Uncle Humphrey was not in his rooms, nor in his club, but fortunately Demetrius ran into a man he recognized as one of his uncle's cronies.

"Swinton? Heard he was dining with Mannlius this evening."

Further questioning elicited directions to Lord Mannlius's town house, which was in Hanover Square. Since the night was balmy and his destination not too distant, Demetrius elected to walk instead of taking a hack.

He found the correct house without difficulty, but gaining entrance was another matter altogether.

"I regret, my lord, but I cannot allow you to interrupt the gentlemen," the butler said quite firmly. "If you would care to wait in the library until the dinner is over?"

"I only wish to speak with my uncle briefly," Demetrius replied.

"I am afraid you do not fully understand the circumstances. His Royal Highness, the Prince of Wales, is also dining with my lord, and it would simply not do for someone to burst in upon them uninvited."

"Could you not simply take a note in to my uncle, asking him to step out into the hall for a minute?"

Clearly shocked, the butler drew himself up even more stiffly. "Lord Thorverton, how can you even suggest such a thing? No one is permitted to leave before the Prince departs. Now, if you wish to wait in the library, you may, but under no circumstances whatsoever can you disturb our royal guest. The wait should not be overlong, since the port has already been taken in."

The house being quite stuffy and grossly overheated, Demetrius chose to wait in the little park in the center of the square. The butler willingly agreed to inform Uncle Humphrey that his nephew wished to speak to him.

After slightly more than half an hour, an ornate coach pulled by six horses drew up in front of Mannlius's residence, and four liveried outriders sprang down to assist the portly gentleman who ponderously descended the steps and with great difficulty managed to climb into the carriage. Then the lackeys took their positions again, the coachman cracked his whip, and the carriage rolled away.

A few minutes later another man appeared in the doorway, and Demetrius recognized his uncle. The butler, who was pointing toward Demetrius, was obviously telling his uncle that he was waiting to speak with him.

Pushing himself away from the fence against which he had been leaning, Demetrius started toward the street. He had gone only a few steps when a low voice behind him whispered hoarsely, "Lord Thorverton?"

Demetrius started to turn, but before he could see who was addressing him, a bag was thrown over his head and twisted tightly around his neck, choking the breath out of him.

Desperately he clawed at the cloth, trying to relieve the pressure on his windpipe before he passed out from lack of oxygen, but it was an unequal contest. Not only was his assailant incredibly strong, but he had also attacked from behind, which gave him all the advantage.

Despite his best efforts to break free, Demetrius could feel his arms beginning to weaken, and he knew that the darkness closing in on him was not entirely owing to the hood covering his eyes.

5

Slowly and relentlessly Demetrius was forced to his knees, and his situation became so desperate that it took him a moment to realize the pounding in his ears was actually the sound of running footsteps.

Suddenly the man holding him gave a grunt of pain, and the pressure on Demetrius's neck was gone. Barely conscious, he fell forward on the ground, gasping for breath.

Rough hands pushed him over on his back, and the hood was jerked off his head. Kneeling beside him, staring down at him with horrified looks, were his uncle and Lord Mannlius's butler. The assailant was nowhere to be seen.

"Are you all right? Speak to me!"

Uncle Humphrey shook him, but Demetrius was still unable to talk. All he could do was nod his head, but that was apparently enough to reassure his uncle, who pushed himself ponderously to his feet.

"I cannot believe such a dreadful thing could have happened right here in Hanover Square," the butler wailed, wringing his hands. "Oh, my, suppose he had attacked His Royal Majesty!"

Hearing that remark, Demetrius abruptly remembered the words that had come out of the darkness—*Lord Thorverton*—and he knew the Prince had been in no danger.

A more immediate puzzle was how his two rescuers had managed to fight off the attacker so easily. Feeling his breathing and heartbeat gradually returning to normal, Demetrius sat up, waited until his head was no longer dizzy, and then got to his feet.

"How the devil did you stop that giant?" were the first words he uttered.

"Slashed his arm," his uncle replied, which did nothing to explain what had happened. Uncle Humphrey bent over and picked up a sword from the grass and waved its bloody tip in front of Demetrius's face.

"Where the deuce did you get that thing?"

"Found it in a little shop in Italy—Florence, I believe it was. The shopkeeper had a collection of the most fiendishly clever weapons. Poison rings, chairs with daggers that would spring out and kill whoever was sitting in them, gloves with poisoned needles worked into the leather, so that if you shook a man's hand, he would die hours later without even knowing anything was wrong. Typical of the Italians to be so devious."

The butler produced a white handkerchief, and Uncle Humphrey carefully wiped the blade clean. Then the butler handed over a long object of some sort, and Humphrey slid the sword into it, there was a click, and suddenly Demetrius was looking at his uncle's cane.

"A concealed sword? All the years you have carried your cane, and I had no suspicion there was anything out of the ordinary about it."

"That's the beauty of it. Can't very well go around with a regular sword and scabbard strapped to my waist. I'd look a proper fool, and doubtless it would cause my jacket to hang crooked."

"You amaze me, Uncle."

"Pish tosh, there is nothing to it. I was happy to have a chance to use the sword after all these years. Of course the cane is quite sturdy and rather stylish too, but I have long wished for an opportunity to try the sword. In any event, I hope this has taught you a lesson, my boy."

"Indeed, I shall procure passage to Italy as soon as may be. Where did you say that shop was located?"

His uncle snorted. "In Florence, but I was not suggesting you try to find another concealed sword; I was referring to this attack. I hope you are now ready to admit that wretched woman's niece is cursed."

Again the words of the attacker echoed in Demetrius's mind—*Lord Thorverton*. Only two words, but they were enough to let him know that this had been no coincidence. Neither fate nor a fatal curse had been behind this brush with death. It had been deliberate, well-planned, directed specifically at him, and it would have been successful if Uncle Humphrey had not unexpectedly produced his sword.

That being the case, the question that could not be avoided was: who was behind the attack?

He was about to explain everything to his uncle, when he realized the butler, having brushed all the bits of grass off Demetrius's coat, was now trying to repair the damage done to his neckcloth. Prudence demanded that he wait until he and his uncle were private before continuing the discussion.

With great difficulty Demetrius managed to persuade Mannlius's butler that the crisis was over, that his assistance, although it had been most welcome, was no longer required, and that he could therefore return to his post.

"I told you that woman is poison—as deadly to associate with as one of the Borgias, don't you know," Humphrey said as they walked along in the direction of Demetrius's house. "I hope you will not be so foolhardy in the future as to ignore the curse."

"There is no curse, Uncle, and I was not a random victim. That bruiser knew my name."

Uncle Humphrey mulled over this new bit of information for a few minutes, then said, "I still say this attack was a direct result of your hanging around that Prestwich woman."

"I am afraid you are correct. The only other explanation is that Fabersham is mad at me for outbidding him for the filly at Tattersall's this morning."

"Nonsense. Fabersham may be hotheaded, and he would probably challenge you to a duel if you outbid him for an opera dancer, but not for a four-legged filly. No, no, it is bound to be the curse."

"Not a curse, I am afraid, but a flesh-and-blood villain. It is not fate that is disposing of Miss Prestwich's suitors. As insane as it sounds, it would appear that some *person* is determined to keep her unwedded. Which brings up the interesting question: did Fellerman fall into the Thames after imbibing a few too many, or was he pushed?''

"Pushed? Whatever are you talking about?''

"I am talking about a murderer,'' Demetrius said. "Was it truly a highwayman who waylaid Arleton, or was it perhaps our oversize friend who is now sporting a sore arm?''

"Now that I think on it, I recall that the driver of the dray that struck down Thurwell was reported to have been an excessively large man. But how could Miss Prestwich have earned the enmity of such riffraff?''

"You miss the point, Uncle. That man was undoubtedly well-paid for his efforts this evening.''

"The devil you say! Well, if that is the case, I trust I have put him out of business for a good while. And with a little luck, the wound will become infected, which will dispose of him for good.''

"But the question remains: who hired him?''

The mist was rising from the grass, and the park was virtually deserted except for a few grooms exercising their masters' horses. It would have been quite pleasant were it not for the fact that Demetrius's neck was still sore enough to keep him constantly reminded of the events of the night before.

"So who do you think is behind the attack?'' Hennessey asked after hearing the whole story.

"I confess, I have not yet got the vaguest suspicion,'' Demetrius replied.

"It could be any one of the men who have wagered large sums of money on your early demise.''

"That thought had occurred to me, and if it is true, then it is exceedingly unlikely that we shall ever identify the culprit. On the other hand, there is some circumstantial evidence to indicate that the same assailant may have been used on previous occasions, which, if true, would eliminate anyone involved merely because of a current wager.''

Hennessey nodded his agreement. "So what do you propose to do?''

"Try to discover a more plausible motive, I suppose. What else can I do?"

"In that case, I shall see what I can do about finding your overlarge friend. I have some contacts in Soho who may be able to provide us with a name. There cannot be too many men his size residing in London, and even fewer who have sword wounds in their arms."

"I thank you for your help, and I wish you luck."

"And if you think you would be needing a bit more protection, I've a couple of stout lads with me."

"Are you suggesting bodyguards? Thank you, but that will not be necessary. I think merely taking reasonable precautions will suffice. I shall take care not to wander around London alone at night, of that you may be sure. And I am seriously considering the purchase of a brace of pistols."

"Actually, the only real solution is to discover the villain, and you may count on me to do all I can."

Greed . . . revenge . . . ambition . . . expediency . . .

Sitting alone at his desk, Demetrius looked down at the list he had written. There were not actually very many motives for murder. One by one he considered them.

"Expediency"—was it possible that someone wished to marry Miss Meribe himself, and so was permanently eliminating all of his rivals? Rather a farfetched idea, since there did not appear to be any spurned suitors lurking about. Also, the method was a bit more drastic than necessary. Flowers and poetry were usually more effective than murder.

Drawing a line through "expediency," Demetrius turned his attention to "ambition," but no matter how he racked his brain, he could not come up with a single area where Miss Meribe might conceivably be standing in the way of someone else's goals.

She was not the reigning beauty—the Incomparable— of this Season or any previous Season, nor was she engaged in trade. She was not attempting to corner the market in wool or control the trade routes to China, or any such thing. Which meant he could eliminate thwarted ambition.

"Revenge" . . . that was a bit more difficult to determine. He could not, of course, say for sure if she had seriously harmed or even deeply offended anyone, although it seemed highly unlikely. To begin with, she had spent most of her life in a small town in Norfolk. If she had acquired an enemy, it would most likely have been there. But nothing untoward appeared to have happened to her in Norfolk, which meant the problem was centered in London. If she had done something horrible here, doubtless the gossips would have long ago spread every detail all over town.

Second, unlike her sister, Miss Meribe was such a gentle person, he could not picture her deliberately slighting anyone. Which meant the offense, if it had happened, would have been unintentional. Motive enough for the cut direct, but scarcely adequate for murder.

Which left "greed." The love of money is the root of all evil, or so the Bible said. So how much money was involved? And was Miss Meribe already rich, or did she merely stand to inherit a fortune? And more important, who would benefit if she died?

No, he was forgetting. None of the attacks had been directed against her. The question was better stated: who would benefit if she remained single?

He was still considering the possibilities when the door to his study was thrown open and Collier came storming into the room.

"Why did you not tell me this morning that you were attacked last night? Ecod, but I wish I had been there." Striding around the room, he made wild slashing motions with his arm, as if wielding a sword. "I would not have settled for wounding his arm, I would have run the blackguard through and through and left him lifeless on the ground."

"It needed only this," Demetrius muttered. Throwing down his quill, he said quite firmly, "Do cease this ridiculous posturing, Collier. I have no time for such childish nonsense."

"Childish!" Collier drew himself up and glared down at Demetrius. "I am not a child! I am nearly one-and-twenty."

Demetrius rubbed his forehead, where the beginning of a headache was announcing its presence. "I should have instructed Uncle Humphrey not to tell you, but I assumed he had more sense."

"I have not seen Uncle today," Collier said, his voice icy. "But the story of the attack against you is all over town. The talk in the clubs is of nothing else."

"The devil you say! Uncle cannot have been that indiscreet." To his chagrin, Demetrius abruptly remembered the second man who had rushed to his aid. The butler would naturally have told his employer, Lord Mannlius, who in turn would not have hesitated a moment to tell a hundred or so of his nearest and dearest cronies, who in turn . . .

With mounting horror Demetrius realized that if the story was indeed all over town, doubtless it had spread even to the Prestwich household. "Meribe," he said on a whisper. "What must she be thinking?"

Without stopping to soothe his brother's ruffled sensibilities, Demetrius dashed from the room. Hurrying to the mews behind the house, he saddled his horse and set off at a headlong gallop through the streets of London.

"Well, I hope you are satisfied."

Meribe looked up to see her sister enter the room and remove her bonnet, which she cast down onto a convenient chair.

"You are late for tea," Aunt Phillipa said crossly.

"It could not be helped," Hester replied. "You could hardly expect me to take my leave before I heard the entire story."

"What story?" Meribe asked, although in the deepest part of her soul she knew what Hester was about to say— and knew also that she did not want to hear even one word of Hester's tale.

"It is all your fault, you know," Hester said, sitting down and accepting a cup of tea from her aunt. "Goodness knows, you have been warned enough times that you were playing with fire."

"No, no," Meribe whispered, feeling her hands begin to shake, rattling her teacup in its saucer.

"Lord Thorverton was attacked last night in Hanover Square," Hester said bluntly.

"It is disgraceful that such a thing should have occurred, and in Hanover Square no less. It is the outside of enough that we in Mayfair pay good money to hire watchmen, and yet when one is needed, there is nary a one to be found. Still and all, it is nothing more than a relative of that horrible Humphrey Swinton deserves, I am sure," Aunt Philippa commented coldly. "And I am sure I told him on numerous occasions to stay away from you, Meribe. You cannot be blamed for that young man's death."

"Death?" Meribe croaked out, at once as chilled as if the blood in her veins had turned to ice water. "He is dead, then?"

Hester shrugged. "I heard he is still clinging to life by the skin of his teeth, but his family is in hourly expectation of bidding him a final farewell. They say he was set upon by three giants who beat him unmercifully and then hacked him to pieces. Would you please pass that plate of macaroons, sister dear?"

Feeling as if she were about to shatter into a million pieces, Meribe set down her teacup and rose to her feet. Without saying a word, she walked out of the room.

Behind her Hester called out, "Of course there are others who are insisting that his injuries are not really serious."

Demetrius galloped up to the Prestwich residence, sprang from his horse, tossed the reins and a shilling to a street urchin who was loitering nearby, and ran up the five steps leading to the front door. Banging on it vigorously with the knocker brought the butler, but not quickly enough to suit Demetrius.

As soon as the door was opened, he pushed past the servant and took the stairs two at a time. Behind him the butler cried out, "Here, now, you may not come barging in this way," but Demetrius ignored him, finding his own way to the drawing room that he had visited once before.

Throwing open the door, he entered quite unannounced. Only two women were in the room, both of whom stared at him in complete astonishment.

"You are looking remarkably fit for one who is reported to be on his deathbed," the eldest Miss Prestwich commented rather acerbically.

His worst fears confirmed, Demetrius felt his heart begin to race, and not from his recent dash up the stairs. "Where is your niece—Miss Meribe?" he asked.

"My niece is no concern of yours," Aunt Phillipa snapped out. "Smucker, throw this impertinent young jackanapes out of my house!"

The butler actually went so far as to lay a hand on Demetrius's arm, but one fierce scowl, and the little man jerked his hand away again as if he had been burned.

"I am not leaving until I speak with Miss Prestwich," Demetrius said resolutely. "So if you will not tell me where she is, I shall be forced to find her myself."

Hester began to giggle. "Oh, this is too delicious! The corpse walks! Tell me, kind sir, are you perchance a specter risen from the grave to terrify all the maidens?"

Ignoring her, Demetrius turned on his heel and started down the corridor, throwing open doors, checking each room for Miss Meribe. By the time he went up the stairs to the second floor, there was quite a procession behind him—the aunt, the sister, the butler, a footman, and two maids. All of them were protesting vigorously, and together they sounded like nothing so much as a gaggle of irate geese.

When he finally found the right door, his heart ached at the sight of the girl standing so still in the middle of the room, her arms wrapped tightly about herself, and her face as white as death. She did not move, not even when he entered the room.

"Meribe," he said softly, and she turned blind eyes toward him. "I am all right. I was not seriously hurt." To his relief, he saw recognition gradually bring color back to her face.

"Lord Thorverton? They said you were near death," she whispered. She reached out a hand to him, then started to sway.

He caught her in his arms before she could collapse,

and she clutched him desperately. "They said . . . they said . . ." She began to cry, great wrenching sobs.

Leaving the rest of the onlookers gawking in the doorway of the room, Aunt Phillipa stormed up to Demetrius and glared at him. "How dare you call my niece by her given name!"

He did not bother to reply. Staring impassively at the older woman, he continued to stroke Miss Prestwich's head where it rested against his chest. Finally, with a snort of disgust, the aunt stalked from the room, muttering her usual imprecations against the male of the species and salting her speech with curses against Humphrey Swinton and all his assorted relatives.

Miss Hester next attempted to interfere. "Really, Meribe, you are acting like the veriest watering pot. I vow you will quite ruin his lordship's waistcoat if you continue in this way."

"I suppose you are the one who brought home all the gossip?" Demetrius said, not doubting for a moment the truth of his assumption.

"And if I did? What business is it of yours?"

"A word of warning, Miss Prestwich. If you continue along the path you have chosen, someday you will come to regret every unkind word that you have ever uttered."

"Hah! You make me laugh," she replied, but her laughter sounded forced, and after a moment she turned her back on her weeping sister and left the room.

The butler, when he took over, showed more sense than the two women. "Move along now, all of you," he said. "The show is over. Go about your business."

He managed to shoo away all the servants except Jane, Miss Prestwich's abigail, who walked into the room and planted herself firmly on a chair by the window. Folding her arms across her chest, she glared at Demetrius, as if to say that wild horses could not make her abandon her mistress in such a compromising situation.

With the distractions removed from the scene, Demetrius turned all of his attention to the poor girl sobbing in his arms. His waistcoat was indeed already ruined, but he would gladly have sacrificed a dozen waistcoats if it would have saved her such pain.

He murmured little soothing words, and after an eternity—which was probably only five minutes or so—he was rewarded by a lessening of her tears.

"They said . . . you were attacked . . . by three men . . . last night," she finally managed to say.

For a moment he debated whether or not to tell her the truth. A lie would be so much kinder—but also so much more dangerous, were she ever to discover the truth.

"I was set upon by a single man, who did seem determined to dispatch me, but my uncle and a servant were nearby, and they managed very efficiently to rescue me. For my part, I cannot claim to have cut a very heroic figure."

His attempt at humor failed, and she pulled herself out of his arms, but only far enough that she could check him for injuries. With desperate fear in her eyes, she began feeling his arms and running her fingers over his chest, as if checking for injuries or bandages.

Catching her hands in both of his, he said in what he hoped was a reassuring tone, "Other than a few bruises on my throat, I am none the worse for the attack. And no, you may not rip off my cravat to see for yourself. You may ruin as many waistcoats as you wish, but I fear I must draw the line when it comes to my neckcloth."

Meribe stared up at him in disbelief. How could he make jokes at a time like this? Why, every minute he was with her increased the chances that the next time he would in truth be struck down by the fatal curse.

Trying to pull her hands free, she protested, "But you must leave here at once. Your life is in great danger."

"But not from you," he said, refusing to release her.

"From being with me," she corrected him. "Please, please, you must not come near me again. I cannot allow you to continue your foolhardy attempt to disprove the curse, not when it has already almost cost you your life. I could not bear it if anything happened to you."

"Miss Prestwich, listen to me!" His voice was so intense, she ceased her struggling. "The man who attacked me knew my name—it was not a random act of violence."

"What are you saying?"

"I strongly believe that the man was paid to attack me."

There was a gasp from the maid, and Meribe became as still as if she had been turned into a pillar of salt.

"Do you understand what that means?" Lord Thorverton continued. "It means that someone is determined to keep you unwedded—determined enough to resort to murder."

"That . . . that cannot be true!"

"It is easier to believe that someone wishes you harm than to believe that you are afflicted with a fatal curse. As I have mentioned on numerous occasions, I am not a superstitious man, but neither am I a naive fool. Long ago I learned that there is much wickedness in this world."

Meribe stared at him in shock, her mind trying to assimilate what he said. Had those other nice young men been . . . murdered?

"In this case, the villain has chosen the wrong victim. I swear on my father's grave that I shall discover his identity."

There was no laughter in his eyes, and Meribe saw again a ferocity in his expression that should have frightened her. But somehow, she could never be afraid of him. Even while she stared at him, his expression softened.

"Your bedroom, I regret, is not the proper place to discuss this matter. I must go home and change my waistcoat, but I will return in an hour with my carriage. Can you be ready to drive out by then?"

"Drive out? Surely you cannot wish to—" Seeing the fierce look return to his eyes, she stopped abruptly.

"The easiest way to put paid to the gossip that is currently flying around London is to appear in public so that everyone—including the murderer—can see with his own eyes that I am unscathed."

"But if what you say is true, then if I am seen with you, whoever has done this will doubtless try again."

"Exactly," he said, and his expression almost made her pity the murderer, ruthless villain though he was.

* * *

One time around Hyde Park was all that Meribe could endure. If she had thought she attracted attention earlier, it was nothing compared to the way people stared and pointed at her today. To her relief, Lord Thorverton said, "Well, I think we have given these rudesbies enough opportunity to gawk, do you not agree?"

Attempting to keep her tone as light as his, she said, "You are right. I believe enough eyes have popped and enough jaws have dropped that it is safe to say all of London will soon be talking of your miraculous recovery. And of your foolishness in continuing to associate yourself with me," she added.

Deftly maneuvering his pair through the gate leading out of the park, he did not, as she had anticipated, turn his horses' heads toward her house. "Where are we going?" she blurted out.

"St. James's Park should be quieter and more conducive to conversation, and we have not yet made any definite plans for discovering the identity of the murderer."

"I still find it difficult to believe that someone is deliberately plotting against me. Surely such things happen only in novels."

"Mrs. Radcliffe and others of her ilk may contrive elaborate and rather unbelievable plots, but not all villains are figments of an author's imagination. Napoleon himself is ample proof that there really are people who choose to be villains, although we may count ourselves lucky that few work their evil on such a grand scale as he does." He deftly steered his horses through a narrow gap between a brewer's dray and a greengrocer's cart.

Although the day was warm, Meribe could not completely repress a shiver. "I think I would almost prefer to have it be a curse," she said finally, wishing she could clutch Lord Thorverton's arm and hide her face against his shoulder. But with the example of bravery that he had been displaying, she could not act in such a cowardly manner. "And truth to tell, I find it quite unbelievable that I have made such an enemy."

"As a matter of fact, I have already been considering the possible impulses that might lead someone to commit murder," Lord Thorverton said as calmly as if he were discussing the weather. Then he explained the reasoning that had led him to the conclusion that greed was the most likely motive. By the time he finished, they had arrived at St. James's Park.

"There is one other thing I think we should consider," Meribe said in a faint voice. "My aunt has often expressed the wish that both my sister and I remain single so that we three can all live together in harmony with no men to disrupt our lives. Perhaps she . . ." But such thoughts were too appalling, and Meribe found she could not accuse her aunt of such dastardly deeds.

"There is one major flaw in your reasoning," Lord Thorverton said with a smile.

"And what is that?"

"As virulent as your aunt's prejudices are against the male of the species, I cannot picture her enlisting the aid of a man in her plot. Now, if a very large *woman* had attacked me last night, I might be inclined to think that your aunt had had a hand in the matter."

"Or a smallish, easily intimidated man," Meribe said with a smile of her own. "You may have noticed that neither our butler nor any of our footmen are even of average stature. Where men are concerned, the bigger they are, the more offensive Aunt Phillipa finds them."

"Which brings us back to greed as the motive," Lord Thorverton reminded her. "Was your father a rich man?"

"Certainly not. At least," she amended, "I have never considered us to be rich. We always lived very simply in Norfolk, and Aunt Phillipa delights in finding a bargain. On the other hand . . . Papa did find it necessary to come to London once a month to look after his affairs, although he never explained what kind of business he was involved in. And I am afraid I never thought it was my place to ask him questions about such things."

"I assume you and your sister are the major beneficiaries of his will?"

"Well, I have always assumed so. Until I arrive at the age of one-and-twenty, everything remains in a trust, and Hester and I receive quite generous allowances. But as far back as I can remember, it has always been understood that as the elder, Hester would inherit our estate in

Norfolk and I would inherit the smaller property in Suffolk that came into the family with my grandmother. I have also heard my father mention investments, but I do not know the extent of them, nor how they may be devised.''

"Then you do not know how much money you stand to inherit from your father, or who will benefit if anything happens to you?''

"I am sorry, but the only other thing I know is that I am required to have a Season every year until I am of age. Aunt Phillipa has grumbled enough about that clause, and I confess that I would sooner stay in the country.''

Which was not the whole truth, nor yet was it exactly a lie, since it involved mere supposition on her part. So often and so vehemently had her father expressed the opinion that blood was thicker than water, that she could not believe he would have left any of his estate away from his family.

Which in turn meant that the only one who might possibly benefit was Hester. But surely her own sister could not have resorted to murder, no matter how she delighted in cutting other people down to size?

The mere idea was so horrible, so sickening, that Meribe could not bring herself to tell Lord Thorverton her suspicions.

6

"Before we proceed with our attempt to discover the identity of the person or persons who hired the assassin," Demetrius pointed out, "we must find out the terms of your father's will so that we may discover if it does indeed provide a motive for murder. Are you perchance acquainted with your father's solicitor?"

"I have met Mr. Wimbwell several times when he came to visit us in Norfolk, bringing papers for Father to sign, but I have never had an occasion to converse with him beyond the usual social amenities."

"But his place of business is here in the City?"

"Oh, yes, I am sure of that."

"Then I shall discover his direction and arrange an appointment for us to speak with him. Will your aunt object, do you think?"

"Undoubtedly," Miss Prestwich replied. "But I no longer feel the slightest desire to worry about what she will approve of or disapprove of."

Demetrius smiled. "You sound quite fierce. What has happened to cause this display of independence?"

"When Hester told us about the assault on your person, Aunt Phillipa displayed a . . . a singular lack of compassion and concern for your well-being." Miss Prestwich glanced away, as if ashamed to look him in the eye.

"I would imagine she said something along the lines of, 'Well, it serves him right, the obstinate fool.' "

"How did you know?" Miss Prestwich asked.

"Your aunt has not made much effort to hide her opinion of me or of my uncle. But you must not let her bother you. I am not exactly proud of everything my relatives

say and do either.'' He was thinking specifically about
his mother, whose prejudice against the Prestwich family
was almost as irrational as Miss Phillipa Prestwich's
opinion of his Uncle Humphrey.

"Well in any case, since it lacks only a few weeks
until I am of age, I have decided it is high time I started
ordering my own life rather than letting my aunt decide
what I may and may not do.''

His curiosity thoroughly aroused, Demetrius inquired
as to exactly what she had in mind.

"Well, to begin with, I hereby resolve never to do
another stitch of needlework, which my aunt loves but
which I have always detested. For my part, I much prefer
raising plants, but she has always insisted that gentle-
women do not grub about in the dirt, so the most she has
allowed me to do is supervise Bagwell, our gardener, and
that is not at all the same as growing flowers and vege-
tables myself. When we return to Norfolk, I intend to
alter that situation to my own satisfaction.''

Demetrius thought about his estate, where no one cared
enough even to supervise the gardener, who tended
therefore to be a bit lackadaisical about his work. Demetrius's paternal grandmother had had a passion for
growing things, and had laid out elaborate flowerbeds
and had planted many varieties of shrubs, some quite
exotic. But after her death, the grounds around Thorverton Hall had rapidly begun to show signs of neglect,
which he had never made any attempt to correct after the
estate passed into his hands. Like his father, his interest
and attention had been restricted to the stables.

"And another thing,'' Miss Prestwich continued, "I
am quite determined to have a pet of my own. Once,
when I was much younger, I found a kitten. So tiny and
sweet it was, I could not help but love it. But my aunt
called it a 'nasty little beast' and ordered the gardener to
drown it in the pond.''

"How terrible for you!''

"Bagwell did nothing of the sort, of course,'' she said
quite fiercely. "He would never do such a cruel thing.
Indeed, he is the only one who shares my interests in any
way, and he was quite my best friend when I was growing

up. At my suggestion, he took the kitten to Farmer Simpson's wife, who was more than happy to give it a home. I am able to play with it whenever I visit their farm, and it has grown up to be quite a splendid mouser. Its kittens are in high demand in the neighborhood, and I am sure if I asked, Mrs. Simpson would allow me to have my pick of the next litter.''

Again Demetrius thought about his own home, where he had three house dogs, twenty couple of foxhounds, plus innumerable cats that kept both the house and the stables free of rats and mice, while producing the inevitable litters of kittens. In contrast, it seemed to him that Miss Prestwich had been cruelly deprived during her childhood and youth. He had a strong desire to invite her to visit him and meet his menagerie, which brought to mind his latest four-legged acquisition.

''As part of your push for independence, have you considered learning to ride?'' he asked, trying not to sound too hopeful. After being so long under her aunt's domination, he did not, on his part, wish to coerce Miss Prestwich into doing anything she did not truly wish to do.

''To ride? Oh, I would dearly love that, but . . . where would I get a horse? And how would I take care of it? I am afraid my pin money would not stretch to cover the initial purchase price, much less the cost of feed and stabling. As frugal as my aunt is inclined to be, still she insists we must have our own carriage, since her father— my grandfather—always maintained that a true lady would never dream of utilizing public transportation. Despite that, she complains mightily every time she receives a bill for hay or oats or straw. Under no circumstances would she ever countenance the added expense of a riding horse, of that I am sure.''

''A not insolvable problem. As it happens, I have recently purchased a mare—for my mother to ride when she is in Devon,'' Demetrius said mendaciously. ''You could borrow it while you are here in London, and I would be happy to teach you to ride. We can go to the park early in the morning, when no one except for an occasional groom will be on hand to witness your initial efforts.''

"I would love to." Miss Prestwich started to accept, but then her face fell. "But I had not considered. I would also need a saddle—"

"I have a sidesaddle you could use," Demetrius interrupted.

"But there is still the problem of a riding habit. And do not attempt to convince me that you *happen* to have a lady's riding habit that just *happens* to fit me, for I shall not believe you."

"I could—"

"And you cannot possibly buy one for me, for that would be most improper. In fact, now that I think on it, I would likely incur the censure of all the high sticklers were I to ride one of your horses. My aunt would also be doubly against such an activity, since it combines horses and men, both of which she detests."

"I had thought you were determined to make your own decisions without worrying about her prejudices."

When Miss Prestwich did not immediately respond, he continued, "I was about to say that I have a friend whose wife is approximately your size. She may have an old riding habit that you could borrow."

"I shall think on it," was all that Miss Prestwich would say. But he did manage, before he returned her to her aunt's house, to persuade her that they must see her father's solicitor without delay.

Descending the stairs, Meribe was pulling on her gloves and feeling a tingle of excitement at the thought of seeing Lord Thorverton again, even though their errand was of the most mundane. He had sent a note around that morning, informing her that Mr. Augustus Wimbwell was willing to see them that afternoon at two of the clock.

"And where do you think you are going?" Aunt Phillipa inquired, scowling up at her.

"Lord Thorverton and I are driving out again this afternoon," Meribe replied calmly.

"Bah, I do not know why you persist in seeing that wretched man," Aunt Phillipa muttered, turning aside to stalk into the library.

Instead of letting her aunt's remark pass without comment, Meribe followed her, shutting the door behind them. "I see that 'wretched man' because he is the only person in London who is concerned about my happiness. Indeed, you are the one who is being totally unjust to condemn him solely on the basis of his uncle. People do not necessarily resemble their relatives, after all." Taking a deep breath, she continued, "For example, you have a great talent for stitchery, and I have none at all."

She paused, but Aunt Phillipa did not make any attempt to deny that Meribe was totally lacking in aptitude for all handicrafts. "Moreover, since I find as much pleasure in growing plants as you do in plying your needle, when we return to Norfolk you may embroider whatever you wish, and I shall grub about in the dirt to my heart's content, and you will stop trying to turn me into a replica of yourself. Is that understood?"

"I had not realized you felt this way," Aunt Phillipa said, rather taken aback.

"Well, then, you have not listened adequately," Meribe said, still feeling rather heated, "for I have told you over and over—"

"In your meek little voice," Aunt Phillipa pointed out in a voice that was not at all meek.

Meribe smiled, but when she answered, her voice was just as firm as her aunt's. "Perhaps you are right. I admit I have not always shown much resolution in expressing my likes and dislikes. But if I have not made myself clear on this occasion—"

"I believe I have understood you." Aunt Phillipa eyed her as if estimating the degree of Meribe's determination. Finally she said, "Very well, as much as it pains me to see you working like a common field hand, I shall not kick up a fuss if you engage in your chosen pursuit. Although I must insist that you wear gloves and a proper bonnet, for if I see even one freckle, I shall withdraw my permission. And you will not, of course, come into the drawing room reeking of compost unless you wish to give me spasms."

"There is more," Meribe said firmly, wishing to make full use of her present opportunity. "Lord Thorverton is going to teach me to ride. He is letting me use one of his horses, and can provide me with a saddle. In addition, he thinks one of his friends can lend me a riding habit—''

''No, no, it is not to be considered! I positively forbid it!''

Aunt Phillipa was so vehement, Meribe could feel her newfound self-confidence begin to erode.

''Do you think I want it bruited about London that I am too clutchfisted to provide my niece with proper clothes? Indeed, missy, if you insist upon perching on top of a horse like the rest of those witless fools, then Madame Parfleur shall make you a riding habit in the finest stare, and I shall not listen to any arguments on the subject.''

With great relief at her aunt's unexpected capitulation, Meribe inquired, ''And may I borrow Lord Thorverton's mare?''

''Well,'' Aunt Phillipa said dubiously, ''it is not exactly proper for a young lady to ride a horse provided by a man who is not a near relative.''

''But on the other hand, you know perfectly well that horses inevitably eat their heads off,'' Meribe pointed out, being careful to suppress a smile at her victory, ''and we would doubtless have to engage the services of an additional groom, who would be an unnecessary expense.''

''There is that to consider. I could wish that it was a female friend who was providing you with a mount. Still and all, I think my consequence is adequate to keep people from talking too much.''

''Besides which, with four deceased suitors to my account, what can the loan of a horse signify?'' Meribe wished she could tell her aunt it was four *murdered* suitors, but she remembered Lord Thorverton's admonition to reveal to no one what they had discovered so far, since more than one person might be involved in the plot.

Aunt Phillipa sighed deeply. ''I cannot help but wish your father had not been so determined that you should have a Season every year until you are one-and-twenty, although now that I think on it, when I was younger, he was continually trying to persuade me to go to London or even to Bath. But ever since my first Season, it has remained a puzzle to me why any woman would wish to tie herself to a man.'' She eyed Meribe speculatively. ''And I think it is high time you told me what Lord Thorverton's purpose is in pursuing you. Are his intentions honorable?''

For a moment Meribe was tempted to lie, but in the end, when Lord Thorverton did not come up to scratch, that would only make her aunt think the worse of him. ''He has told me quite openly that he is offering nothing beyond friendship.''

Her aunt's countenance brightened, but only for a moment, since Meribe continued, ''But if he should offer for me, however, I fully intend to accept, and you shall *not* refuse me permission.''

''Or I suppose, as determined as you appear to be, that you would elope?''

Meribe nodded, knowing all the time that she could never do anything so shocking. And knowing also that the chances of Lord Thorverton ever offering for her were virtually nonexistent.

''Then if such is the case, I suppose I shall have to become better acquainted with your young man. I must say I would prefer it if he took Hester off my hands, but then, I suppose he is no more fond of her sharp tongue than I am.''

Meribe was finding it increasingly hard not to blurt out all her dreadful suspicions concerning her sister. But surely at the solicitor's office they would discover that her fears were totally ungrounded. When they were children, Hester had been so kind to her, and they had played so contentedly together. Of course, that had been before Hester had cancelled her betrothal and had begun to use her tongue like a rapier.

There was a tap on the door, and Smucker stepped in to inform them that Lord Thorverton was waiting outside.

''You are looking remarkably pleased with yourself,'' Demetrius commented when Miss Prestwich was seated in the carriage. And you are looking extraordinarily pretty today, he added to himself. He was not sure of the cause, but every day he saw her, she seemed to grow more beautiful.

"I *am* quite pleased," she replied. "I have had a discussion with my aunt—or an argument, if you prefer—and for the first time in my life I have emerged a winner from the confrontation. She has given in on all points. Henceforth she will be civil toward you, I may work in my garden, and you have her permission to teach me to ride."

"Then I shall speak to my friend's wife at once."

"That will not be necessary," she said with a gleam of mischief in her eyes. "My aunt was most adamant that if I wish to ride, I must purchase a proper habit from Madame Parfleur. In fact, now that I think back on our conversation, I suspect that it was the mention of borrowing clothes from a total stranger that so incensed my aunt, she forgot to protest as vigorously as she might have about the riding lessons."

She looked so delighted—and so delightful—that Demetrius was almost overcome by the impulse to seize her in his arms and rain kisses all over her face. Unfortunately—or perhaps fortunately—a carriage being pulled through crowded London streets by two fresh horses was not the best place for such activities.

Nor, now that he thought about it, would such rakish behavior be consistent with his offer of friendship. Still, he could not help wondering if her lips would taste as sweet as they looked.

It took considerable effort to pull his eyes away from her charms and force his mind back to his driving, especially since moments later she trustingly tucked her hand in the crook of his arm.

"Do you know, in all the months I have been in London, this is the first time I have ever been to the City," Meribe commented when they had turned off Fleet Street into a narrow lane where Mr. Wimbwell had his offices.

"And what is your opinion of it?" Lord Thorverton asked.

"Everyone seems to be in such a hurry. Or perhaps 'hurry' is not the right word—'purposeful' would be a better way to describe them. No one is strolling along aimlessly."

He reined his pair to a stop in front of a three-story building, and a liveried employee of the law firm hurried down the steps to attend to the horses. Assisting her to descend, Lord Thorverton whispered in Meribe's ear, "Are you ready to beard the lion in his den?"

"Yes, but ever since I awoke this morning, I have been wondering what we will do if Mr. Wimbwell refuses to tell us anything," she murmured.

Lord Thorverton shrugged. "I shall do my best to persuade him, and if he refuses, we shall merely have to think of some way to manage without that information."

They were met at the door by an employee, who bowed and led them to another, more dignified personage, who in turn passed them on to a junior partner, who handed them over to a somewhat less junior partner, who with a flourish ushered them into the presence of the senior partner of the firm, Mr. Augustus Wimbwell.

The solicitor was quite old and bent, and the few remaining hairs on his head were snow white. Moreover, he regarded Meribe in such a kindly and benign fashion that she was reminded of how he had been in the habit of bringing her and her sister each boxes of sweets when he visited their father in Norfolk. Consequently she no longer felt the slightest bit of trepidation at the upcoming interview, for surely he would do everything in his power to assist them.

After introductions were made and tea was called for, Lord Thorverton explained succinctly why they were there.

"Murder?" Mr. Wimbwell asked, his eyes widening. "I am sorry, but our firm has nothing to do with criminal cases. We limit our business to legal contracts and civil suits."

"But that is why we are here," Meribe said, smiling in what she hoped was a persuasive manner. "We need to know the terms of the trust my father set up for me in

his will, so that we will know who has a motive for keeping me from marrying.''

At her words the solicitor looked even more shocked
than he had when Lord Thorverton had uttered the word
"murder." "But, my dear child, surely you are not asking me to break the law? Your father's will stated specifically that the terms of the trust are to remain confidential
until you come of age.''

"Which will be in less than a month," she reminded
him.

"Of course," he replied. "I have it entered on my
calendar already. On that date I shall be happy to explain
everything to you. You will not find me the least bit tardy
in the execution of my duties.''

"Mr. Wimbwell," Lord Thorverton said firmly, "with
all due respect, this is a matter of life and death. As I
explained, we fear that four young men have come to
untimely ends for reasons contained in that trust. I myself was attacked the night before last by someone I believe was hired to kill me.''

"Then by all means, my lord, you must take your proof
and lay it before a magistrate, and he will see to it that
the proper person is apprehended. But I repeat, we do
not handle criminal matters.''

"As of this moment, I have no proof, only suspicions,
but reason tells me that the motive for the murders is
contained in the terms of the trust," Lord Thorverton
said so fiercely that it was obvious to Meribe he was in
imminent danger of losing his temper.

The solicitor did not appear to be the least bit intimidated by Lord Thorverton's temper. Smiling benignly,
Mr. Wimbwell said in an equally firm albeit still mild
voice, "If I am to understand you correctly, you are asking *me* to break the law myself.''

"Only because we wish to prevent another murder,"
Meribe interposed, trying not to think about the fact that
if there was another murder, Lord Thorverton would be
the victim.

"I am afraid you do not understand, my child," Mr.
Wimbwell said, turning to her. "If we once begin to
make exceptions to the law—even if we feel we are fully

justified—then after a short time, everyone will think he can decide for himself which part of the law he will obey and which part he will ignore. There would be total anarchy—utter chaos would ensue. No, my child, I must hold myself to the letter of the law.''

"Even if you ignore the intent?" Lord Thorverton asked, his voice now icy.

"I am perfectly aware of what Sir John's intent was, my lord. I drew up the deed of trust myself, and it exactly expresses Sir John's wishes.''

"I cannot believe that Miss Prestwich's father wished for all her suitors to be murdered.''

"If such is the case, and I am certainly not admitting it is, then I am sure the blame lies elsewhere, for I am well-known in the City for my ability to draw up legal contracts that will stand up in court.''

Despite continued attempts at persuasion, the solicitor refused to admit the validity of their arguments, and finally Lord Thorverton stood up and announced that they were leaving.

He appeared to be taking their defeat quite calmly, but Meribe was angrier than she remembered ever being before. She was still fuming when Lord Thorverton's carriage had been fetched and they were on their way back to Mayfair.

"I am sure," she said finally, "that if he had called me 'my child' one more time, I would have screamed right in his face.''

But she had not sufficient practice at remaining angry, and before they had gone very far, she felt the tension drain out of her body, leaving only a slight headache behind. "Since Mr. Wimbwell refuses to assist us, what do you propose we do now?"

"There is still the possibility that we can find my assailant. A friend of mine, Thomas Hennessey, is communicating with certain people he knows to see if he can discover the man's identity.''

"But how can you hope to achieve success when no one saw the rogue's face?"

Lord Thorverton smiled. "I am not exactly a small man, and my uncle swears that the man who tried to strangle me was at least a full head taller than I am. There are not many men so large, and the one we are looking for also has a sword wound on his right arm. Consequently I have reasonable cause to think that I shall soon be able to confront the blackguard and discover who hired him.''

Alone in his office, Augustus Wimbwell pulled open a drawer of his desk and removed a flask that was hidden under some unimportant papers. Using his teacup, since he had no glass readily at hand, he poured himself a goodly measure of brandy, which he did not hesitate to gulp down.

He was shaking so much, he had to use both hands to hold the cup, and even then he spilled a few drops.

Why, oh why, had he ever done it? One tiny slip—one slight deviation from the strait-and-narrow path—and the consequences were more serious than his worst nightmares!

It had seemed so insignificant when he had done it. Never before and never after had he yielded to temptation. Only once had he not held himself strictly to the letter of the law, and if Lord Thorverton's suspicions were correct, the results had been completely out of proportion to the offense.

In the course of their rather heated discussion, Lord Thorverton had accused him of lacking compassion, which was patently untrue. It had been compassion—misguided, but well-intentioned—that had so disastrously loosened his tongue all those years ago.

If only there were some way to go back in time! Given another chance, he would never have uttered those seemingly innocent words.

But surely Lord Thorverton's theories were not well-founded? There must be some other explanation. But in his heart, Augustus knew that he had indeed committed an unforgivable sin—the worst offense a solicitor could possibly be accused of. He had betrayed the confidence of one of his clients. Only once, to be sure, but that was one time too many.

* * *

Arriving at his house in a less-than-congenial mood, Demetrius was somewhat cheered up by finding Thomas Hennessey waiting for him. His pleasure was tempered by the discovery that the Irishman had taken Collier into his confidence.

That was a minor irritation, however, and quickly forgotten when Demetrius heard the distressing news his friend had discovered.

"I have located your assailant—or rather, a watchman found him this morning. Besides the cut on his arm, which—and you may compliment your uncle on his swordplay—was to the bone, the man was also shot through the head."

"Shot!"

Hennessey nodded. "I questioned the watchman, but apparently nothing incriminating was found on the body. The man was well-known in certain circles, however. He went by the name of Black Jack Brannigan, and a thoroughly nasty character he was. The authorities have long suspected him of committing various acts of violence, but they were never able to establish proof."

"Where was the body found?" Collier asked.

"In Bruton Mews."

Turning to Demetrius, Collier said excitedly, "But that is directly behind the Prestwich residence in Berkeley Square."

"Which leads me to wonder who was employing him," Demetrius replied. "Because if it were simply a matter of his attacking another innocent person, surely any person who shot him in self-defense would have reported the attack to the proper authorities."

"The same thought occurred to me," Hennessey said. "But it appears that having sought out his employer, Mr. Brannigan received a bullet through his head in lieu of whatever money he was promised. Most unfortunate for us—although as things have turned out, he undoubtedly regrets as much as we do that he is unable to testify against the person who hired him. But tell us, did you fare any better at the solicitor's office?"

Briefly and succinctly Demetrius related the events of their interview with Mr. Wimbwell.

''What a stupid old man,'' Collier blurted out.

''I would not call him that,'' Demetrius corrected him. ''I can well understand his position. As he said, where would we be if everyone felt free to bend the law to suit his own requirements?''

''That is quite generous of you,'' Hennessey said, ''but in this case his rigid adherence to the letter of the law may well cost you your life.''

7

Hester surveyed herself in the cheval glass. She was not entirely pleased with the new gown Madame Parfleur had sent over.

"Amaranth is a most flattering color for you," Jane commented beside her. "You should wear it more often."

"But the neckline is much too high," Hester said crossly. "I cannot imagine what Madame was thinking about. She must have mistaken me for an old lady of ninety who is afraid of drafts."

Jane experimentally folded under a bit of the fabric at the neckline. "Perhaps it could be lowered by an inch or so."

"There is no perhaps about it," Hester replied. "The dress is entirely unacceptable as it is now. It will have to go back for alterations."

They were interrupted by a light tap at the door. It was Smucker, come to inform her that she had a gentleman caller below.

"Tell Lionell he can wait until I am done trying on my new gowns," Hester replied automatically.

"It is not Mr. Rudd, Miss Hester. I believe it to be your father's solicitor, Mr. Wimbwell."

"Dear old Wimby? How delightful. I have not seen him since shortly after Father died. Put him in the library and tell him I shall be down directly. Oh, and, Smucker, fetch him some tea and a plate of bonbons. Wimby dearly loves chocolates, especially ones with cream centers."

"As you wish." Smucker bowed himself out.

"I shall wear this dress, Jane. As old as he is, Mr.

Wimbwell will doubtless approve of its excessive modesty. But hurry and fix my hair.''

A quarter of an hour later she joined her father's solicitor. He had aged shockingly since the last time they had met, and he looked as if he already had one foot in the grave. He struggled to get up out of his chair, but she laid her hand gently on his shoulder.

"Do not get up, dearest Wimby." She kissed him on the cheek, then seated herself in the chair next to his. "It has been so long since you visited us. I am sorry Meribe and my aunt are out shopping. They would have also been delighted to see you.''

At the mention of the others, a shadow passed over the old man's face, and he turned his head away slightly. "That is all for the better, since I need to speak with you privately. I do not quite know how to say this.''

Hester could not imagine what business had brought Mr. Wimbwell to speak to her rather than to her aunt. "Is it something to do with the trust?''

"Yes," he said, but his expression became even more hangdog. "I am afraid I have done something quite wicked.''

Hester gasped. "Never say you have embezzled from my father's estate!''

Now it was Mr. Wimbwell's turn to look shocked. "My word, nothing of the sort! All the assets are most properly invested in government consols, and as long as there is an England, no harm can come to your . . . er, to your father's money. It is just . . .''

"It is just what?'' Hester was getting so impatient to discover why he had come that she wished she could shake the information out of him.

"I should never have revealed to you the terms of the trust," he blurted out in a rush. Then he looked directly at her, and his eyes were filled with great sorrow.

"But you told me all that years ago. Why is it now become such a problem that you have needed to come see me about it? Not that I am not happy to have this opportunity to visit with you, of course.''

After a bit more persuading on her part, Wimbwell finally said, "If your sister marries in the next few weeks, your income will be only a tenth of what it would be if she remains single."

"Yes, yes, that is what you told me," Hester said impatiently. "Please go on."

"I do not know any delicate way to put this . . ." he continued to hedge.

"Tell me at once!" Hester snapped out, her patience at an end.

Startled, the old man blurted out, "Have you been hiring someone to murder all your sister's suitors?"

"Murder?" Hester looked at him in astonishment. Did he actually suspect her of having hired someone to kill Meribe's suitors? His question was so unexpected—and so preposterous—that she could barely keep herself from bursting out laughing. Poor old thing, he had apparently become completely senile.

Tears of pity now filled her eyes, so upset was she that dear old Wimby had been reduced to this pathetic, paranoid old man. And all those years ago he had been such an intelligent man, awake on every suit, or so her father had always said.

"There, there, my dear child."

Now he was patting her hand, trying to comfort *her!* She had to bite her lip to hold back the hysterical laughter.

"It was silly of me to think you could ever do such a thing."

By digging her fingernails into her palms, she was able to control her emotions enough to say calmly, "Indeed it was. I would not even know where to find a . . . a murderer for hire, were I to want to employ such a person, which I assure you I do not."

The relief on his face made her angry. Who did he think he was, coming to her with his ridiculous accusations? And what kind of a person did he think she was? Even making allowances for his apparent senility did little to lessen the hurt.

"I do apologize for my suspicions, my child, which I see were completely unfounded." He continued to beg her pardon, but she scarcely heard what he was saying. When she was a child, he had held her on his knee and allowed her to play with his watch, and yet he had thought her capable of murder?

It was all of a piece—first Peter had betrayed her; then her father, and now even Wimbwell, who had always liked her the best, had turned against her.

It required an immense effort to remain civil until she finally managed to usher the old man out of the house. But it did not take long after that for her to see the possibilities for humor in the whole episode. As she had always done, she hid her pain behind a sharp tongue and a sarcastic wit.

"Me? Why should I dance with her?" Uncle Humphrey looked at Demetrius in dismay.

"Because I am determined to disprove this supposed curse once and for all," Demetrius replied. "Therefore I have been enlisting some of my friends—Thomas Hennessey, Collier, and a few others I am sure I can trust to hold their tongues—to dance with Miss Prestwich."

"But . . . but . . . but . . ." Humphrey looked around as if wishing he could flee from the spot, but Demetrius had him cornered between a pair of potted palms, and there was no way for him to escape except by climbing over one or the other of them.

"And do not try to convince me that you are still afraid some supernatural power will strike you down," Demetrius said, keeping his voice low so that none of the other guests would overhear them. "You know as well as I do that Black Jack was undoubtedly a paid assassin and that he is by now already rotting in a pauper's grave."

"But . . . but . . . I don't . . ."

"And do not try to persuade me that you do not dance, for I have seen you leading out any number of ladies."

"*Married* ladies only, I assure you, my boy."

"You need not worry. I can vouch for Miss Prestwich; she will not set her cap for you."

"But the problem is her aunt. I cannot abide that woman, don't you know."

"No, I do not know," Demetrius said crossly. "I have been trying to find out what unforgivable thing you did to her all those years ago, but so far my mother refuses to divulge your secrets, and you are also proving quite impossible to pin down.''

"I? I? I did nothing to her—you should rather ask what she did to me!''

"What did she do to you?'' Demetrius asked.

"She . . . Oh, blast it all, Nephew, as much as I despise that woman, as a gentleman I cannot reveal what she did, not even to you, else I could not hold up my head in public any longer. Now, stop berating me, for it will do you no good.''

"I am not asking you to dance with the aunt,'' Demetrius said in a low, menacing voice. "You may give her the cut direct for all I care. But you will be civil to the niece, or you will answer to me.''

Humphrey tugged his waistcoat down over his rounded paunch, brushed an imaginary speck of lint off the sleeve of his jacket, eyed Demetrius consideringly, then finally said sulkily, "Very well, I shall dance with the chit.''

"Thank you, Uncle, I knew I could count on you. You will find she is quite light on her feet. I do not think you need worry about your toes.''

"Bah!'' was all the reply his uncle vouchsafed.

"And then he asked me if I had hired someone to kill my sister's suitors! Can you imagine such impertinence? Really, he was too droll.'' Hester looked at her friend expectantly, but instead of smiling, Lionell raised his hand to cover a yawn.

"My dear, if you will persist in telling these boring stories about senile old men, I shall be forced to take myself off to the card room.''

"Well, I found him quite amusing.''

"Old people are never amusing, only tedious. I should prefer it if no one over the age of fifty were allowed in London.''

Hester did not even smile at his feeble attempt at wit, although her lack of response did not appear to bother Lionell in the slightest. He began to tell her the current *on-dit* about Lord Westerholme's wife, which was so titillating that Hester abandoned her affronted pose and related to Lionell the equally scandalous—and even

possibly true—story she had heard concerning the third
Baron Edgeford, father of the present baron.

It was amazing what one could accomplish by greasing
the right palm, Collier thought with a smile. Moving
soundlessly through the darkened rooms of the solicitor's
premises, he soon reached the door he had been seeking.
Taking a second key from his pocket, he inserted it in
the lock, turned it, and heard the telltale snick of the
bolt.

Once inside the room, he checked to see that the heavy
curtains were tightly closed, then raised the shutter on
his lantern only far enough that he could inspect the contents of the file drawers.

Finding the correct folder was more difficult than he
had anticipated, since there seemed to be no logic to the
order of the files.

After a wasted hour he suddenly realized that they were
after all arranged logically—not alphabetically, as might
be expected, but by the rank and importance of the various clients. Going back to the first drawer, he quickly
flipped past one duke, three earls, a half-dozen or so
viscounts, innumerable barons, until he finally found the
proper drawer containing records for baronets.

Moments later he was extracting the papers concerning
Sir John Prestwich's estate. Without any qualms he seated
himself at the desk and began to copy the pertinent ones,
using Mr. Wimbwell's own quill and ink for his purpose.

The documents were long and full of legal terminol-
ogy, and the sky was exhibiting a rosy tinge in the east
by the time he was finished and the original documents
were restored to their proper place.

Tucking the copies inside his jacket, he quickly and
noiselessly left the premises, locking the doors behind
him and hiding both keys in the crevice where he had
been instructed to leave them.

A good night's work, he thought with satisfaction. And
the contents of the papers were damning enough to justify the risk he had taken. Demetrius would be very
pleased to have his suspicions confirmed.

* * *

Looking around Tattersall's for his brother, Collier spotted his uncle instead. Humphrey Swinton was patting the neck of a flashy black gelding, whose groom was talking rapidly and earnestly.

"Good afternoon, Uncle," Collier said, inspecting the beast with a jaundiced eye.

"Ah, Collier, my boy. How lucky for me that you have turned up at such an opportune time. Give me your opinion of this fine fellow—should I buy him or not?"

"That would depend, of course, on whether you were wishing to put him in your stables or in your stewpan."

Collier's answer did not please the groom overmuch. With a disgusted snort he led the horse away, no doubt seeking a less discerning customer to diddle.

Casting one last look at the departing pair, Humphrey said, "Are you sure, Nephew? It seemed like such a pretty horse—its coat was so shiny and healthy-looking."

"Boot blacking," Collier muttered, still checking the crowd for his brother.

"Really? How odd."

"Only thing odd about it is finding it here at Tatt's. It's an old trick, but if one of the Tattersalls discovers it is being used here, the owner will have to take his business elsewhere. By the bye, have you seen Demetrius? I was told he was here."

"Saw him not ten minutes ago down at the kennels. Told me he's considering picking up some Welsh foxhounds. Wants to try running them with the English hounds—maybe even try a little cross-breeding. Can't say I approve, but your brother always was determined to go his own way."

A few minutes later Collier spotted his brother talking with old Mr. Tattersall. Moving through the group of men inspecting the various hounds, he waited impatiently while Demetrius finished his conversation. "Got something you will be interested in," he said out of the corner of his mouth when Mr. Tattersall finally excused himself to talk to another customer.

"What is it?" Demetrius asked impatiently, his gaze

and his attention still on a fine couple of hounds being exhibited.

"Can't tell you here. Need to find someplace more private." Sliding his hand inside his jacket, Collier pulled the papers out just enough that his brother could see the corners.

After eyeing them with some displeasure, Demetrius looked around, then led the way to a quiet corner, where he took the documents and flipped through them quickly, his face gradually turning an alarming shade of red. "Where the devil did you get these?"

Gleefully Collier explained how easily he had managed to acquire them. Instead of praising him for his resourcefulness, however, Demetrius continued to scowl at him.

"How could you have done such a childish trick?"

"Childish? There was nothing childish about it," Collier snapped back, thoroughly incensed at his brother's attitude. Demetrius was always determined to hog all the glory for himself; he never wanted Collier to receive credit for anything.

"You are correct—it was merely illegal, or had you considered that? Bribery, breaking and entering, stealing documents—is that the full extent of your criminal activities, or have you neglected to tell me the whole of it?"

"I should have known you would not appreciate the trouble I have gone to on your behalf."

"Trouble? You do not seem to understand just how serious the consequences will be if anyone discovers what you have done."

"No one suspects a thing."

"And pray tell me how you can possibly know that."

For the first time, Collier began to feel a trifle uneasy about his nocturnal adventure. "Well, and why would they suspect something? I left everything exactly the way I found it."

"Did you? Are you absolutely positive? Is this another of your 'sure things'?"

"Even if they suspect someone was there, I know I did not leave any evidence behind that would point to me."

"You said you bribed a clerk to give you the keys. Can he not identify you?"

"Of course, but what does that signify? If he accuses me, then he accuses himself at the same time. I hardly think that likely."

"Do you not? And how long do you think it will take for him to break down under persistent questioning? Will he not attempt to save his own skin by accusing you?"

"But there is no reason for anyone to question him," Collier insisted, beginning to feel a bit more nervous.

"Unless you left some sign of your entry."

In his mind Collier could already hear the clang of the bars shutting behind him when they locked him up in Newgate Prison or wherever they kept condemned felons. "The risk seemed justified to me, since this is a matter of life and death," he finally said.

"I strongly doubt you considered the risk at all," Demetrius said. Then, taking the papers with him, he stalked away.

Someday, Demetrius decided, he would have to let Collier suffer the consequences of his rash actions. But not this time—not when Collier's entire future hung in the balance.

Signaling a hack, Demetrius gave the driver instructions to drive him into the City. Jouncing along, he gradually became convinced that he was riding toward a disaster that he would not be able to prevent.

When he entered the solicitor's office, it was as bad as he had feared. Instead of the solemn decorum of his previous visit, this time nobody greeted him or asked him to state his business. Instead, all the employees, from head clerk to lowest office boy, as well as the junior partner, had left their desks and were clustered around the door to Mr. Wimbwell's inner office.

Expecting the worst, Demetrius shouldered his way through the crowd until he could see into the adjoining room. The junior partner, who two days before had been so dignified, now had tears streaming down his cheeks.

Kneeling on the floor was a man who appeared to be a doctor. He was checking Mr. Wimbwell, who was lying on his back on the carpet. Even to Demetrius's un-trained eyes it was readily apparent that the doctor's services were no longer required.

While everyone else's attention was focused on the body, Demetrius glanced quickly around the room. He could spot no evidence of his brother's visit, but something about the room jarred him.

The box of bonbons on the old man's desk, he realized, coupled with chocolate smears on the deceased's fingers.

"Apparently he has suffered a heart attack," the doctor said, rising to his feet. "Hardly surprising, considering his age."

"If I might have a word with you in private," Demetrius said. Then, as if it were his own office, he directed the junior partner to clear the room and then shut the door.

"I'm Stephen Jamison, my lord," the man said as soon as the others had returned to their desks. "As junior partner, I suppose I am in charge here now until Mr. Wimbwell's son can be sent for. He is senior to me, but unfortunately he left yesterday morning to attend to some pressing business in Edinburgh. I fear it will be most difficult to send word to him."

"The possibility exists that Mr. Wimbwell may have been poisoned. I suggest you have the candy analyzed," Demetrius said quietly.

"Poisoned?" Mr. Jamison collapsed weakly onto a chair.

"What candy?" the doctor inquired, looking around. "Ah, yes, *that* candy."

"It seems likely that the deceased was eating it just before he died," Demetrius pointed out. "Where did it come from?"

"A m-messenger boy b-brought it an hour ago," the partner stammered.

"And who sent it?" the doctor asked, picking up the box to inspect it.

"I couldn't say, sir," the partner replied.

A search of the room revealed nothing more than a card with Mr. Wimbwell's name and direction on it.

"Now, then, sir," the doctor asked sharply, "I should like to know what your interest in this matter is."

"B-begging your pardon, sir," Mr. Jamison interposed, "but this gentleman is Lord Thorverton. And this is Dr. Creavy, my lord. He has the offices directly above us."

Demetrius extended his hand, and after a brief hesitation the doctor took it, although there was still a hint of suspicion in his eyes.

"Four days ago," Demetrius explained, "I was set upon by a hired assassin. The day before yesterday I called upon Mr. Wimbwell in these offices to question him about that attempt."

"Surely you did not think that old man capable of such a deed—no, of course you did not. Excuse me for interrupting, I am afraid my nerves are a bit on edge. Pray continue," the doctor said, wiping his forehead with a large handkerchief.

"I believe the attempt was connected to a trust that Mr. Wimbwell is administering, and that documents in his files will reveal the killer's motives," Demetrius said, only with difficulty managing to keep his hand from automatically reaching up to check the incriminating papers now reposing in his inside jacket pocket.

"Killer? But you are obviously still alive, my lord."

"But four other men are dead, and quite likely at the hands of the same assassin, who has been identified as Black Jack Brannigan."

"If you know who attacked you, why do you not question him directly?" the doctor asked.

"Because he has also been murdered," Demetrius said. "Which leads me to think that Mr. Wimbwell may also have died an unnatural death."

Jamison gave a moan and covered his face with his hands, but the doctor picked up the box of bonbons. "I cannot like the implications, but I believe your suspicions are well enough founded that I shall certainly arrange to have these candies checked for poison."

"And if they have indeed been tampered with, will you please send me word?"

"Of course," the doctor agreed, taking Demetrius's

card and sticking it in the pocket of his waistcoat. "And I appreciate your assistance in this matter, my lord. Although I am still hopeful that the chemist will find nothing more dangerous than cream fillings."

Meribe's sister and aunt were just setting out on a shopping expedition when Demetrius arrived at the Prestwich residence.

"Good afternoon, my lord," the aunt said in what was for her a remarkably civil tone. "If you are looking for my younger niece, she is in the garden. I suppose I have you to thank for encouraging her in this madness she has for dirtying her hands?"

"I regret that I cannot take credit for her interest in plants," Demetrius replied.

The aunt snorted. "And her ridiculous desire to learn to sit on the back of a horse without falling off—I suppose you will try to convince me you had nothing to do with that either?"

"Why, no, madam, I will claim full responsibility for putting that idea in her head."

With a look of disdain the aunt set off down the street at a fast pace. Apparently her supply of civility was easily exhausted. As for the sister, she had managed the entire time to ignore Demetrius as completely as if he were invisible.

On the other hand, the butler had mellowed considerably since the last visit. "Good afternoon, my lord. Miss Meribe will be so pleased to see you. She is working in the garden. If you will be so good as to follow me?"

Reaching a door at the back of the house that apparently led to the outside, the butler paused before opening it. "I must tell you, my lord, how pleased some of us are that the restrictions against gentlemen callers have been lifted. I understand we have you to thank for that."

With a smile Demetrius corrected him. "No, I rather think that was all Miss Meribe's doing. She has acquired enough resolution to face down the dragon, as it were."

"Ah, but when one asks how she acquired that resolution, then one must clearly look to you," Smucker said, opening the door with a flourish.

Spotting a figure kneeling on the ground at the end of the garden, Demetrius headed in that direction. Wearing a bonnet to protect her face from the sun, Miss Prestwich was kneeling on a folded cloth, but the gloves she should have had on her hands were lying beside her on the ground. At his approach, she looked up.

Her face was glowing with such pleasure, he felt his heart leap within his chest. But then he remembered the bad news he was bringing her. Once he told her what had transpired, her adorable smile would fade, her dark eyes would again become sad . . .

He did not think he could bear it.

"Oh, my lord, it is so wonderful to be able to work in the garden again." She held up her hands and smiled ruefully. "My aunt insisted, of course, that I wear gloves, but I could not resist running my hands through the dirt, although the soil here is not the best. I would dearly love some compost to work into it."

"Can you not get all you need from the stables?"

Shaking her head, she explained with a smile, "Horse manure must be aged a year before it is safe to use. Besides which, it is so full of grass seeds, I would be forever at my weeding. But our groom says he knows a man who raises rabbits, and their droppings make the best possible fertilizer. He is confident he can get me all I need for such a small garden."

Demetrius tried to smile also, but the knowledge of how hurt she would be when she found out the contents of the trust made it difficult.

Reaching over, she picked up a clod of dirt with scraggly green things sticking out of the top. "Is this not disgraceful? These poor little bulbs should have been transplanted years ago. They have multiplied until they are so tightly squeezed together it is all I can do to separate them. You will be amazed when you see how beautifully they will bloom once they have room to grow."

She looked up at him so trustingly, he wished there were some way to postpone the inevitable. But there was not.

"I have brought you a copy of the trust your father established for you and your sister," he said, and the smile faded from her face. Without further explanation he held the papers out to her.

She started to reach for them, but then she paused and held up her hands for him to see. "I am afraid I am every bit as grubby as my aunt predicted I would be. Could you perhaps read it to me?"

"It does not contain good news," he warned.

"No," she said, picking up a clump of bulbs and beginning to separate them, "I did not think it would."

"The original will was substantially as you had understood it to be, but shortly before his death your father wrote a second will."

Tears rolled down her cheek, and she reached up and rubbed them away with the back of her hand, leaving a streak of dirt in their place.

Wishing he could take her in his arms again, he instead unfolded the papers, found the pertinent section, and began to read. " 'I, John Prestwich, being of sound mind and memory, praise be to God, do hereby revoke any and all previous wills made by me.' There follow some instructions concerning proper burial, payment of debts, and bequests to servants; then he goes on, 'Item: Since it appears unlikely that my elder daughter, Hester, will ever marry, my will is that she shall have her grandmother's estate in Suffolk and all the income therefrom for her own use and behoof for as long as she shall live, and at her demise it shall descend to my eldest grandson, to be held in trust for him until he shall arrive at the age of twenty-one, and failing that, it shall descend to my eldest granddaughter, to be held in trust for her until she shall arrive at the age of twenty-five, and if neither of my daughters shall leave issue legally begotten of her body, then this estate shall pass to my nearest legal male heir.

" 'Item: To my younger daughter, Meribe, I leave all my property in Norfolk and all the income therefrom for her sole use and behoof as long as she shall live, and at her demise . . .' and there he gives the same terms as for your sister, but at the end he adds also, 'provided she, my younger daughter, Meribe, shall marry before the age of twenty-one, and if she does not, then she shall have her grandmother's estate in Suffolk and her sister, Hester, my elder daughter, shall have the estate in Norfolk whereon I now live.' ''

''Well,'' Meribe said, smiling up at him, ''that is not at all bad news. Even though the property in Norfolk is greater than the one in Suffolk, the difference is not sufficient to warrant murdering anyone.''

''There is more,'' Demetrius said simply. ''He leaves you the lifetime income from all the rest of his property under the same conditions—that if you do not marry before the age of twenty-one, it shall go to Hester.''

''All the rest? I know of no other property.''

''Your father had extensive investments—government consols, shares in the East India Company, and shares in various other commercial ventures—and the income from them is ten times the amount from the properties in Norfolk and Suffolk. If you do not marry in the next month, your sister will be a very wealthy woman.''

Meribe's shoulders were shaking now, but not a sound came out. Raising a tear-streaked face to him, she said, ''But she is my sister—I love her so much. How could she have done such wicked things? No, I cannot believe she could be so cruel, not even for money.''

With a heavy heart Demetrius said, ''I am afraid that the income we are talking about amounts to over twenty thousand pounds per year.''

Shaking her head, Meribe cried out with such anguish, he felt as if his heart were also breaking. ''I do not want her to be the one!''

8

"Hester must have been terribly hurt when she discovered how our father had virtually disinherited her," Meribe said. She was seated beside Lord Thorverton on a little bench at the very back of the garden, and she could not help wishing his arms were around her. She needed comfort now more than anything else, and the memory of the last time he had held her in his arms had not faded in the slightest.

"Hester was even more grief-stricken than I was after Father died, which was understandable since she was closer to him than I was. But then a week or so later she changed—and now that I think back, it was about the time Mr. Wimbwell came to visit us that Hester changed: she started letting Aunt Phillipa and all the servants and me feel the sharp edge of her tongue, which she had never done before.

"Really, I cannot imagine why Mr. Wimbwell did not make a greater effort to persuade Father not to alter his will. Granted, it is probably a well-written document, but it is patently unfair, and so I shall tell him when next I see him."

Beside her Lord Thorverton was silent. Looking up into his eyes, she saw great sadness. He started to speak, but she shook her head, not wanting to hear more. Then his arm was around her shoulders, but as comforting as that was, every word he said added to the pain in her heart.

"I stopped by Mr. Wimbwell's office just before coming here. I am afraid he is . . . dead."

"Oh, that poor old man. I should not have spoken so harshly of him."

"There is more."

Meribe felt her heart skip a beat. "More?"

"There is a possibility that Mr. Wimbwell did not die of natural causes. Someone sent him a box of bonbons, and he was eating them just before he collapsed. At my suggestion, the doctor is having them analyzed for poison."

"Bonbons? Were they perhaps . . . ch-chocolate with . . . with cream centers?"

His hand, which had been stroking her arm, became quite still. "Yes, as a matter of fact, they were. How did you know?"

"They were his favorites. For as far back as I can remember, he always brought us that kind."

"Us?"

She did not want to say the words that would condemn her sister.

"Who besides you knew what kind of candy he preferred?" Lord Thorverton asked, not letting her evade the knowledge she was trying desperately to deny to herself.

"My sister knew. My aunt may have, but she was not living with us until after Father died, so I am not sure she ever met Mr. Wimbwell in person."

Lord Thorverton did not speak for a long time. Finally he said, "There is, of course, always the possibility that the chocolates were not poisoned."

"You said no one knows who sent them?"

He was quiet for a long time, then said, "Yes, they were delivered anonymously."

"Which in and of itself makes them highly suspect, does it not?"

"But on the other hand, why would your sister have sent them now?" he asked, calmly and casually putting into words what Meribe was most afraid of—that her sister was behind these terrible deeds. "It occurs to me to wonder why—if we are to assume that she has known the terms of the trust from the beginning, and that she has been responsible for the 'accidents' that have befallen your suitors—why would she suddenly, after all these years, have decided today to poison that poor old man?"

Relief flooded Meribe's heart. Yes, it was true: Hester had no motive for killing Mr. Wimbwell—at least not at this particular time.

"Unless, of course, you told Hester we spoke with him this week?" Lord Thorverton added, a question in his voice.

"No, no, I did not," Meribe said eagerly. "I told her nothing of our suspicions—nothing of our visit to the City. Oh, of course she could not have done such a vile thing, and it was wicked of me to suspect her even for a minute. Now I am sure the chemist will discover that nothing was wrong with the chocolates either."

Lord Thorverton did not immediately answer. When he did speak, his voice held no conviction. "Doubtless you are correct."

Meribe stayed in the garden after Lord Thorverton took his departure. She found a measure of comfort working with the plants, and did not put away her tools until the last of the bulbs were transplanted.

Entering the house, she met Smucker, who gasped when he saw her. "Miss Meribe, you have been crying! Has Lord Thorverton done something to upset you? Perhaps I should not have left him alone with you in the garden?"

"No, no," she said, wishing she had had a chance to wash her face before anyone saw her. "He brought me news that my father's solicitor, Mr. Wimbwell, died today."

"Oh, what a shame. And he looked quite healthy when he came to speak with your sister. But then, none of us can know the number of our days upon this earth."

His words caught her completely by surprise, and Meribe felt her knees weaken and her heart begin to race. "When . . . when did Mr. Wimbwell come here?"

"Why, yesterday, Miss. He wished to speak privately with your sister, but I have no idea what they discussed."

Meribe had a very good idea what Mr. Wimbwell had said to Hester. Doubtless he had told her of their attempt to discover the terms of the trust, which meant that Hester had indeed had a motive to remove him from the scene—permanently. In her heart of hearts, Meribe no longer had any doubt but that the chemist would discover the candy had been poisoned.

"You dance very well . . . for an ogre," Miss Prestwich said with a smile.

Humphrey could not hold back his own smile. He no longer had any trouble understanding why his nephew was infatuated with the chit—she did have a certain appeal. "Ogre?" he asked with a chuckle.

"So my aunt has led me to believe. Alas, I fear she has wronged you, for I find you quite charming and a delightful partner."

At her words, Humphrey felt himself completely in charity with Miss Prestwich. Actually, he *was* charming—there was no need for him to have false modesty—and quite in demand as a dance partner. It was unfortunate that this sweet young thing was burdened with such an aunt and that her sister was likewise not to be endured. But at least the child was perceptive enough to see through her aunt's poisonous lies.

"Indeed," she continued earnestly, "when one stops to consider that my aunt hates all men, and that she hates you most of all, one would have to assume then that you are more . . . more manly than most." She lowered her eyes quite demurely.

Humphrey puffed out his chest. Really, there was a great deal of logic in what this young lady said, and he, for one, was more than willing to do everything he could to aid and abet his nephew. Indeed, now that he thought on it, Demetrius was being remarkably slow to put an end to all this nonsense about a curse.

Well, he would just have to have a word with the lad . . . point out his responsibilities . . . see to it that the boy did not waste any more time before bringing the assassin to account.

Meribe stared down at the words in the *Morning Post:* "SOLICITOR MURDERED IN HIS OFFICE." Yesterday she had sent Lord Thorverton a note telling him that her sister had, after all, spoken with Mr. Wimbwell just the day before he died. And by return messenger Lord Thorverton had informed her that the chocolate candies had in truth been poisoned. But somehow, seeing the facts laid out in print gave the murder a reality that Meribe could no longer deny, no matter how desperately she did not wish to believe it.

Across from her Hester continued to eat and converse with their aunt as if she, Hester, had not a care in the world. Was she perhaps secretly gloating at the success of her scheme? Did she feel she was completely safe from detection? Was she so selfish, so hard-hearted, that she felt no remorse for what she had done?

If her sister had looked the least bit nervous, Meribe would have held her tongue. But the sight of Hester chattering away about the new gowns she had ordered while poor Mr. Wimbwell was not yet even properly buried was too much to endure.

Carefully watching her sister's expression, Meribe said, "Oh, my, how dreadful."

"What is that, my dear?" Aunt Phillipa asked.

"Mr. Wimbwell died the day before yesterday."

"Mr. Wimbwell? The name sounds familiar, but I cannot place him. To whom is he related?" Aunt Phillipa inquired.

Meribe paused, but her sister made no effort to explain. In fact, Hester was so still, only the trembling of her hands served to differentiate her from a statue carved of marble.

"Do you not remember him, Hester?" Meribe asked, keeping her voice bland, when all she wanted to do was shriek with rage.

Quickly tucking her hands out of sight below the edge of the table, Hester replied, "I? Why, no, I do not recall the name either." She uttered the blatant lie in a most casual voice, as if she were declining an invitation to walk in the park.

"Do you not? I am surprised. He was our father's solicitor, and I remember him quite well," Meribe said, still watching her sister's expression most carefully. "It is quite shocking to read that he was murdered by eating some bonbons. Some anonymous person sent him choc-olates with cream centers that were laced with poison.''

What was the expression on her sister's face? Horror, to be sure, but was there also guilt? Or was it only fear? Fear of being discovered? Only one thing Meribe was sure of: whatever the emotion causing her sister to be-come pale as death, it was not remorse for what she had done.

"How dreadful," Aunt Phillipa said. "First Thorver-ton was attacked right in Hanover Square, then this Wimbwell person was murdered at his office in the City. Whatever is this world coming to?"

Without responding to their aunt's comment, Hester excused herself and left the room, her breakfast barely touched.

"I do not know, Aunt," Meribe said. But she did know. She could no longer pretend that her sister was not involved in the murders. Why else would Hester have lied about remembering Wimbwell, when she had seen him only two days before?

Climbing the stairs to her room, Hester felt so weak she clung to the banister to keep from falling. The news in this morning's paper made her feel positively ill, and she was not at all sure she could make it to her room before collapsing.

Thoughts raced through her head at a dizzying speed: Wimbwell had suspected her of murdering Meribe's suit-ors, and now Wimbwell was dead . . . Wimbwell had suspected, and Wimbwell was dead . . .

As if that were not appalling enough, no matter how she tried not to listen, a little voice in the back of her mind kept repeating, "You told Lionell Rudd that Wimb-well suspected you of being a murderer, and now Wimb-well has himself been murdered. You are to blame for his death. . . .''

No, she had had nothing to do with it! She had just told Lionell as a joke, because the ridiculous fancies of a senile old fool had seemed so amusing. But murder was never a laughing matter, and poor old Wimby, who had always favored her over Meribe—dear Wimby, who had been like a kindly old uncle to her—was dead, poisoned by eating his favorite chocolate candies with cream centers.

Reaching her room at last, she closed the door behind her, turned the key, then leaned back tiredly against the panels. Would that she could lock up her thoughts as easily! But there was no way to deny that she was the one who had been a fool, thoughtlessly turning the solicitor's visit into an amusing anecdote.

Had she at any time told Lionell about Wimbwell's partiality for that particular kind of bonbons? She could not remember for sure.

There was, however, no question but that she had told him the terms of her father's trust. All those years ago, when she had discovered how her father had virtually disowned her, she had poured out her misery and anger into Lionell's ear.

He had been the only one who had known how bitter she had been when Meribe's first betrothal was announced.

To make matters worse, she had even joked with him about her good fortune after Collingwood was killed in a riding accident. Joked? No, if she were to be honest with herself, she had secretly gloated, actually reveled in the knowledge that she would inherit the greater portion, which should by rights go to the elder daughter.

Lord Thorverton's words echoed in her mind: "Someday you will come to regret every unkind word you have ever uttered."

Regret? She covered her face with her hands, remembering the thoughtless way she had used words to wound other people's sensibilities . . . the way she had delighted in the cutting phrase, the maliciously amusing story . . . always egged on by Lionell to say something even more unkind.

Suddenly the most appalling realization struck her, and her heart began racing in her chest. She had told Lionell of Wimbwell's suspicions, and now Wimbwell was dead. If, as she suspected, Lionell had killed the old man, then what would Lionell do to her if he knew *she* suspected *him?* Would he again resort to murder?

Hester began to shake all over, and then in a blind panic she darted across the room and climbed into her bed, pulling the covers over her head. Huddled there in the soft darkness, she tried to reason away her fears.

Lionell could not possibly have done anything so monstrous as poisoning an old man—Lionell could not have. Not only had he been her friend all these years, but he was the consummate dandy, worrying about nothing except the cut of his waistcoat or the polish on his boots.

But *was* he her friend? To be sure, he was always at hand when she needed a dance partner, and he frequently took her up in his phaeton for a turn around the park. But if she were in trouble, could she turn to him for help? No, the mere idea of asking Lionell for even the slightest favor was ludicrous. A more self-centered person she had never met.

Could he have been so altruistic as to have killed someone just so that she could inherit a fortune? Hester felt herself relax. Whatever her suspicions had been, she found it impossible to believe that Lionell would be willing to exert himself in the slightest to help her or anyone but himself.

On the other hand, might it not be to his benefit if she inherited a fortune? He was far from well-off, and in her first Season he had made a push to capture an heiress, who had ended up marrying a pair of broad shoulders. Had Lionell had an ulterior motive for cultivating her friendship all these years? Might he not think it possible that she would share some of her inheritance with him? That if he played his cards right, he would be able to dip his fingers into her purse whenever he wished?

No matter how hard she tried to believe he was not guilty of murder, there was still that damning coincidence: she had told Lionell of Wimbwell's suspicions, and the next day Wimbwell was poisoned.

If there was a chance that Lionell had used poison on one occasion, how could she drink champagne if he were the one to fetch it for her? Knowing how Fellerman had fallen into the Thames, how could she be brave enough to step out on a balcony with Lionell when a ballroom became too stuffy? After what had happened to poor Lord

Thurwell, how could she accept Lionell's escort when shopping without fearing every moment that he might trip her up—might "accidentally" thrust her under the wheels of a passing vehicle?

Even more crucial, how could she talk to him normally, how could she look him in the eye, without inadvertently revealing that she knew his evil secret?

Shivering from fear rather than from cold, she pulled the covers more tightly around her, wishing she could leave London and never see Lionell again . . . wishing Wimbwell had never told her the terms of her father's trust . . . wishing she had had the good sense to keep a civil tongue in her head all these years.

As usual, Tattersall's was crowded, but most of the men were in the yard where the auction was being conducted, and Demetrius had easily managed to find a quiet corner where he could meet with the only three men in London whom he trusted completely. Having informed them of the recent developments, he was hopeful that one of them could suggest a plan for catching the murderer.

"I say we should *do* something," Uncle Humphrey said indignantly as soon as he heard the full story of the poisoned candies.

"I think we are all agreed on that. But the question is, *what* should we do?" Demetrius said irritably.

"I don't know, but we cannot let that blasted, sharp-tongued female succeed with her infamous plan."

"The worst of it is," Hennessey pointed out, "if we do nothing, then in a few short weeks the older sister will simply inherit the fortune, and that will be that."

"Well, I think the best thing would be for you to marry the young lady," Collier said emphatically.

"Splendid idea," Humphrey said. "You should marry the gel, Nephew."

Amazed by his uncle's total change of heart, Demetrius said, "Are you seriously suggesting I should ally myself with that family? That I should take one of those dastardly Prestwich females for a wife?" Then he could not keep from grinning at the older man's immediate discomposure.

"Well, we're certainly not suggesting you marry the older sister!" Humphrey blurted out, obviously appalled at the mere thought of such a union. "But the younger Miss Prestwich is not a bit like the other two, don't you know. She doesn't appear to hate men in the slightest, and moreover, she keeps a civil tongue in her head. Pleasant sort of female, in fact. Remarkably discerning too," he added, but did not explain in what way she was discerning.

"I think it is a perfectly good plan," Collier said. "Marry Miss Prestwich and with one blow you will foil her sister's infamous plan."

"And find myself leg-shackled for life," Demetrius said. "No, thank you. We must think of another plan to unmask the villain."

"Can't understand why you don't want to marry the gel," Uncle Humphrey muttered. "Wonderful gel like her needs a husband, don't you know."

"She can inherit her father's estate without marrying anyone if we can prove her sister is a murderer," Demetrius replied.

"Wasn't referring to the trust," Uncle Humphrey said indignantly. "I meant it would be a pity if that sweet little thing were left on the shelf. She'll be a loving mother and a warm armful in bed, I can tell you." Becoming aware that the other three were staring at him in astonishment, Humphrey added rather lamely, "There's passion in her, don't you know. Just because I'm a bachelor doesn't mean I don't know females."

"I agree with your uncle wholeheartedly," Hennessey said, an imp of mischief in his voice. "She's just the wife for you, Thorverton. That makes it three to one in favor of the marriage. You'd best see about getting a special license."

"I do not find your attempt at humor amusing," Demetrius said. While Miss Prestwich was indeed a pleasant sort of female—not given to chattering or having the hysterics—she did not at all resemble his neighbor's wife, and he had long ago decided that if he ever got married, his wife must be just as intelligent and knowledgeable, just as resourceful and ingenious, just as fearless and bold, and just as competent and capable as Anne. Surely that was not asking too much—was it?

"I was not joking in the least," Uncle Humphrey said, and his tone was indeed quite serious. "You had best marry the girl, and the sooner the better. Once you are hitched, you can forget all this murder nonsense and get on with producing an heir."

"Are you forgetting my mother—your sister? Since you are so in favor of this marriage, I shall leave it to you to persuade her to accept the young lady in question." Not that Demetrius intended to marry Miss Prestwich, but he had promised to be her friend, and it would be an easier task if his mother were at least minimally civil.

"I?" Humphrey said, beginning to edge away. "Much as I would like to help, Nephew, I am afraid I am otherwise occupied for the foreseeable future."

To Demetrius's amusement, Hennessey caught Uncle Humphrey by the arm and said firmly, "Listen carefully. By tomorrow we expect to hear that Lady Thorverton is calling upon the Misses Prestwich, do you understand?"

Humphrey opened his mouth, but no bluster came out. The Irishman could be most intimidating when he made the effort, although Demetrius knew his friend was quite mild-tempered by nature.

"You have twenty-four hours, Uncle," Demetrius said with a smile.

Humphrey was not amused. Jerking his arm free, he departed without a backward glance.

"And as for you, my friend," Hennessey said, turning to Demetrius, "I think you would do well to consider your brother's suggestion seriously. It appears to me that Miss Prestwich would be an ideal wife for you."

"And it appears to me that too many people are trying to mind my business," Demetrius said, his temper flaring up.

Watching his friend stalk away in a huff, Thomas Hennessey grinned to himself. He should not—really he should not—but he knew he was going to. "That was a good idea you had, Baineton. It is too bad your brother would not listen to you."

Beside him the boy muttered angrily to himself, then

said, "He never listens to me. Doubtless if you had suggested it first, he would at least have considered it carefully, rather than rejecting it out of hand."

"Do you know, it has occurred to me that it is not necessary for your brother to marry the lovely Miss Prestwich." Thomas paused, then added, "All that is really necessary is that the murderer *think* that the two of them are going to marry."

Collier Baineton looked at him with dawning comprehension, but then he frowned. "My brother would be in an absolute rage if anyone—especially me—did something contrary to his expressed wishes. In fact, I would not be surprised if he were driven to physical violence."

Thomas shrugged. "He would get over it. One would only have to lie low until the initial explosion had occurred. And besides, had you considered that if the plan works and the murderer is exposed, your brother would have to acknowledge that he was wrong and someone else was right?"

"And if the plan works too well? If the murderer is successful? I am not all that eager to take over my brother's title and estate."

"I brought several stout lads with me from Ireland, and I can vouch for their loyalty. I have already offered them to your brother as bodyguards."

"He said nothing to me about them."

"Well, you see, he refused to consider using them—said he could protect himself."

"There, you see, Demetrius is so devilishly determined to have his own way, he will not listen to anyone else's suggestions, no matter what their merit."

Thomas grinned. "But you see, my boy, some of the rest of us are equally determined."

"Do you mean . . . ?"

"Exactly. There have been two of my men following your brother ever since the first attack."

The boy laughed, obviously pleased to discover that for once his brother had not gotten his own way.

"Had you heard about the boxing match being held in a little village near Reading this week?" Thomas asked casually.

Baineton was no dummy, that was obvious. "Do you know," he replied at once, "I have just become an ardent fan of pugilism." Grinning cheekily, he took his leave and strolled away, whistling softly under his breath.

Collier inspected the brief note he had just written. "Betrothed: Miss Meribe Prestwich and Demetrius Baineton, Lord Thorverton." Well-satisfied with his efforts to imitate his brother's hand, Collier sanded the note, then folded and sealed it. After clearing away all signs of his presence in Demetrius's study, Collier sought out one of the footmen and gave him instructions to deliver the missive to the offices of the *Morning Post*.

An hour later, after packing the necessaries in a small portmanteau, he slipped out of the house and went cheerfully off to meet Charles Neuce and Ernest Saville, with whom he was driving down to Reading.

It was unfortunate that he could not be a fly on the wall and hear the thunderous oaths that were bound to be uttered when his brother found out what he had done. But it was more prudent to be absent until Demetrius's wrath had cooled to manageable levels.

9

Aunt Phillipa lowered her newspaper and glared over the top of it at Meribe. "Well, missy, I see your splendid lord has come up to scratch."

Hester gasped, and Meribe looked at her aunt in bewilderment. "Whatever are you talking about?"

"The list of betrothals in the *Morning Post* includes your names: Miss Meribe Prestwich and Demetrius Baineton, Lord Thorverton. Well, I cannot say that you did not warn me, but it is still rather shabby of you not to have apprised me of the agreement between the two of you before I read about it in the *Post*. But it is all of one piece, since I have long known that the younger generation has no respect for the proper way of doing things. It has become such a helter-skelter world, there is no telling where it will end. In my day, gentlemen had the decency to cover their heads with wigs, or at the very least they powdered their hair, but now they lark about with their hair clipped indecently short."

As much as she hated deceiving her aunt, Meribe could not reveal that the betrothal was nothing more nor less than a hoax—undoubtedly a trick on Lord Thorverton's part to catch the murderer. Would that Lord Thorverton truly wanted to marry her—how wonderful it would be in that case!

Except she was forgetting: by announcing their betrothal, whether legitimate or a clever bit of deceit, Lord Thorverton was making a target of himself—setting himself up for another assassination attempt.

If only he had asked her permission first! Not that she would have given it, of course. Not even the income from her father's investments was great enough to warrant tak-

ing such a foolhardy risk, and so she would tell Lord
Thorverton when she saw him.

Aunt Phillipa rattled her paper indignantly, then said
crossly, "And as for you, Niece, you would have done
better to take my advice and shun the company of men.
Well, that is all I shall say on the subject, except for this:
you have made your bed, and now you must lie in it."

Meribe felt her face grow hot at the thought of lying
in bed with Lord Thorverton. It had been uncommonly
pleasant to have him hold her in his arms . . . what would
it be like to sleep beside him? To see his face on the
pillow beside her? To wake up in the morning in his
embrace?

"You are assuming, of course, that nothing untoward
will happen to his lordship between now and the wedding," Hester said, interrupting Meribe's pleasant day-
dreams. "I am surprised he is willing to risk being struck
down by the curse."

"There is no curse," Meribe blurted out. She almost
said it had been a hired assassin who had killed her other
suitors, but fortunately she bit back the words in time.
Under no circumstances could she allow Hester to learn
that they had discovered her wicked machinations.

Hester's expression was now so icy, she seemed a complete stranger, and Meribe wondered if she had ever truly
known her sister.

"If I were you," Hester said, "I would cry off before
it is too late to save Lord Thorverton's life."

She is threatening me, Meribe realized with amazement. She is actually warning me that she will have him
killed if I do not jilt him. Was Hester really the heartless
monster she appeared to be? Was there nothing left of
the kind older sister who had helped Meribe with her
lessons? Who had tucked Meribe in at night after their
mother had passed away? Who had smuggled food up to
Meribe when she was sent to bed with no supper? Was
that sister gone forever?

The love of money is the root of all evil. Did Hester
want to be rich so badly that she was willing to con-
done—no, to solicit—murder?

"If you are quite done picking at your food, then I

suggest we call for the carriage," Aunt Phillipa said, interrupting Meribe's thoughts. "Madame Parfleur is expecting us at eleven so that we can pick out the fabric for your riding habit. Unless you have come to your senses and given up such ridiculous notions?"

"No, I have not changed my mind," Meribe said, although she could no longer feel the slightest excitement at the thought of learning to ride. She doubted, in fact, that she could find enjoyment in any activity—even gardening—so weighed down was she by fear for Lord Thorverton's life.

"Do you come with us, Hester?" Aunt Phillipa asked, rising to her feet.

"No, I have made other plans," Hester replied, her voice betraying no emotion.

Humphrey Swinton rehearsed his speech while he walked along with jaunty step toward his sister's residence. As head of the family, he would say, it is my decision who—whom?—we shall recognize and whom we shall turn our backs on. And I have decided that Miss Meribe Prestwich is a delightful young lady, quite worthy of Demetrius's attentions.

We should be thankful, he would point out, that Demetrius's affections have been engaged by someone whose manners are above reproach, whose countenance is pleasing, and whose station in life is commensurate with that of Demetrius.

A firm tone, that would be best. Override Dorothea's objections before she had a chance even to utter them. And he would project his voice the way Babette, an opera dancer who had been under his protection for a delightful two years, had taught him.

One must be open-minded, he would explain—though actually, as the head of the family, he owed his sister no explanation. To condemn an innocent young girl because she has the misfortune to have a harridan for an aunt is not only unfair but also . . . also . . . What was the word he needed?

Unjust . . . pernicious . . . reprehensible . . . That was not quite what he wanted to say. He stopped walking and scratched his head with the end of his cane, almost knocking his hat off in the process.

Shameful—that was the word he was looking for. To exhibit such prejudice brought shame upon the fair name of Swinton.

Satisfied at last, he began walking again, muttering his speech over and over, lest the proper words escape into the ether.

He could not help smiling. He could see it all in his mind: himself, standing straight and dignified, laying down the law; his sister cringing back in her chair, fearful of arousing his ire.

Yes, yes, he would have no trouble carrying out his assignment. Demetrius would be quite proud to have such a noble uncle who did his duty in the face of forceful opposition, who did not retreat abjectly when under enemy fire.

Arriving at the Thorverton residence, he mounted the steps, rapped on the door with his cane, greeted Mc-Dougal with great bonhomie, then commanded majestically, "And tell my sister that I wish to speak with her at once."

"Begging your pardon, sir, but that would not be wise."

"What's that?"

"Lady Thorverton is in a perishing temper. I cannot say what has touched her off, but she threw her breakfast tray at the wall this morning, and then she boxed the maid's ears—and my lady has never before been given to physical violence. If I were you, I would come back another day."

The picture of himself as a general, fearlessly leading his troops into battle, stayed with Humphrey, however, and he said in a firm voice, "Nonsense. I am not now, nor have I ever been, afraid of my sister." Which was bending the truth considerably, but the new, resolute Humphrey was not afraid of any woman—or any man, for that matter.

"But—"

"But me no buts, my good man. I wish to speak to my sister without delay."

"Very well, if you will wait in the drawing room, I shall inform her that you are here."

The look on the butler's face was not exactly admiration, but that would change after Humphrey had bearded the lion—that is to say, the lioness—in her den. McDougal would be struck dumb with awe, in fact, when he saw how easily Humphrey handled his sister.

"Lioness" was not quite the word for Dorothea, he discovered to his own consternation. "Avenging angel" was a better description, and he could only be thankful she had seen fit to leave her flaming sword in her dressing room.

Before he could even open his mouth, she rolled over him like a calvary charge, screaming imprecations—although luckily not directed at him—spouting nasty threats, uttering dire warnings. Relentlessly she forced him to retreat, until he found himself with his back to the wall.

Glaring up at him like one of the Furies, she said, "I expect you to do something about this *immediately.*"

"D-do something? About what?"

"Have you not been paying attention? About the betrothal!" She shook a piece of newspaper in front of his face, and with relief he grabbed it.

It was not easy to read, since it had already been savagely mangled, crumpled, torn, twisted up . . .

"There—there! Read the announcement for yourself! Oh, that any son of mine should have done such a deceitful thing! Betrayed by my own child! Does a mother not deserve even a modicum of respect? Have I nursed a viper at my bosom all these years?" To Humphrey's relief, she moved away from him and began to pace around the room.

He immediately started breathing again, and his heart slowed down to merely double its normal pace. Then, with fingers that trembled only slightly, he smoothed out the offending piece of newsprint and scanned it quickly. In the middle of the list of betrothals recently entered into, the names Miss Meribe Prestwich and Demetrius Baineton, Lord Thorverton, popped out at him.

By Jove, but his nephew had bottom! He'd actually

done it—thumbed his nose in the murderer's face. Demetrius was a credit to the Swinton family, even though
technically he was a Baineton and not a Swinton. Still,
the boy was his nephew, and Humphrey was quite proud
of him.

"I demand that you put an end to this nonsense! You
will go at once to the newspaper offices and threaten them
with a lawsuit if they do not print a retraction, do you
hear me?"

Stiffening his backbone, Humphrey glared down at his
older sister. For years she had pushed him around—
browbeaten him unmercifully—but no longer. "I hear
you," he said in a calm but firm voice. "And I doubt
not but that all the servants can hear you also." He took
a step forward, and staring up at him in amazement, Dorothea took a faltering step backward.

Pressing his advantage, he advanced remorselessly.
"As head of the family, I order you not to meddle in this
business in any way."

"How . . . how *dare* you talk—" she attempted to
say, but he cut her off ruthlessly.

"Furthermore, you will not only welcome Miss Prestwich into the family but also give a party for her *and* for
her aunt."

Losing ground rapidly, Dorothea still essayed a de-
fense. "Never," she said, but her voice quavered weakly,
and it was obvious to Humphrey that he almost had her
routed, foot, horse, and gun.

"Do not say 'never' to me—say, 'yes, sir, at once,
sir.' " His voice now sounded menacing even to his own
ears.

Her mouth moved, but not a sound came out.

"Say it!" he bellowed, and so well did he project his
voice that had he been onstage at Covent Garden, he
could have been heard even in the back of the farthest
balcony. Babette would have been proud of him.

Tears welled up in his sister's eyes, and he felt all his
energy and determination leak away. "Now, don't cry,
Dorothea. I am sorry I yelled at you."

"Nobody cares about my feelings," she said, snif-
fling. "The only reason I did not like Miss Prestwich in

the first place was that her aunt treated you so abominably. I am sure she is a very sweet girl if you say so.''

''I do, and I think you will agree with me once you get to know her better.''

He was very satisfied with himself when he left the Thorverton residence a short time later. Really, it was not at all hard to manage his sister. All that was required was a little gumption.

Watching McDougal show her brother out, Lady Thorverton was in such a towering rage she could hardly contain herself. So, Humphrey thought he could strut in here and dictate to her whom she must recognize—bah! The silly fool had not even noticed that she had promised him nothing.

He would be a graybeard before she would allow that contemptible Phillipa Prestwich to set foot in *her* house. And as for the niece, if Demetrius married that scheming hussy, then he could say good-bye to his mother, because she, Lady Thorverton, would never live in the same house with the pair of them. Not that Demetrius would mind if his mother had to eke out a meager existence in some shabby rented house in Bath. Such an unnatural son he was—so lacking in the proper filial respect.

Thinking about the injustice of it all, Lady Thorverton began to feel quite sorry for herself. But at least she had one son who behaved as he ought. Of a certainty, Collier would never desert his dearest mama. Perhaps he might even be willing to accompany her on her errands this afternoon. Having him for an escort would do much to soothe her jangled nerves.

Ringing for McDougal, she instructed him to inform Master Collier that his mother wished to speak with him as soon as it would be convenient.

''Beg pardon, my lady, but your son is not here at present.''

''Not here? But he would never go out without stopping to wish me a good morning and to inquire about my health.''

The butler cleared his throat and so far forgot what he owed to his position that he actually shuffled his feet.

"The maid has just informed me that Master Collier's bed was not slept in last night."

"Not slept in? Has that ridiculous boy taken rooms at the Albany again? If he has, be sure that Demetrius will bring him back directly."

Again McDougal looked uncomfortable. "Master Collier's things are quite untouched, my lady, so I do not believe he has gone so far as to move out."

"Then when did he leave? And why did no one ask him where he was going? Surely you have not taken it upon yourself to disobey my instructions?"

"I regret, my lady, but no one saw him leave the house. It would appear that he slipped out secretly."

Tears filled Lady Thorverton's eyes, and this time they were not the crocodile tears she had cleverly produced in order to win the confrontation with her brother. "Slipped out? Rubbish! My dearest son would never have sneaked away like a common thief. How dare you suggest such a thing!"

"But, my lady—"

"Oh," she wailed, clasping her hands to her bosom, "he has been kidnapped, I just know he has. And it is all the fault of the Black Widow. No matter how often he was warned—and I pleaded with him myself on numerous occasions—Demetrius *would* associate himself with her. And now the curse he scoffed at has struck down his innocent little brother! My sweet Collier has been snatched out of my loving arms—more than likely murdered most foully! Oh, was ever a poor mother treated so insensitively, so callously, so shabbily as I?"

Demetrius had never before been scolded more thoroughly—or quite so delightfully. From the moment his carriage had pulled away from her house, Miss Prestwich had been ringing a peal over him: he was foolhardy in the extreme; he had made a target of himself; he should have consulted her, and she would have urged caution; if he were killed, she would never forgive him.

He did not think she was at all well-practiced in the art of browbeating a man, however, since in lieu of making him feel cast down, her lecture was only making it difficult for him to suppress a grin.

Glancing down at her was definitely a mistake. One look at her dark eyes glistening with unshed tears, and his urge to smile was replaced by a strong desire to hold her in his arms and kiss her tantalizing lips, which were quivering sweetly.

"You might at least have warned me. I felt a positive fool when my aunt congratulated me, not that it matters, but Hester was sitting right there, and I might have accidentally said something to betray our plan. Really, I cannot think what you were about to send that announcement to the newspaper."

"You err in your assumption," he replied, directing his horses to St. James's Park. He was not in the mood to run the gauntlet of curious, prying, meddling gossips who at this hour were driving, riding, and promenading along Rotten Row. "I sent no announcement to the *Morning Post.*"

"You . . . But who . . ."

"I visited their offices, and they informed me that a servant wearing my livery brought them the note. By their description of the fellow, I recognized him as one of my mother's footmen."

"Your mother? But surely she would not have done such a thing. Why, she will not even acknowledge me in public."

"My uncle has spoken to her about that, and he assures me that she will no longer dare to give you the cut direct. But in any event, you are correct. It was not my mother, but rather my brother who instigated this scheme."

"Without consulting you?"

"Oh, he consulted me, all right. He suggested that I marry you so that your sister would not inherit your father's estate. When I rejected his plan, he deliberately disobeyed me."

There was a soft sound beside him—a sudden intake of breath—and he instantly wished that he could call back his intemperate words. But how could he explain away the hurt he had obviously caused her by mentioning marriage, while at the same time making it obvious that he did not wish to marry her? He could not very well say, "I would be happy to marry you, but you do not meet the standards I have set for my future wife." Nor could he say, "It is not that I do not like you. I am indeed quite fond of you. Unfortunately, I do not love you."

"You need not worry, you know," she said quietly. "When this is all over, I shall release you from any obligation. I shall not take advantage of your brother's foolishness to trap you into a marriage not of your liking."

She sounded calm enough, but when he looked at her, her head was lowered and all he could see was her bonnet. Blast it all! Why had he not thought before he brought up the subject of marriage? He was proving to be as heedlessly rash as Collier.

They drove in silence for what seemed like an eternity. "Would you like to stroll a bit?" he finally asked, unable to think of anything else to do to heal the breach between them.

"No, thank you," she said, her voice still barely above a whisper. "I think, if you do not mind, I should like to return home now. The sun is really quite hot, and I forgot to bring my parasol."

The drive back to Berkeley Square was uncomfortably tense, and to add to his disquiet, Demetrius spotted two men following them. Big bruisers, they looked as if they had been cast from the same mold as the late Black Jack Brannigan. It would appear that Miss Hester Prestwich had found herself a pair of hired assassins this time.

Demetrius had learned his lesson well enough, however, that he did not mention the two ruffians to his companion. She was already worried enough about his safety that she did not need additional cause for alarm.

With a little luck—and with the help of his friends—he should be able to capture one of the brutes and force him to disclose who had hired him. Once the plot against Miss Meribe Prestwich was made public, he, Demetrius, could return to his horses and allow her to announce that their betrothal was called off. Which would make it twice that he was jilted—enough to make any woman wonder about his suitability as a husband.

On the other hand, there was bound to be a scandal when the elder Prestwich sister was arrested for murder. Could he in all decency take himself off to Devon and leave Miss Meribe to face the malicious gossip alone?

In fact, now that he thought about it, it would be better for all concerned if her sister were not arrested and tried for murder. With a little judicious handling of the situation, Miss Hester could undoubtedly be persuaded to immigrate to Jamaica or Canada or some other suitably distant part, after first signing over to her sister all her rights to their father's estate.

Clearly it behooved him to stand by Miss Meribe until everything was settled. Then she could jilt him.

He was frowning when he returned his horses to the stables.

She had to convince Lionell it was all a hum—that some prankster had inserted the announcement of the betrothal in the newspaper. Hester looked around the crowded ballroom trying to spot the dandy whom she could no longer dismiss as nothing more than a posturing, conceited fop.

Finally espying him dancing with Miss Quailund, Hester waited impatiently for the music to cease. Then she moved as unobtrusively as possible around the room, so that she would be properly positioned to intercept him when he returned the young lady to her chaperone. For the first time in her life, Hester felt self-conscious, and she found it difficult to believe that everyone in the room was not watching her when she "accidentally" bumped into Lionell.

"Excuse me, my dear, are you all right?" Lionell took her arm to steady her, and his words were all concern.

Fixing a smile on her face and desperately hoping he did not mark how false it was, she giggled nervously, then blurted out, "The most amusing thing—you will positively die when I tell you." *Die*—whatever had possessed her to use that word?

Resolutely she continued, "Some prankster has inserted an announcement in the *Morning Post* that my s-sister is betrothed to Lord Thorverton." With difficulty she kept smiling, praying that he had not noticed her stutter—that he did not suspect she was trying to mislead him.

"Hartwell, who stands to lose five thousand guineas if his lordship is still alive on the first day of July, informed me that the announcement was delivered by a footman wearing the Thorverton livery. How odd," Lionell commented absently.

"A disgruntled servant," Hester improvised quickly. "The insolent jackanapes has, of course, been let go."

Raising his eyebrows in mock astonishment, Lionell said, "But you are singularly informed about the doings of Thorverton's household. I had not realized the two of you were so close."

"He s-sent a note to my sister—an apology, as it were."

"There is another possibility, you know." Lionell looked at her speculatively.

Hester felt her gorge rise up into her throat—surely he did not, like Wimbwell, think that she had anything to do with promoting the curse!

"One of the numerous gentlemen who have wagered small fortunes on the early demise of my Lord Thorverton may have bribed the servant."

He had accepted her explanation! She was flooded with relief. "Yes, of course, that is more than likely the case," she agreed, then quickly, before he could question her further, she changed the subject and began talking about the outrageous gown Mrs. Gilmoreton was wearing, which made her look like the veriest ladybird.

Her feelings of relief did not last out the evening, however. Lord Thorverton, with blithe disregard for his own safety, danced not twice, but three times with Meribe, acting the entire time as if he did not notice how everyone was staring at him in ghoulish anticipation—how they were all waiting for him to be struck down by the fatal curse.

The only thing she could be thankful for was that Lionell had left the party before the newly betrothed couple danced with each other a third time. With a little more luck, by the time he heard any gossip, she would have come up with another prevarication with which to soothe his suspicions.

If indeed he was in any way connected with the assassinations. Perhaps it was, as Lionell had suggested, the work of someone who had wagered a large sum on the shortness of Lord Thorverton's life expectancy. Men, especially ones cursed with the gambling fever, were known to behave rashly on occasion.

Was it not more likely that one of them—one of the Corinthians who were willing to risk life and limb in a curricle race or to watch with glee while two men pounded each other's faces into bloody pulps—was it not more likely that someone like that had hired some ruffian to attack Lord Thorverton?

Indeed, now that she thought on it, that attack was not necessarily even connected with her sister, despite what the gossips around town were so quick to whisper. The deaths of the other suitors had undoubtedly been nothing more dreadful than the accidents everyone assumed them to have been. And Lord Thorverton, at an earlier period in his life, might easily have aroused the enmity of someone who now was seeking vengeance.

If such were the case, then all that remained unexplained was Wimbwell's murder, which had happened the day after he visited her. But other than the time element, was there any reason to connect one event with the other? Doubtless Wimbwell had a great number of clients, one of whom might have cause to hate the old man.

For all she knew—and despite his assertions of innocence—Wimbwell might very well have embezzled money from some other client. Then again, she had seen signs of incipient senility; perhaps he had merely made an innocent but costly blunder with someone's investments?

There was, of course, the fact that the killer had sent chocolate bonbons with cream centers—the *poisoned* chocolate bonbons—but then, Wimbwell had made no secret of his fondness for the sweets. Dozens of people, including all of his office staff, must have known he would gobble them down immediately.

More than likely, when the authorities investigated, they would discover a disgruntled employee, a dissatisfied client, a plethora of other suspects, any one of whom was a more likely candidate for Tyburn than Lionell, who was too involved with his own person—with the polish on his boots and the folds of his neckcloth—to worry himself with the ramblings of a silly old man.

It must have been the shock of hearing about the murder that had made her suspect Lionell in the first place, because now that she thought about it, the very idea was absurd. If Lionell had poisoned Wimbwell, then that would mean he was also behind the attack on Lord Thorverton, and that was where her suspicions faltered and failed.

While she could be brought to believe Lionell might have poisoned some bonbons, she could not, with the best of efforts, picture him consorting with a scapegallows from Soho. Although Lionell prided himself on knowing the best supplier of snuff in London, she could not imagine that the dandy would have the slightest idea where to go to find an assassin for hire. Even the thought of it now made her smile, so amusing it was.

Around Hester people were whispering, and she could hear scattered snatches of conversations—"wouldn't wager a groat he'll see his next birthday" . . . "that'll make five dead, won't it?" . . . "the devil's mark is on her" . . . "I wouldn't be in his shoes for all the tea in China" . . . "the Black Widow" . . . "how long?" . . . "doomed" . . . "the curse will bring him down, you mark my words"—

"Good evening, Miss Prestwich."

Hester recognized the man addressing her. Mr. Hennessey was an upstart Irishman who five years ago had astounded everyone by winning the hand of Lady Delilah. "I do not believe we have been introduced," she said coldly, but instead of bowing politely and moving on, he took a seat beside her.

"Since Lord Thorverton is one of my dearest friends," he said glibly, "I am sure we are destined to become well-acquainted once he is your brother-in-law."

"I am willing to wait until after the ceremony," she

said, keeping her eyes averted from his face. She did not at all like the knowing way he was looking at her—the open appraisal in his glance.

Did he, like Wimbwell, suspect her of hiring an assassin? But no, he could not possibly have any knowledge of the terms of her father's will, and so he would have no reason to connect her with the death of the old man.

She glanced at the Irishman out of the corner of her eye, but was not reassured. He looked like a fox ready to pounce . . . and he was making her feel like a rabbit about to be gobbled up.

"So you believe there will actually be a wedding ceremony?" he asked. "The majority of the people here think Thorverton will be struck down by the fatal curse, but I would like your honest opinion. Is Lord Thorverton brave or merely foolhardy? Tell me, Miss Prestwich, are you superstitious enough to believe in such things as fatal curses?"

Turning to look at him, she said coldly, "What I believe, Mr. Hennessey, is that people who play with fire often get burned. And now, if you will excuse me, I fear I have torn my flounce." She stood up and hurried from the ballroom, pursued by the whispers of the crowd.

10

"Do not look behind you, but we are being followed," Demetrius murmured to Hennessey as soon as they had left the dance and begun walking the few short blocks to the Thorverton residence. "I have spotted the pair of ugly bruisers several times in the last few days, but so far they have not made any attempt to waylay me."

Ignoring Demetrius's warning, the Irishman casually looked over his shoulder, then broke out in a large grin. "Malone and Mulrooney," he said. "I would have to agree with you that they have no pretensions toward beauty, but on the other hand, each is virtually strong enough to pick up a horse and throw it over a fence if the beast refuses to jump."

"So they are the stout lads you mentioned earlier? And without my permission, you have set them to follow me like a pair of watchdogs. I remember quite distinctly telling you I have no need of bodyguards."

"Since you have seen fit to thumb your nose at the murderer—I refer, of course, to the announcement you sent to the *Morning Post*—it will be small comfort to your friends if we catch the culprit after he has already dispatched you to a cold and solitary grave," the Irishman said. "Trapping the villain is a laudable pursuit, but I intend to see that the bait does not get gobbled up in the process."

"I did not write that announcement."

"Wheesht, and here I thought you'd come to your senses and asked that lovely girl to marry you."

"My brother took it upon himself to interfere yet again. This time, however, he has gone too far, and it will probably take both your stout lads to keep me from wringing the boy's neck when I find him.''

Turning the corner onto Grosvenor Square, Demetrius asked, "Will you come in for a bit of brandy? I am sure that if we put our minds to it, we can find a more enlivening topic of conversation than my younger brother.'' So saying, Demetrius began to describe a new colt he had—a promising two-year-old he was considering keeping for his own use.

The discussion of horses came to an abrupt end when the butler opened the door to admit them. ''Your mother is waiting to speak to you in the drawing room,'' McDougal informed him, his face haggard. "It is Master Collier—he has totally vanished. His bed was not slept in last night, and your mother is most distressed. She fears he has been kidnapped or even murdered.''

''What nonsense is this?'' Demetrius said, pushing out of his mind a fleeting fear that his brother might actually have met with skulduggery.

''I know your mother has a penchant for dramatics, my lord,'' the butler said, wringing his hands, ''but this does appear to be serious. No one saw Master Collier leave the house, and he told no one where he was going or when he would be back, which is most unlike him. Lady Thorverton has sent footmen to all the clubs, inquiring after him, but they have all denied knowledge of his whereabouts.''

Demetrius gave a bark of laughter. "As my mother should have expected. Does she not realize that the doormen in all the clubs have standing instructions to say that a member is not present even if he is? More than likely my brother is at this very moment ensconced in a comfortable chair in White's playing cards with his cronies. My mother would do better to worry about the gambling fever that seems to have infected Collier's brain, for I tell you flat out, I shall not open my pockets to him again until he shows signs of having developed at least a modicum of common sense.''

''Well, old friend,'' Hennessey said, clapping Demetrius on the back, ''I believe I shall decline your offer of brandy and conversation. Perhaps another day.''

''Deserting under fire?'' Demetrius asked with a rueful smile.

''Knowing when to retreat is ofttimes more crucial for success than charging blindly ahead,'' his friend said before departing.

A short time later Demetrius found himself in the unaccustomed position of defending his brother's actions. ''Collier lacks but a few days of being one-and-twenty, Mother. I find nothing odd about it that he has neglected to account to you for his every movement.''

His mother rose up out of the chair where she had been reclining in a tragic pose and advanced on him in a complete rage. ''Since you have never shown me the slightest consideration, I can well believe that you have been encouraging my darling boy to cast me aside like a . . . like a discarded neckcloth!''

''Well put, Mother, since you will persist in hanging around the poor boy's neck. Collier will never become a man if you continue to treat him like a child.''

At his mocking words, she puffed up like a broody hen protecting her chick from a marauding fox. ''I do not wish to hear a lecture from you about the proper way for a mother to act. You are not now—nor will you ever be— a mother. Knowing your attitude, I find it in me to *pity* that wretched Miss Prestwich. Did she know how cold-hearted you are, she would jilt you tomorrow and count herself lucky to have escaped. And as for your brother, I *demand* that you hire a Bow Street runner to find Collier, and we can only *pray* that the runner is in time to save my darling child's life—a life that *you* have endangered by consorting with a young lady who everyone *knows* is afflicted with a fatal curse.''

''A Bow Street runner? Surely you jest. I can think of nothing that would alienate Collier more surely than having a runner sent after him to drag him home like a naughty child.''

''It is all your fault, you know. If you had not given that announcement to the papers, your brother's life would not now be in jeopardy, but you have refused to take the advice of your elders and avoid that wretched woman. Perhaps you will believe in fatal curses when you discover your brother's lifeless body—or will you even then deny responsibility?''

With those parting words his mother stalked out of the room, her rigidly straight back proclaiming her displeasure with her elder son.

Little did she know that her angry words had reminded Demetrius of the bone he had to pick with his brother. Collier was undoubtedly—and very wisely—hiding out until Demetrius might be expected to have forgotten all about that infamous betrothal announcement.

Left in peace, Demetrius rang for some brandy, then settled himself in front of the fire. His thoughts were far from peaceful, however. As much as he was convinced that he understood perfectly why Collier had felt it necessary to sneak out of the house, still the possibility existed that Miss Hester Prestwich might have found herself another hired assassin—who in turn might have snatched the wrong brother.

Now he was being as foolish as his mother, seeing villains behind every bush. He took a sip of brandy, but found it tasteless. Finally he admitted to himself that he could not rest easy until he made an effort to find his brother.

With regret he abandoned his comfortable chair and set out to check at the clubs for his brother. He was not best pleased when he heard footsteps behind him. Looking over his shoulder, he recognized Malone and Mulrooney, and their presence did nothing to improve his mood.

By the time the sun was up, Demetrius had made a thorough check of all the clubs to which he belonged, and he had also gone to several of the more notorious gambling hells. Unfortunately, he was not an ardent gambler himself, which meant he was woefully ignorant about the innumerable smaller places where one could go if one wished to lose one's money rapidly.

Likewise, if he had only known who his brother's special friends were, his search would have been easier, since he could have asked them for news of Collier. But to his chagrin, Demetrius could not remember any name except Charles Neuce, whose face he was not even sure he would recognize. Although it was painful for him to admit, Demetrius began to suspect that during the last year or so he should have been paying less attention to his horses and more attention to his brother.

Returning home, he was met at the door by his mother, who had obviously not been to bed either. When she saw he was alone, grief clouded her face. If she had had the hysterics, Demetrius could have dismissed her fears and gone to bed, but her haunted look was not part of her normal dramatic repertoire.

"Very well, Mother," he said tiredly, thinking with longing of his bed, "I shall go at once to Bow Street and engage the services of a runner."

Lady Thorverton stared with hatred at the young lady her elder son was dancing with. The Black Widow was smiling and talking as if she had not once again more than likely caused the premature demise of an innocent young man. Dorothea's feelings for Demetrius were not much pleasanter. How could he act as if he had not a care in the world, when his brother might even at this moment be lying dead in a ditch somewhere, struck down by the fatal curse?

But perhaps it was not too late to save Collier. Although the Bow Street runner had been duly hired the day before, he had not yet reported back, which to her way of thinking only proved that even a runner was helpless against an evil curse.

No, the only way to break the power of the curse and save Collier's life was to end the relationship between Demetrius and that wretched Miss Meribe Prestwich.

Perhaps if she spoke with the girl directly, Miss Prestwich might be willing to release Demetrius from her clutches. But no, the chit was undoubtedly enraptured with the idea of having ensnared an earl in her coils.

On the other hand, she might be amenable to a bribe. Given a sufficiently large offer of money, she might—

But no, Dorothea had heard that Sir John Prestwich had been well to grass. Doubtless neither of the two Prestwich sisters was lacking in sufficient funds.

All things considered, there was only one thing to be

done. Tomorrow—no, tonight—she would send a notice to the *Morning Post* that they had erred in publishing the betrothal announcement, and she would demand that they print a retraction. Demetrius would, of course, be in a rage, since he appeared to be totally blinded by Miss Meribe Prestwich's charms, but Dorothea had endured his blustering on earlier occasions. And this time, at least, she had right on her side, which would make it ever so much easier to withstand Demetrius's wrath.

"Have you ever seen such a game fighter as the Manchester Marvel?" Collier asked his friends. He was still feeling quite intoxicated with the excitement of the boxing match he had just witnessed, and he could not settle down with a glass of brandy like the others. Moving around the private parlor they had rented at the Painted Boar, he jabbed at the air with his fists. "I was quite sure he would go down in the twenty-seventh round, and with the pounding he was taking from the Bedford Bruiser, I'd never've believed that the Marvel would be able to stay on his feet for another twelve rounds."

"Game he was," Charles Neuce agreed, his tone lugubrious, "but I could wish he'd exhibited a bit more science. I'd two hundred guineas riding on him to win, and the devil only knows how I shall pry that much out of m'father."

"Only lost a hundred myself," Ernest Saville put in mournfully, "which is not an enormous sum, but I expect my brother won't see it that way. He'll ring a peal over me and threaten me with the Fleet, but if I look properly chastised, in the end he'll pay. He always does. And what about you, Baineton? Is Thorverton going to fly up into the boughs when he discovers your losses, or are you plump enough in the pocket that you don't need to ask him for any brass?"

For a moment Collier was tempted to lie, but then he confessed, "I didn't lose anything."

"You don't mean to tell me you put your money on the Bedford Bruiser?" Charles Neuce gave him a look of disgust. "If that don't beat all. Not sure I should have given you a place in my carriage."

"Actually, I didn't even make a wager," Collier admitted. "Thing is, my brother made it quite clear he disapproves of my gambling with money I don't have."

"So what's that to the point?" Saville asked. "My brother is not keen on it either, but I don't let that stop me from having a bit of fun."

"The point is, any money I get from Demetrius tends to have too many strings attached. Besides which, I'm still hoping that if I play my cards right, I may be able to persuade him to buy me my colors as soon as I am one-and-twenty."

"Give over," Neuce said scornfully. "Thorverton will never go against your mother's wishes, and you told us that she's dead set against a military career for you. Why, she has the hysterics every time you even mention the army, and I swear I have seen her have palpitations when she just catches sight of you standing next to someone wearing a scarlet jacket."

"Be that as it may," Collier said, "if I can prove to my brother that I am grown-up, I am sure he will be able to arrange something. When he makes up his mind, not even my mother can make him change it."

Neuce and Saville exchanged glances. "Don't mean to cast a damper on your hopes," Neuce said, "but you did mention that you sneaked out of the house without telling anyone where you were going. Can't think that's any way to bring your brother around. Bound to be annoyed when he discovers you've kicked over the traces and gone off to a pugilism match."

Collier smiled sheepishly. "The thing is, before I left London I did something I knew would make him mad as hops. I can't tell you what it was, but I'm hoping if I stay away long enough, he'll be over the worst of it before he sets eyes on me again."

"You're daft," Saville said. "Seems to me Thorverton'll be doubly angry at you—once on account of whatever rig you pulled, then again because you didn't stand and face the music."

With a sinking heart Collier realized his friend was right: nothing so enraged Demetrius as a person refusing to take his punishment like a man. Why had he not remembered that when Hennessey had made his suggestion to play least-in-sight?

They'd had a trainer once—a man from Dorset who'd had a wonderful way with horses—but on one occasion he had been having a nip in his room when he should have been attending a mare in labor, and when Demetrius had confronted him, the man had whined and dragged out any number of excuses, each one lamer than the one before. Demetrius had had the man packed up and off the estate in less than an hour.

"Well," Collier said, throwing himself down into a chair beside his friends, "if Demetrius doesn't come through for me, I can always take the king's shilling."

"You wouldn't!" Saville said. "Being an enlisted man ain't a proper thing for a gentleman. Don't think it'd suit you at all."

"Well, it certainly doesn't suit me to be kept dancing attendance on my mother. And if she has her way, she'll keep me on leading strings for the rest of my natural life," Collier said with a scowl.

"He's got a point," Neuce said. "Count myself lucky my own mother don't want to stir a foot out of Bath. Visit her twice a year for a week or two and escort her to the Pump Room like a dutiful son, and that's all she expects of me. Fact is, after a few days she's usually hinting that I must have pressing business elsewhere. Once told me to m'face that I'm too resty to suit her. Got so much energy, it makes her tired just being around me."

"Well, I don't see why Baineton here even puts up with his mother's whims and crotchets. From the sound of it, he needs to show a little more backbone," Saville said, shaking his head in disgust. "Already under the cat's paw, and he ain't even leg-shackled yet."

"Well, I'd like to see you do better," Collier retorted, springing to his feet. "I suppose you'd just laugh it off if your mother looked at you with tears in her eyes and accused you of no longer loving her. Blast it all, she's my mother—I can't just tell her to go to the devil!"

Before Saville could answer, there was a rap at the door, and Collier went to answer it. A heavyset man of middling height wearing a dirty gray-brown overcoat stood there. His nose looked as if at some earlier time he might have gone a round or two in the ring himself. "Mr. Collier Baineton?" he asked.

"Yes, I'm Baineton," Collier replied impatiently. "What is it you want with me."

"My name is Stevens—Josiah Stevens. Your brother hired me to find you," the stranger replied.

"Hired you? What nonsense is this?" Collier was too stunned to think properly.

Coming up behind him, Neuce clapped him on the shoulder. "It's clear as daylight, Baineton. This gentleman has the shifty-eyed, implacable look of a Bow Street runner."

The man did not deny it, and from his seat by the table Saville spoke up, deliberately making his voice high and prissy. "After all, Mama's widdle boy mustn't wun off on his own to pway wif his widdle fwiends. Go along wif this nice man, now; he's come to take 'ou home like a good widdle boy."

Both of his friends were grinning like fools, and Collier knew it would take only a few hours after they arrived back in town for this story to be spread all over London. Blast it all! How dare Demetrius embarrass him like this! If it was meant to be punishment for the betrothal notice in the *Morning Post,* it was rather extreme.

"If you'll collect your things, sir," the runner said deferentially, "we'd best be on our way."

Turning back to face his friends, Collier said, "If you breathe one word of this affair to anyone I shall . . . I shall be forced to call you out."

Unfortunately, both his friends were laughing too hard to pay any attention to such a threat.

Meribe stared at the newspaper, unable to believe the words she was reading. "The *Morning Post* regrets to inform its readers that one pair of names was erroneously included in the list of betrothals appearing on its pages the day before yesterday. Lord Thorverton has informed us that he is not at this time betrothed."

It was what she had wanted: by announcing to the

world that there was nothing between the two of them, Lord Thorverton was more than likely saving his own life. Yesterday she had herself urged him repeatedly to cancel their sham betrothal.

So why did she now feel so miserable? When she should have been rejoicing in her heart that he was safe, why did she feel as if she would never be happy again?

"Why the stricken look, Niece?" Aunt Phillipa inquired, daintily picking up a triangle of toast and inspecting it carefully. "Is the news in the *Morning Post* so terrible this morning? Has Wellesley suffered a defeat in Spain?"

With difficulty Meribe managed to speak. "It appears that I have been jilted."

"Jilted?" Hester asked. The look of relief on her face was quickly masked, but not before Meribe had seen it. "Well, it is doubtless for the best. Although one would not choose to be jilted, it is better than attending the funeral of still another suitor."

"Mind your tongue," Aunt Phillipa snapped out. Then, turning to Meribe, she said in a conciliatory voice, "But Hester is right, my dear. Breaking the betrothal without first informing you shows a decided unsteadiness of character on Lord Thorverton's part. You are doubtless better off without him, and I can only hope you will do nothing so foolish as to go into a decline."

"No, I shall not do anything so foolish," Meribe replied, but despite her calm assurances to her aunt, she could not quite rid herself of a foolish feeling of regret that the betrothal—even though it had been a hoax—was now officially ended. Indeed, it had been quite pleasant for the last forty-eight hours to pretend that they were truly betrothed—that they would one day marry.

For her own reputation, she cared nothing. She could hardly sink lower in the estimation of society, no matter what she did. And she could not fault Lord Thorverton for sending in the retraction. But now that she thought about it, he had behaved in a rather high-handed manner. As her aunt had pointed out, it would not have hurt him to have informed her in advance of his intentions.

With deliberate effort Meribe fanned the tiny sparks of

anger that flickered feebly inside her. It was not so much what Lord Thorverton had done as the way he had done it. After all, the wording of the announcement could have been improved by the simple expediency of saying, "Lord Thorverton *and* Miss Prestwich have informed us . . ." There had been no need to make it quite so obvious that he was jilting her. That could hardly be called the act of a friend.

But perhaps even their friendship was now over. Perhaps Lord Thorverton had deliberately chosen this method of informing her that he no longer wished to have anything at all to do with her.

Hester watched the play of emotions across her sister's face. Keeping her own countenance suitably impassive, she nevertheless rejoiced inside. Although she felt pity for her sister, Hester could not entirely suppress the feeling of relief that she herself felt.

Now, at least, Lionell—if indeed he was responsible for the deaths generally attributed to the fatal curse— would have no cause to harm Lord Thorverton. And in a fortnight Meribe would turn one-and-twenty, and then Hester would inherit not only the estate she had always been promised but also the income from her father's vast investments.

Once the money was hers, she would, of course, give a generous portion of it to Meribe so that they could both be happy. Really, it would work out much better this way. If Meribe inherited everything, doubtless she would *wish* to give Hester her rightful share, but the only way Meribe could inherit was by marrying, and in such a case her husband would control all her money. And such were the ways of the world that very few men would be willing to give half their wives' dowries to their sisters-in-law.

No, all in all, things were working out for the best. There was nothing wrong with Lord Thorverton as a husband for Meribe, and Hester would do everything possible to promote his courtship of her sister. But only after Meribe was one-and-twenty.

* * *

It was becoming quite obvious, Demetrius realized, that he could remonstrate with his mother until he turned blue in the face, and she would still not admit that she had committed a heinous offense against an innocent young lady.

Therefore, as much as he hated to do it, he could think of no other way to put a stop to her machinations than to threaten her where she was most vulnerable. Waiting only until she paused in the recital of her grievances, he spoke in a calm, firm voice.

"I warn you, madam, that if you ever again interfere in my affairs, I shall immediately buy Collier his colors."

"You would not dare!" his mother said, her voice rising to a shriek.

"You would be amazed at what I will dare," he replied. "And do not delude yourself that I am making an idle threat."

Clasping her hands to her bosom, she declaimed, "Oh, that you could hate your own brother so much, that you would ruin his life by forcing him into the military!"

"No coercion would be required; he has already begged me to buy him a lieutenancy in a cavalry regiment. And as for hating him, I have come to realize that if I wish to do what is in his best interests, I would do well to remove him from your influence."

For once his mother was rendered speechless, and before she could recover her voice, he bowed politely and left the room.

Unfortunately, even though he had achieved a measure of success with his mother, he still had to face Miss Meribe Prestwich and tell her what had happened. "It is all my mother's fault," he would explain. But no, he could not put all the blame on her, lest he be guilty of the same kind of childish behavior for which he had earlier scolded his brother.

Indeed, having once left Devon, he had set in motion a train of events that seemed to have developed a momentum of its own. Would his mother have sent the retraction to the *Morning Post* if Collier had not first sent the announcement? And would Collier have sent the notice if he himself had not asked for suggestions as to how to trap the murderer? Would Wimbwell have died if he and Meribe had not gone to speak to him?

Walking briskly to Berkeley Square, Demetrius gradually came to realize that by his efforts to help, he had caused grave injury to the young lady he was attempting to protect. Owing to his relatives, she had become betrothed against her will, and then had been callously jilted.

If he wished to call himself a gentleman, there was nothing for him to do but ask her—persuade her, if necessary—to marry him. It mattered little that she was not the type of woman he would have chosen for a wife if he'd had the freedom of choice. What mattered was that he do whatever was needful to undo the pain he had caused her.

It was not as if she were an antidote, of course. She was quite pleasing to the eye and she had no serious faults that he could think of. She was not headstrong or flighty, nor did she chatter incessantly. More important, she had kept her sweetness of disposition under conditions that were distressing enough to have caused even a saint to become bitter and resentful.

To be sure, her knowledge of horses was nonexistent, but at least she liked animals and appeared willing to learn to ride. He might even see about teaching her to drive.

Yes, now that he thought about it, they should be able to rub along rather well together, and the chances were that even if he waited a lifetime, he would never meet another woman like his neighbor Anne, and since that was the case, Miss Meribe Prestwich would do well enough.

Which meant all he had to do was propose to her in a suitable romantic way so that she would not notice when he never actually avowed enduring love. Women, he had learned through various friends' experiences, were funny that way; the female sex were not especially keen about treating marriage like any other business merger. But he had confidence in his own ability to pull it off.

Of course, a proper proposal was not actually all he

had to do—he also had to trap a murderer. Luckily, the two tasks could be easily combined.

Much to his mortification, he was not given the opportunity to speak with anyone except the butler.

"I regret to inform you that the Misses Prestwich are not at home," Smucker said nervously.

"It is only Miss Meribe Prestwich that I need to speak with," Demetrius explained. "Perhaps I might wait? When do you expect her to return?"

Looking even more ill-at-ease, the butler said, "The Misses Prestwich are not at home *to you.*" The emphasis was subtle but definite.

Demetrius cursed under his breath, and for a moment he toyed with the idea of forcing his way past the butler. Such uncivilized behavior would hardly advance his cause, but it was tempting, considering that the young lady he wished to marry was undoubtedly in her room crying her eyes out. Or more likely she was in the garden finding consolation among her plants.

He smiled at the mental picture of her with her gloves discarded on the ground, her hands and likely her face streaked with dirt.

Before he could quiz the butler further, the door was shut in his face, and he heard the sound of the bolt being slid into place.

Walking toward Tattersall's, he could not help contrasting this day with that idyllic day only a few weeks ago, when he had watched Dolly's foal be born. Lawrence had indeed been correct when he had prophesied that misfortune was bound to follow their months of good luck.

It was almost enough to make Demetrius superstitious, but despite everything that had happened since he had come to London, he still clung to his belief that a man could make his own luck, whether good or bad.

11

"I still say you oughtn't to be calling on a gentleman like this," Jane protested.

"Lord Thorverton lives with his mother," Meribe replied, lifting the heavy knocker and letting it fall. "I am sure not even the highest stickler would find anything to criticize me for, since they can assume that I am calling on Lady Thorverton."

"But you don't want to speak to *her*," the maid continued to remonstrate.

"Well, I certainly cannot tell the butler that I wish to speak with *Lord* Thorverton," Meribe replied, although she could not look forward to a confrontation with her aunt's sworn enemy, and she could only hope that Lord Thorverton would happen to be with his mother.

Her wishes were not to be granted. Finally opening the door after an unconscionable time, the butler looked down his nose at the two of them, as if they were Gypsies come to steal the family silver.

Handing him her card, Meribe said bravely, "I wish to speak with Lady Thorverton," while Jane attempted to hide behind her back.

With a total lack of civility the butler shut the door in their faces and left them standing on the stoop while he carried the card to his mistress.

When he returned after a good ten minutes, he looked as if he had eaten an unripe persimmon. Without meeting her eyes, he said stiffly, "Lady Thorverton has instructed me to tell you that you are not welcome in this house and that if you ever come here again, she will have charges laid against you at the nearest magistrate."

"Here, now," Jane said, "you don't have no cause to

be so disrespectful to my mistress, no matter what that old harridan told you to do.''

''Her ladyship has also instructed me to tell you that it is all your fault that Master Collier has been kidnapped and likely murdered.''

At Meribe's look of horror, most of the stiffness went out of the butler's spine, and he seemed almost wistful when he said, ''He has quite vanished, and her ladyship is beside herself with worry. She fears that he has also been struck down by . . . by . . .''

''By the fatal curse?'' Jane asked contemptuously.

The butler nodded miserably, and Meribe realized there was nothing for it but to admit her true purpose in coming here. ''Would you please inform Lord Thorverton that I wish to speak to him?''

Again the servant became the quintessential butler. Straightening his back, he said quite formally, ''His lordship is not home.'' Then, after a furtive glance over his shoulder, he hurriedly shut the massive oaken door in Meribe's face for the second time.

''Well, and I hope you have learned a lesson from all this,'' Jane said crossly once they were well away from the Thorverton residence. ''No good ever came of a woman chasing after a man. It's unnatural, that's what it is.''

She continued to animadvert on the foolishness of young girls who wore their hearts on their sleeves, but Meribe hardly heard what the maid was saying.

Guilty thoughts frantically chased each other through Meribe's mind. Whyever had she not been more resolute in turning down Lord Thorverton's offer of friendship?

Did it really matter whether she was afflicted with a fatal curse or whether she had acquired a mortal enemy? In the end, the results were the same—another innocent young man had been struck down in the prime of life.

Oh, but she wished she had never accepted Lord Thorverton's initial offer of assistance, nor any of the subsequent offers! She had been selfish in the extreme, thinking only of her own happiness. It was no wonder Lord Thorverton wanted nothing more to do with her.

* * *

With the end of the Season fast approaching, Almack's was crowded with young ladies, their hopeful expressions looking a bit desperate. None of them looked as desperate as Meribe felt, but she was not trying to catch a husband, she was only attempting to avoid speaking—or dancing—with Lord Thorverton lest the murderer make another attempt on his life or on the life of one of Thorverton's friends.

This was not as easy as she might have wished, because Almack's did not provide a plethora of places for a young lady to hide. After her third visit in the space of one hour to the room set aside for ladies who wished to freshen up, her aunt asked her if she was coming down with something.

"No, I just do not wish to dance with Lord Thorverton," Meribe confessed, feeling quite ill at the sight of the aforementioned lord approaching her yet again.

"Then for heaven's sake tell him so to his face. Men do not understand hints the way women do. You have got to be firm, otherwise he will continue to trifle with your affections."

Instead of heeding her aunt's advice and showing resolution, Meribe bolted back to the ladies' room, where she huddled miserably for a good quarter-hour, wishing she could again find comfort in Lord Thorverton's arms, but knowing it was too dangerous for him.

If only her birthday would come more quickly, before anyone else's life was shattered. She would not mind eking out an existence on the meager pittance she would receive from her father's will, if only her sister would be satisfied with her ill-gotten gains and would call a halt to this evil conspiracy she had instigated.

"Next time she bolts, you could lie in wait for her and catch her the moment she emerges from that blasted retiring room," Hennessey suggested.

Demetrius looked at him in disgust. "What a gentlemanly thing you're suggesting. And I suppose that once I have 'caught' her, I should throw her over my shoulder and make off with her as if she were one of the Sabine women. A proper heathen I would look."

"Just trying to help," Hennessey said, his cheerfulness intact. "Would you like me to ask her to dance? Perhaps I can find out what's bothering her."

"I know what is bothering her. She is upset that I—or so she thinks—canceled the betrothal. I cannot say that I blame Miss Prestwich for being annoyed with me. She did not want the announcement put into the newspaper in the first place, and now she is probably disgusted with me for blowing hot and cold like the veriest feather-headed wigeon."

"Still, she should give you a chance to explain that it was your mother who sent in the retraction, and not you."

"As if that makes a difference to the gossips. Have you seen the way they are whispering? And they are avoiding her as if she has the plague."

"They were whispering about her and avoiding her before she even met you, and they have never stopped since. The only thing that will put an end to all the speculation and gossip and wagering is for you to marry the girl."

"Which is a bit hard to do if I cannot get her even to speak to me."

Hennessey raised his eyebrows in mock surprise. "So, you've come to your senses at last. I congratulate you."

"Congratulations are a bit premature, don't you think? At the moment she is unwilling even to dance with me, much less entertain an offer of marriage."

"But I am sure you will be able to persuade her." Hennessey clapped him on the back. "And now, if you will excuse me, I have someone I need to talk to."

Demetrius caught him by the arm. "You are not going to bother Miss Prestwich—I forbid you to talk with her."

"Forbid? My, we are feeling rather crotchety this evening, aren't we?"

"Understand me, Hennessey, I am not joking about this. Give me your promise that you will not approach her this evening."

"Very well, if that is what you wish, I promise to stay away from her."

There was something about the look in the Irishman's

eyes that Demetrius did not quite trust, but he could hardly call his friend a liar. "Thank you," he said, releasing the other man's arm.

Hennessey strolled away as if he had not a care in the world, and a few minutes later Demetrius saw him in earnest conversation with Humphrey Swinton. Muttering an oath, Demetrius started toward his uncle, but before he could make his way through the crowd, Uncle Humphrey had approached Miss Prestwich and bowed.

With a tremulous smile she stood up and laid her hand on his arm and allowed him to lead her out to join the set that was forming.

Demetrius felt such intense frustration, he wanted to bang his head against the wall, but knowing how many people were watching him and waiting to see what he would do, he carefully kept his expression impassive.

As much as he had been against Hennessey's interference, now that Miss Prestwich was talking with Uncle Humphrey, Demetrius felt impatient to discover what was being said.

The music dragged on and on, and when the final chord was played, instead of returning Miss Prestwich to her seat, Uncle Humphrey led her over to a pair of chairs that were positioned somewhat apart from the others, and they continued their conversation.

"You could approach her now, no doubt," Hennessey's voice came from behind his shoulder.

Without turning, Demetrius said, "I suggest you leave before Almack's is treated to the sight of two grown men brawling and brangling like a couple of schoolboys."

"Keep in mind that I am only trying to help," Hennessey said, a smile in his voice. "And don't forget to send me an invitation to the wedding."

"The way it looks, she'd sooner wed my uncle."

"Fustian, the young lady dotes on you."

"She has a strange way of showing it." Demetrius could not possibly be feeling jealous—not of his uncle, who was a portly, middle-aged bachelor more fond of food than of women. But even the most confirmed bachelor could take a tumble for a pair of soft brown eyes.

Strangely enough, now that he had decided he wanted

to marry Miss Meribe Prestwich of the oh-so-kissable lips, he felt quite impatient to get the matter settled.

"Do you know," Hennessey commented, "it might look a little less odd if you were to dance with one or two of the other young ladies. Standing here scowling at your uncle will only add fuel to the gossip."

"Do you know," Demetrius retorted, "I am beginning to find your helpfulness a bit tedious. Perhaps if you tried very hard, you could find someone else who would appreciate your advice more than I do."

"Ah, but the lady patronesses won't allow Malone and Mulrooney inside these sacrosanct portals, so I must keep my place here beside you."

Demetrius turned to his friend in amazement. "Surely you do not suspect that there will be an attempt on my life in here?"

"Why not? How difficult would it be in this crowd for someone to jostle up against you and at the same time to slip a dirk between your ribs? Or to drop some poison into your glass of orgeat? That stuff already tastes nasty enough to kill a man."

"I hardly think it likely that Miss Hester Prestwich is skilled with a knife, and she cannot very well bring another like Black Jack in here to do the job. As you have pointed out already, the patronesses are particular as to whom they allow inside. Besides, why would a hired assassin go to so much trouble to gain admittance to Almack's, when he can simply use a gun some night and shoot me down in cold blood? Of what use would you or Malone or Mulrooney or my uncle be in such an event?" Demetrius asked.

He wished he could hear what Miss Prestwich was saying. No doubt she was busily enumerating all his various and assorted shortcomings for his uncle's edification.

"To begin with, not everyone is a good-enough shot to hit a moving target in the dark. Second, since the murderer might be expected to want to escape with his own life, he would not risk attempting to shoot you when you are accompanied by men who could chase him down."

"You are making it sound as if I am safe on the streets

of London as I would be if I were back in my own stables in Devon,'' Demetrius commented, a touch of sarcasm in his voice.

''Offhand, I would say that the sister has not yet been able to find a replacement for Black Jack, because if she had, another attempt to send you to meet your maker would surely have been made by now.''

Tearing his eyes away from Miss Meribe Prestwich, Demetrius glanced around the room and discovered Miss Hester Prestwich was staring intently at him. As soon as his eyes met hers, she quickly looked away, but it was too late; he had already noticed her look of fear.

''There is one thing more you should consider,'' Hennessey said softly in his ear. ''There is a good possibility that the sister has an accomplice. I don't mean someone she has hired, but someone from our own class. I find it difficult to believe Miss Hester dealt with Black Jack without using an intermediary, nor do I think she would have gone with her maid into a shop to purchase the bonbons or the poison. Therefore, if you wish to expose her, you will have to discover who among these illustrious gentleman has been aiding and abetting her.''

''What is the point of worrying about it if Miss Meribe will not even let me speak with her?''

''She will get over being miffed. She does not strike me as the type of female who can hold a grudge. And as you have pointed out, it would be criminal to allow the sister to profit from her misdeeds.''

Demetrius was about ready to say the devil take Sir John Prestwich's money, all he wanted to do was marry Miss Meribe Prestwich and take her back to Devon and let her grub around in his gardens to her heart's content. He had enough money for both of them—she did not need to bring her father's fortune as a dowry.

But something in Demetrius rankled at the thought of the sister profiting from her wicked deeds.

At long last Uncle Humphrey finished his conversation with the young lady in question and escorted her back to her relatives. Then he casually strolled over in their direction, stopping to chat with friends along the way. Demetrius doubted that his attempt to look casual was fooling anyone in the room.

Casting furtive looks to the right and to the left, Uncle Humphrey sidled up to them. "Meet me outside in half an hour," he muttered out of the corner of his mouth. Then, still nodding and smiling to his acquaintances, he moved on.

"She is not mad at you for jilting her, don't you know," Uncle Humphrey said as soon as the three conspirators met on the street outside Almack's. "Thing is, she went to see you this afternoon, but you were not home, and your mother ordered McDougal to refuse her admittance."

Walking along in the direction of Grosvenor Square, Demetrius caught sight of a figure half-hidden in the shadows and his muscles tensed up. But then with relief he recognized Mulrooney. Doubtless Malone was also lurking about nearby.

"Even that did not upset Miss Prestwich overmuch, because she understands about eccentric relatives, as well she might, living with that aunt of hers. I will admit my own sister is also given to mad starts, but I suppose in this instance one must make allowances for the fact that she is quite beside herself with worry about young Collier, don't you know."

Distracted as he was by the thought of a possible assassin waiting somewhere in the darkness, Demetrius did not immediately grasp the import of what Humphrey was saying. When his uncle's words finally sank in, Demetrius caught him by the arm.

"Wait a minute—if Miss Prestwich is not angry with me because of the retraction, then why will she still not speak to me?"

"Because of Collier, of course. Your mother accused Miss Prestwich of recklessly endangering your brother's life by associating with you. The fatal curse, don't you know."

"Blast it all! I made sure I had finally persuaded Miss Prestwich that there is no curse and that there never has been any curse," Demetrius said harshly.

"To be sure," his uncle replied mildly. "But it doesn't make a ha'porth of difference as far as the results. Whether it's a curse or a murderous sister, you'll have to admit it's dangerous to be around Miss Prestwich."

"Bah!" was all Demetrius could think of to say. As much as he might wish it otherwise, what his uncle was saying made sense. "So what is your opinion, Hennessey? You have been uncommonly quiet this far."

"I was just thinking that meddling in other people's affairs can be risky."

"Et tu, Brutus?" Demetrius asked, feeling very much older than when he had gotten out of bed that morning.

"What's this?" Uncle Humphrey asked. "Have you taken to spouting Latin, Nephew? If that's your pleasure, then here is where we will part company, for if there is one thing I will not tolerate, it is listening to folks jawing on in a heathen language. Speak in English or hold your tongue, that's what I say."

"It appears," Demetrius explained, "that Mr. Hennessey here has also been meddling in my affairs."

"Playing the role of *deus ex machina,* as it were," Hennessey said impudently.

"Blast it all, now he's started it too! Did you not listen to what I just said?" Uncle Humphrey's voice had risen almost to a shout. "Not one word of Latin! Do I make myself clear?"

"Quite clear, Uncle," Demetrius said. "Now, if you would also be a little more clear about what you have been up to, Hennessey?"

"Well, it was nothing much. I merely mentioned to your brother that there was to be a bout of fisticuffs in a little village near Reading yesterday," the Irishman said.

"And you said nothing about this to me when you knew I was worried about Collier? You let me waste hours searching all over London for him?" Demetrius could not keep all the anger out of his voice, but he did manage to maintain a reasonable degree of control until a sudden suspicion struck him. "Wait—when did you mention this pugilism match?"

"Right after I pointed out to him that it was not necessary for you to marry Miss Prestwich, so long as the murderer *thought* you were going to,'' Hennessey replied. Then, holding up his hands in mock surrender, he quickly added, "No, no, you must not strike me! Remember Malone and Mulrooney—in a fight between us, their loyalty would be to me.''

"Ah, but you forget,'' Demetrius could not resist saying, "that I have my uncle on my side, and *he* carries a lethal cane.''

There was a moment of stunned silence; then Humphrey objected, "Now, see here, Nephew, don't expect me to slash up this rogue, for I tell you flat out, I will not do it, even though he is an insolent Irishman too full of blarney for his own good. Why, if I was to start cutting up people right and left, first thing you know, all the young bucks would be calling me out to test their mettle. No, I will not oblige you in this matter, and do not think you can persuade me, for you will find my mind is quite made up.''

Hennessey and Demetrius both burst out laughing. "Relax, Uncle,'' Demetrius said, clapping the older man on the back. "I was only jesting.''

"Well, I must say this is a strange time to be making a joke,'' Humphrey said indignantly.

"When things are looking blackest, what else is there to do?'' Demetrius replied. "My brother has vanished, my mother is prostrate with anxiety, I have threatened her shamelessly, my best friend has just brazenly confessed to meddling, the woman I wish to marry will not even speak to me, and to top it all off, someone is undoubtedly at this very moment plotting ways to kill me. Pray, what can I do but laugh?''

"I could use a stiff drink,'' Humphrey muttered. "Do you still have any of that port your father laid down in '87?''

"I imagine McDougal can find a bottle or two. It is not my favorite tipple, so I have not made vast inroads into it,'' Demetrius replied.

"No, no, you cannot refer to such magnificent port as 'tipple,' '' Humphrey objected. "Disrespectful, don't you know. One must treat such a blessing from the gods with the honor it deserves, don't you agree, Hennessey?''

"To my great regret, I have never had the pleasure of sampling any '87 port," the Irishman replied.

"Never tasted it? But that is shocking! I had not realized Ireland was so uncivilized! You must come in and sample a glass. Demetrius will not object," Humphrey said with assurance. "I will say this for the lad, he'll never offer you inferior champagne or that disgusting swill they serve at Almack's."

Demetrius was about to offer his uncle an entire case of the aforementioned port, when about thirty yards ahead and a little to the right a shadow separated itself from the deeper darkness. Just as he was beginning to realize the import of what he was seeing, a pistol shot rang out.

Instinctively he started toward the assailant, but before Demetrius could take even two steps, his friend and his uncle threw themselves on him and bore him to the ground. As he fell, a second shot whistled over his head, and the two Irish grooms lumbered past the three of them where they lay on the pavement. Strong they might be, but unfortunately they were not notably fleet of foot.

A horse's hooves clattered away down the street, which made it even more unlikely that Malone and Mulrooney could catch up with the miscreant.

"Are you hurt, my dear boy?" Uncle Humphrey's voice boomed out right beside Demetrius's ear.

If Demetrius could have moved, he would have winced, but with both Hennessey and Humphrey lying on him, he could barely wiggle a finger.

"I am . . . in danger . . . of expiring . . . on the spot," he labored to say. "If . . . you both . . . do not . . . get off me . . . I fear my chest . . . will be quite . . . crushed."

Immediately and with profuse apologies his companions rolled off him and stood up. The relief was enormous, and it took Demetrius only a few moments to catch his breath and then get to his feet. Solicitously Uncle Humphrey began to brush off Demetrius's jacket.

"Never mind, Uncle, I fear this garment is now fit only for the dustbin," Demetrius said.

"Well, at least I was half-right," Hennessey said cheerfully, walking back a few paces to pick up their hats and Humphrey's cane.

"How is that?" Demetrius asked.

"Very few people are good enough shots to hit a moving target in the dark. Too bad I did not also consider the possibility that the assassin might think to provide himself with a horse."

Hennessey held out his hat and Demetrius took it and clapped it on his head.

A few minutes later the two Irish grooms returned. Handing Demetrius an antique silver-chased dueling pistol, Mulrooney said, "It appears that the assassin dropped one of his pistols. I found this lying on the pavement."

"I think, Hennessey," Demetrius said after inspecting it in the light of a street lamp, "that you are undoubtedly correct in assuming that Miss Hester Prestwich has a gentleman accomplice. This is not the kind of weapon used by most residents of Soho."

"It is a shame we cannot simply search anyone we suspect, in order to see if he is carrying the mate to this pistol. Of course, there is a chance that some gunsmith might be able to identify it," Humphrey suggested.

"It is possible, but considering its apparent age, it is not likely," Demetrius replied. "In any event, I think we had better come up with a plan that has a higher chance of success."

12

The carriage pulled to a stop in front of the Prestwich residence, and Meribe sighed with relief. As soon as the door was opened and the steps let down, her sister climbed out and hurried into the house without a backward glance. Meribe, however, waited to see if her aunt required any assistance.

Descending from the carriage and taking Meribe's proffered arm, Aunt Phillipa said petulantly, "I wish someone would tell me what is going on. Hester did not utter a single word all the way home, which, although it was quite restful for me, is very much out of character for her. And as for you, young lady, you spent the evening popping in and out of the ladies' room like a veritable jack-in-the-box. The only thing I can conclude from your behavior is that both of you are coming down with something quite dreadful, which is sure to spoil what little pleasure I am able to find in London these days."

Smucker opened the door for them and took Aunt Phillipa's cloak, but Meribe indicated that she wished to keep hers for the moment.

"I can only hope," her aunt continued, "that whatever you are sickening with, it does not involve spots. I cannot abide watching people scratch themselves. It is so very vulgar." With these parting words Aunt Phillipa ascended the stairs and passed from view.

Left alone at last, Meribe wandered out into the garden. Only a few short weeks ago she had thought she could not be more unhappy than she was. Now she knew differently.

Only twenty-four hours had passed since she had last spoken with Lord Thorverton, but it seemed more like an eternity. Over the course of the last few weeks they had been so preoccupied with solving the mystery of who was permanently disposing of her suitors that Meribe had not noticed how she had little by little become accustomed to being with Lord Thorverton every day—relying on him for advice, turning to him for comfort.

Even when she was not with him, her thoughts were centered on him. No matter what she might be doing, she was invariably anticipating their next meeting—planning what she would say to him, wondering what news he might have for her. But mostly just wanting to be near him.

Especially when things went wrong—and they seemed to be going wrong with increasing frequency—she needed him and only him. His strength supported her and gave her the courage to face the unavoidable and the determination to deal with the unthinkable.

Looking back on her life before she had met him, she realized now how empty her days had been. And looking ahead?

Tears filled her eyes at the thought of the endless days . . . the empty weeks . . . the unendurable months . . . the unbearably lonely years. How could she manage without him? How could she even find comfort working in her garden, when everywhere she looked she was reminded of him?

Love was not supposed to make her feel like this—love was supposed to bring happiness and contentment, not soul-wrenching misery.

If only there were some safe way to continue seeing Lord Thorverton—some way to marry him that would not endanger his life or the lives of his family and friends.

In the dark, empty garden, it seemed to Meribe as if her life would always be as bleak and lonely as it was now. For a moment she almost wished her sister had arranged for a fatal accident to befall *her*. But then she resolutely pushed such unworthy thoughts out of her head.

Time, she knew full well, did indeed heal broken hearts. It would not be soon, but someday in the future she would be able to look back on these weeks in London and remember Lord Thorverton without pain. She would be able to feel gratitude for his friendship, for his assistance, for the comfort of his arms.

Someday, but not today. Tomorrow, even, she would try her best to be brave and resolute, but not now. It was too soon—the wound was too fresh, the pain too intense.

Sinking down onto the stone bench where she had sat with Lord Thorverton, Meribe covered her face with her hands and allowed the tears to flow.

How long she cried, she had no way of knowing, but when the tears finally ended, she wiped her eyes, sat up straighter, and began to plan her future—a future in which she would not be Lord Thorverton's wife.

She was still determined to learn to ride, even though he would not be her teacher. She would also get a kitten, and her aunt would just have to accustom herself to it. But most important of all, she and Bagwell, her gardener, would turn the gardens of Prestwich Hall into such a showplace that people would come from miles around just to see the flowers and shrubs. Perhaps her aunt might even agree to having public days. Perhaps three times each year—once during the spring, once in the summer, and once in the fall—they could open the gates to all and sundry.

If only Aunt Phillipa would agree! It would be nice to have a goal in life—to have something to look forward to. And more important, if she and Bagwell were to do such a thing, they would have to work very hard, because there was so much that needed to be done, and consequently Meribe would not even have a moment to think about might-have-beens and if-onlys.

Rising from the bench with the intention of going inside, she happened to glance up and notice that the light was still on in her sister's room. And what, Meribe wondered, would Hester do with her twenty thousand pounds a year? Would she stay in Norfolk or would she want to travel? Would she live here in London, in this house that would belong to her, or would she perhaps buy a house in Bath or Brighton? What kind of plans did she have for the money, to obtain which she had conspired to commit murder?

The words from the Bible came to Meribe then: What shall it profit a man if he shall gain the world and lose his soul?

What is it you want to possess that is worth the cost of another person's life, Hester? she asked silently, staring up at the lighted window. Have you ever stopped to realize the price you are paying in order to acquire the luxuries that you seem to think you cannot live without? Will you be able to enjoy your ill-gotten gains? Is your conscience completely dead, or are you still feeling some twinges of guilt?

Even as Meribe watched, the light went out in her sister's room, and it seemed almost as if Hester had answered her. Even later, when she was curled up in her own bed, the memory of that darkened window stayed with Meribe, as if it were a symbol of the blackness in her sister's heart.

Collier waited impatiently in the library for his brother to return from his evening's entertainment. During the journey back to London, his anger had abated considerably, but he was having little luck curbing his restlessness.

While he could not agree that his brother had acted correctly in hiring a Bow Street runner, still and all, it was understandable that Demetrius had been concerned. As much as he hated to admit it, it had never occurred to Collier that anyone would suspect he had been the victim of foul play. Under normal circumstances, Demetrius would have jumped to the correct conclusion, namely that Collier was playing least-in-sight until he was no longer angry.

But these were not normal times—a murderer was walking the streets of Mayfair, stalking Demetrius, and therefore Collier should not have absented himself from his brother's side.

All afternoon he had, in fact, been picturing all the terrible "accidents" that could have happened to Demetrius while he himself was larking about the countryside with his friends.

He was just starting to run through the possible disasters once again when he heard a commotion in the entrance hall. Hurrying to the library door, he opened it and beheld a strange spectacle.

Uncle Humphrey, Demetrius, and Thomas Hennessey stood there being fussed over by McDougal. Although the three gentlemen were dressed for an evening at Almack's, they looked as if they had gone several rounds with the Bedford Bruiser. At second glance, Collier realized it was mostly their clothes, which had suffered from gross mistreatment, rather than themselves.

"Ecod, what have the three of you been doing—crawling home on your hands and knees?" he said, and instantly there was dead silence and three pairs of eyes turned toward him. Four pairs, actually, if one counted the butler's.

After a long moment, during which Collier could feel his cheeks beginning to heat up, Demetrius said mildly, "Welcome back."

Collier had intended to rebuke his brother for sending a Bow Street runner after him, but now he changed his mind. From the manners of the others it was obvious to him that something untoward had happened this evening, and his own righteous indignation at being treated like a child now seemed . . . seemed, well, rather childish.

"Would someone like to tell me what has been going on?" he said.

"Hum, well, yes." Uncle Humphrey broke the silence. "Well, you see, my dear boy, while we were returning from an evening at Almack's—the usual dismal affair, by the way. You did not miss a thing by staying away, but then, I have learned never to have any great expectations of a good time when I go there. Such an insipid place, I cannot think why it is so popular. But be that as it may, while we were strolling along on our way here—not that I would not have preferred to take a carriage, but then, no one consulted me. And do you know, now that I think on it, we would have been much better off to drive home, because someone took a couple of shots at your brother, and he would have been much safer if he'd been in a closed carriage, don't you know."

"That would explain the hole in his *chapeau bras*, then," Collier said, admiring his own sangfroid.

Demetrius took his hat off and stared at it, then broke out laughing. "Ecod, but the blackguard was a better shot than I've been giving him credit for. It appears I have been remiss in not thanking you gentlemen properly for throwing me to the ground and nearly crushing the life out of me."

Blast it all, Collier thought, he should never have left his brother's side! He gave Hennessey a black look for having made his idiotic suggestions about the betrothal announcement and the prizefight.

The Irishman met his glance and shrugged. Then, looking suitably apologetic, he said, "As much as I admire your hallway, Thorverton, I suggest we retire to the library, and perhaps if it is not too much trouble, we might have a bit of that port I have been hearing so much about."

"Capital suggestion," Humphrey said. "Some of the '87, McDougal, if you please."

A few minutes later they were all seated comfortably, Hennessey and Humphrey sipping the port, while Collier and Demetrius shared a bottle of excellent brandy.

"It seems to me," Collier said, "that this whole affair has dragged on much too long. Something must be done, and done soon, to catch the villain."

"Or villains," Hennessey said. "We suspect that Miss Hester Prestwich has a cohort—someone to act as an intermediary between her and the ruffians she hires."

"You have proof of this?" Collier asked eagerly.

"Not a bit," Demetrius replied. "But the pieces of the puzzle fit together better if we assume that someone of our own class is aiding and abetting her."

"A gentleman?"

"Do not sound so surprised, little brother. You know very well that London is full of so-called gentlemen who have not even a nodding acquaintance with honor," Demetrius pointed out.

"So the question is, what are we to do to trap the villainous pair?" Hennessey asked.

"To begin with," Demetrius said, looking directly at

his brother, "there will be no more announcements in the *Morning Post.*"

Collier started to protest that his intentions had been good, but then he remembered his new resolve to act with more maturity, and he bit back the excuses he had been about to utter.

"The only thing for you to do is go back to Devon," Uncle Humphrey said unexpectedly.

"And leave Miss Meribe alone? Don't be daft," Demetrius said heatedly.

His words were so angry, Collier looked at him in astonishment. What else had happened while he was out of town? Had his brother, who after Diana had jilted him had sworn an oath never to get mixed up with a female again—his brother, who was determined never to be leg-shackled—had his brother done the unthinkable and fallen in love? It appeared that such was indeed the case.

Bravo, big brother, Collier silently applauded.

"No, no," Uncle Humphrey protested, "I did not mean abandon her. Take her along, and her aunt, and her sister, and whoever else we can think of. Do it up right, so it will look like a proper house party, don't you know. The thing is, London is too big—there is no way we can protect you properly here. But Devon is another matter. Out there, so isolated on the moor, the servants would notice in a flash if some stranger was lurking about."

"By Jove, that's a capital idea," Hennessey said. "I propose we drink a toast to your uncle, who has come up with the best plan yet."

Rather than lifting his glass, Demetrius said, "Might I remind you that Miss Prestwich is not speaking to me at the moment?"

"But only because she thought young Collier here had been kidnapped by the assassin," Uncle Humphrey said, and all eyes turned toward Collier, who felt even more ashamed of his earlier behavior. "But now that I think on it, you have only to tell her that your brother is home again safe and sound, and I am sure she will listen to you."

"Your brother plans to propose to Miss Meribe Prestwich,'' Hennessey explained, the light of mischief again in his eyes.

To his amazement, Collier noticed that Demetrius—his calm, mature, always-in-control-of-himself big brother—appeared to be blushing.

"I'll drink to your success," Collier said, his spirits lifting immeasurably. "I never did like the idea of stepping into your shoes. Now you will be able to provide your own heirs."

There was no longer any doubt about it: Demetrius's face was now bright red.

"I think I would rather face the assassin unarmed," Demetrius murmured to Hennessey early the next morning as they rumbled over the cobblestones in the closed carriage Hennessey had borrowed for the occasion from his father-in-law, the earl.

"Rather than what?" Hennessey asked. "Oh-ho, I have it. Rather than ask Miss Meribe Prestwich to marry you." He chuckled. "Are you so unmanned by a pair of soft brown eyes that you cannot find the words that will make her yours? But come now, you have surely done this before—did you not propose to the fair Diana on bended knee?"

"That was . . . easier somehow," Demetrius replied. "I knew she was expecting me to do it, and I knew she intended to say yes." What he did not add was that somehow her answer, whether aye or nay, had not been as important to him as Miss Prestwich's answer was. Had Diana turned him down, he would have been indignant that she had led him on, and cross with her for not letting him know before he made a fool of himself, but even when he had still thought he wanted to marry her—even before he discovered what life would be like as her husband—even then he would not have felt as if his heart were broken if she had declined to marry him.

But if Miss Prestwich said no? He did not want to think about it. But as they proceeded through the streets of Mayfair, he had nothing else to think about, and the more he thought about it, the more determined he became.

If she said no, he would ask her again and again until she said yes. It was that simple. After all, he thought with an inner smile of delight, in the beginning she had repeatedly told him no when he had offered to be her friend, and yet he had managed every time to turn her no into a yes.

Since that was the case, why prolong things? Why not persuade her today, rather than tomorrow or the next day or the day after that?

"You are looking like the cat who ate the canary," Hennessey said, interrupting his thoughts. "Have you figured out how you are going to persuade her to accept you?"

"Not at all," Demetrius replied, now smiling openly. "But I am determined that you will not see me emerge from her house until I am betrothed."

"Then I wish you luck, my friend," Hennessey said as the coachman pulled the team to a halt and the footmen—in this case not the earl's servants, but Malone and Mulrooney—sprang down from their places on the back of the coach and opened the door.

"I do not believe in luck, whether good or bad," Demetrius replied. "Nor do I believe in fatal curses or evil spirits or"—and here he grinned broadly—"or even in leprechauns or other wee folk. What I do believe in is resolution, determination, and persistence. In short, when it comes to stubbornness, Miss Prestwich will discover that I am an expert and she is but a rank amateur."

"Fortunately for you," Hennessey agreed with a laugh. "I should not wish a wife for you who resembles your honorable mother."

Leaving his friend in the coach, Demetrius went up to the door and pounded on it with great vigor. A moment later the butler opened the door and peered up at him.

"Good morning, my lord," Smucker said politely, then launched into what was obviously a prepared speech. "I regret to inform you that Miss Meribe has given orders—"

Demetrius interrupted him. "I do not like to contradict you, Smucker, but I am coming into this house and I am going to speak with Miss Meribe Prestwich."

The butler looked up at him, then down to where Demetrius's rather large foot was firmly planted in the doorway, preventing the door from closing.

"I have no desire to hurt you, Smucker," Demetrius continued, "and you know as well as I do that there is no one in this house who is large enough and strong enough to prevent me from entering." He lifted one eyebrow in silent question, and the butler nodded in confirmation.

"That being the case, let us assume that I have now lifted you up bodily and moved you out of the way. Can we assume that, do you think?" Demetrius purred, his voice like velvet.

Obviously recognizing the steely determination behind Demetrius's polite words, the butler hurriedly opened the door wider. "I think we can assume that," he croaked out. After clearing his throat nervously, he added, "And likewise we can assume that you have forced me to tell you that Miss Meribe is presently in the garden."

"Thank you, Smucker," Demetrius said with a genuine smile.

The butler's smile was more tentative. "And do you wish me to assume also that you have threatened me with severe bodily harm if I mentioned your presence here to Miss Phillipa Prestwich?"

"Oh, the most severe," Demetrius replied, taking a golden guinea from his pocket and flipping it to the butler, who caught it adroitly. "And you may congratulate me, Smucker. I am going to marry Miss Meribe."

"Has she . . . but if . . . then why?" The butler looked more than a little confused.

"No, I have not even asked her properly," Demetrius admitted, "but I intend to remedy that omission as soon as may be. And I am determined that before I leave this house, she will agree to be my wife. I am not sure how long it will take me to persuade her, but if I am still here at noon, I trust you can provide a suitable repast. I should hate to grow weak from hunger."

"No, indeed, my lord, that would not be wise," Smucker replied. "And I shall have Cook prepare something, just in case."

"Which reminds me, not a word of this to anyone," Demetrius said quickly. "No one must know about the betrothal, not the servants or even the sister and the aunt."

"You are planning an elopement?" Smucker looked shocked.

"No, no, nothing of the sort. Only the betrothal needs to be kept secret. The wedding, which will take place quite soon, will be completely open and aboveboard."

"Then you may depend on me," Smucker replied. "If any word of this leaks out, it will not be by any of the servants under my supervision." Bowing formally, the butler vanished into the shadowy nether regions belowstairs, leaving Demetrius to find his own way to the small door leading out into the garden.

At first glance Demetrius could not spot Miss Prestwich, but then he saw a figure in a rose-colored gown kneeling on the ground, halfway concealed behind an overgrown shrub. He approached her quietly, and when he was but a few feet away, she spoke without looking up.

"If my aunt has sent you out here to pester me, Smucker, then you may go right back in and inform her that I am not going to go shopping today or be fitted for a new dress or entertain any ladies for tea. I am going to stay in the garden *all day,* is that clear?" Her voice wobbled a bit at the end, and she raised a rather grubby hand and wiped her cheek.

"Quite clear," Demetrius replied.

"Oh," she gasped, dropping her trowel. She looked up at him, then looked away, then picked up the trowel, then laid it down again. Finally she peeked up at him from under the brim of her bonnet.

Her confusion was delightful, and the tear streaks on her face led him to believe that he would not be needing the repast he had asked Smucker to prepare.

"What are you doing here?" she said. Standing up, she shook out her skirts and tried to look stern. "I gave Smucker specific orders that you were not to be admitted."

Taking out his handkerchief, Demetrius carefully

wiped the tears and other smudges off her face. "In case you have not noticed, I am considerably larger and stronger than your butler. He was quite unable to prevent me from entering."

"You *forced* your way in?" Her eyes grew even bigger and rounder.

"Let us say that since we both agreed that I *could* force my way in if it became necessary, neither of us saw any point in going through the motions." He lifted her chin and tilted her face to the right and then to the left. Satisfied that he had done a thorough job of removing the evidence of her gardening efforts and her tears, he pocketed his handkerchief.

"Well," she said, showing all the determination of a six-week-old kitten, "you might as well show yourself out, because I am not going to talk to you." She crossed her arms and glared up at him, her lower lip pushed out pugnaciously.

Demetrius was sorely tempted to wrap his arms around her and kiss away her pout. Instead he contented himself with running his fingers lightly along the line of her jaw. "My brother sends you his apologies. He regrets very much having caused you concern on his behalf."

"He is safe, then?"

The look of profound relief on her face made Demetrius regret his leniency where his brother's escapade was concerned. The boy should have been horsewhipped for causing Miss Prestwich so many hours of grief and worry.

"Yes, he came home safe and sound. He was never in any danger, other than in my mother's imagination."

"Oh, I am so glad," Miss Prestwich whispered, and then she was in his arms without his quite knowing who had made the first move toward the other.

Not one to pass up a golden opportunity, Demetrius asked, "Will you do me the honor of marrying me?"

Making regretful noises, she tried to free herself from his embrace, but he relaxed his hold only enough to allow her to look up into his face.

"Knowing what danger you would be in as my betrothed, I cannot agree to marry you," she said, regret in her voice and pain in her eyes.

"Last night you would not even speak to me," he pointed out, his voice completely reasonable.

"I only refused for your own protection," she said earnestly. "It was not because I do not still consider you my friend. I explained it all to your uncle, who promised to explain it to you."

"He did that," Demetrius confirmed.

"So you see, you really should not have come here. It is not safe for you to be seen with me or even to be seen entering my house."

He wished he did not have to destroy her illusions of safety. "I understand completely why you acted the way you did," he reassured her. Then he forced himself to say the fateful words. "But I am afraid your efforts were in vain. When I was on my way home last night, someone fired two shots at me."

The blood drained out of her face, but he continued relentlessly. She had to understand that she was living in a fantasy world. "The first shot went through my hat, and the second would more than likely have struck me in the chest, had not Hennessey and my uncle thrown me to the ground."

At his words she fainted dead away in his arms.

13

Sitting on the bench, holding the unconscious Miss Prestwich on his lap, Demetrius had doubts as to his own analysis of the situation. Had shocking her really been the only way to persuade her that she was not going to save his life by refusing to see him? Could he not have glossed over the events of the night before? Made them seem less serious?

A few minutes ago it had seemed necessary to tell her the whole truth in order that she might fully comprehend the ruthlessness of their adversary, but the longer she was unconscious, the more he feared he had acted a little too ruthlessly himself.

Before he could finish berating himself, she began to stir. He had no trouble identifying the moment she became fully conscious, because she stiffened, gasped, and then scrambled off his lap. Backing a few steps away, she looked delightfully confused, and a blush rose up her neck and colored her cheeks a charming shade of pink.

"Will you not be seated?" he said politely, and after a short hesitation she sat down on the opposite end of the bench, quite as far from him as possible. Which was not actually very distant, since it was a smallish bench, obviously intended for two and not for three.

She eyed him nervously, like a skittish foal still unused to the ways of men.

"Your anxieties to the contrary, I am quite able to protect myself," he said mildly, "and I can protect you and my friends and my family."

She said nothing, so he asked, "Do you have confidence in me?" After a long time—or so it seemed to him—she finally nodded.

"In that case, please set aside all considerations of fatal curses and wicked assassins and immense fortunes and poorly thought-out trusts, at least for the moment, and answer me from your heart. I am asking you to marry me for the simple reason that I wish to spend the rest of my life with you."

He was rewarded with a tentative smile, which was encouraging enough that he inched his way closer to her. When she did not immediately spring to her feet, he closed the remaining gap between them completely and took her hands in his. Smiling down at her, he asked, "Miss Prestwich, will you do me the honor of marrying me? Will you come live with me in Devon and take care of me and my sorely neglected garden?"

He could see the remaining doubt and confusion in her eyes. A gentleman would have waited, would have allowed her time to make up her own mind. But at this moment Demetrius was not feeling at all like a gentleman. Without a qualm, he took advantage of her indecision.

Easily pulling her back into his arms, he set out to kiss her senseless. After the first long and thoroughly satisfying kiss, he managed to murmur, "Marry me," and when she did not immediately answer, he kissed her again.

Her arms curled themselves around his neck, and a little voice in the back of his mind pointed out that his uncle had been correct—that his marital bed would not be at all lacking in passion.

The second time they came up for air, she asked him in a weak, breathless voice, "Are you planning to keep on kissing me until I agree to marry you, my lord?"

"Precisely that, Miss Prestwich," he replied quite firmly, delighted with the way his courtship was progressing.

"Then," she said, her winsome dimples peeking out, "I think it only fair to warn you that I expect to be *very* slow to make up my mind."

He gave a bark of laughter, then leaned his forehead down against hers. "And if I refuse to kiss you again until *after* you have agreed to marry me? What then, Miss Prestwich?''

He could feel her tremble against him, and her voice was so soft he had to strain to hear her reply.

''Why, then, I shall be forced to accept your offer, my lord.''

He almost groaned in relief. ''Miss Prestwich,'' he said, holding her as tightly as he dared, ''will you be my wife?''

''Yes, Demetrius, I will.''

''You will not regret your decision, Miss Prestwich. I swear that I shall be a good husband.''

''You may call me Meribe,'' she said softly, ''and I fear I am already beginning to regret my consent.''

In astonishment, he pulled away enough that he could see her face, which wore a serious expression. ''You have changed your mind so soon? What have I said? What have I done?'' His confusion was total.

''Well, so far, being betrothed to you is turning out to be a great disappointment,'' she said, and this time he caught the sparkle of mischief in her eyes. ''You did promise—or at least you implied—that if I accepted your offer, you would kiss me again.''

''Ah,'' he said, ''you are right. That was definitely part of our bargain.''

A considerable time later he thought to ask, ''Just how many kisses do you calculate I owe you?''

''At least a lifetime's worth,'' she murmured.

''Well, never let it be said that I failed to pay my debts promptly,'' he replied before kissing her again.

Relaxed from a countless number of kisses and secure in Demetrius's arms, there was nothing Meribe wanted less than to break the bubble of happiness surrounding the two of them. If only there were some way they could spend the rest of their lives alone together in this tiny walled garden.

But the world outside the walls was still waiting, and the danger there would threaten Demetrius until she turned twenty-one . . . or until she married him.

With a deep sigh she spoke reluctantly. ''You said you

could protect yoúrself from my sister—or rather, from
whoever is trying to harm you,'' she corrected herself.
''Exactly how do you propose to do that?''

''To begin with, no one must know that we are well
and truly betrothed,'' he said.

Disappointment mingled with relief in Meribe's heart.
On the one hand, she wanted to share her present joy
with the entire world; on the other hand, she did not want
to risk losing Demetrius, and with him, her happiness.

''Second, we have decided—''

''We?''

''My brother, my uncle, and my friend Thomas Hennessey. Last night we talked over various possibilities,
and we have decided that it would be safest for everyone
concerned if we all go down to Devon. London offers too
many opportunities for an assassin. We shall, of course,
invite your sister and your aunt, and Hennessey is bringing his wife, so it will look like nothing more than a
normal country party. The advantage is that out on the
moor, where my estate is located, it will be very easy to
spot any stranger lurking about.''

''So you still expect another attempt will be made on
your life? Excuse me, that is a foolish question. Of course
we must be on the alert for any such event.''

''I wish I could truthfully say that I do not think your
sister will try again, but that would only be wishful
thinking.'' They were both quiet for a moment, then Demetrius said, ''There is one other thing I should tell you.
I have a special license, taken out in both our names, in
my pocket, so that we will not have to wait for banns to
be called.''

He did not need to remind her that her birthday was
less than a fortnight away, and that if they waited for the
banns to be called on three successive Sundays, Hester
would automatically succeed with her wicked scheme and
inherit a fortune by foul means.

''You are planning a trap for my sister, are you not?''
Meribe inquired, although she knew what the answer had
to be.

''I wish there were some other way,'' Demetrius said.
''We will do our best to prevent a scandal. And let me

reassure you that it is not my intention to send her to prison. If we can catch her in the act of . . . of attempting something, we do not plan to turn her over to the magistrate. If she is willing to cooperate, we will pay for her ticket to Canada or the West Indies, and we can arrange for her to be paid a quarterly stipend conditional upon her staying out of England.''

''Thank you,'' Meribe said, feeling very sad at the thought of never seeing her sister again. And feeling even sadder when she considered what the future would hold for Hester, alone in a strange country. But perhaps in the Americas Hester might also find a man who would love her, and perhaps she might, over the years, become less bitter.

Thinking about bitterness reminded Meribe of her future mother-in-law. ''And what of your mother? I know she does not approve of me.''

''My mother has made so many threats and vows about what she will and will not do that she has quite talked herself into a corner,'' Demetrius said with a smile. ''With a little encouragement from Collier, she has decided that she needs to go to Bath and take the waters. He will be joining us after he escorts her there and sees to it that she is comfortably settled in.''

''I am sorry to come between you and your mother,'' Meribe said.

''Do not be. We have never been close, and she is always getting in a miff about something or other that I have done—or that she imagines I have done—that does not please her. When it suits her, she will come about. More than likely, as soon as you produce a grandchild for her to dote on, she will fall on your neck and proclaim you the most perfect daughter-in-law in all of England—that is, so long as you allow her to dictate to you every aspect of the babe's care. In addition, when you get to know my mother better, you will discover that she has a very flexible memory, and once she is a grandmother, she will deny under oath that she ever uttered the slightest word of censure against you. And she will believe every word of it.''

Meribe could feel her cheeks getting hot at the thought

of bearing Demetrius's child, and she tried to hide her face against his chest, but instead he tipped her chin up, grinned down at her, and kissed her gently.

"Do you have any more worries you need to discuss?" She shook her head.

"Then let us go in and inform the others of our plans," he said, standing up and holding out his hand to her. Without hesitation, she grasped it, wishing she never had to release it again. Wishing . . . wishing they were already married and he was leading her to their bed. Looking up into his eyes, she rather suspected his thoughts were following the same path hers were. In a word, he looked every bit as frustrated as she was feeling.

After changing her dress and having Jane arrange her hair, Meribe joined Demetrius in the drawing room. She was not best pleased to discover that Lionell Rudd had also come to call. Although she knew she should be grateful to him for not abandoning her sister during these last several years when the other gentlemen had stayed away in droves, Meribe had never quite managed to feel at ease around the dandy. Too often it seemed to her that she could hear more true maliciousness in his comments than in the cutting remarks Hester was fond of making.

"Oh, there you are at last," Aunt Phillipa said acerbically. "Thorverton here has been telling us about the proposed expedition to Devon."

"I hope you are agreeable," Meribe said, taking a seat beside her sister on the settee. "I am quite determined to go, but you may come with us or stay in London as you see fit."

Aunt Phillipa eyed her with displeasure, then turned to Demetrius. "This is all your fault, Thorverton. Before she met you, she was the most biddable young lady one could wish for. She never displayed the slightest bit of impertinence, and now she is so set on having her own way about things that I think she would argue with me if I said the sun came up in the east."

"She may not care one way or another if you accompany us," Demetrius said smoothly, "but I for one will be vastly disappointed if you and your elder niece do not come for a visit at Thorverton Hall.''

"Gammon," Aunt Phillipa retorted. "You must think I have just cut my eyeteeth if you are expecting me to believe such a whisker. A *man*"—she invested the word with loathing—"never wants a chaperone along, no matter how he may pretend to be a gentleman. In this case, since you will doubtless encourage my niece to defy me if I refuse to jump to your bidding, I suppose we shall have to go along to Devon with you. What say you, Hester? Do you wish to express your opinion, or are you still not feeling like talking?''

Her head bowed and her hands folded in her lap, Hester said softly, "Whatever you decide to do is fine with me, dear aunt.''

Her meekness was so patently false that Meribe wanted to grab her sister and shake her and ask why. Why had she done the terrible things it appeared she must have done?

Aunt Phillipa snorted in disgust. "Now you are become as mealymouthed as Meribe used to be.'' Turning to Demetrius, she inquired in what was for her quite a civil tone, "When are you planning to go down there, and whom else have you invited?''

"I should like to depart the day after tomorrow if that will give you time for your packing," Demetrius replied. "And as to others, my friend Thomas Hennessey is coming with his wife, Lady Delilah. My brother will be joining us later, and''—Demetrius paused, then said with a touch of defiance in his voice—"and my uncle, Humphrey Swinton, will be accompanying us also.''

At the mention of that abhorred name, Aunt Phillipa went rigid, and everyone in the room stared at her. How would she react, Meribe wondered, to the information that her despised enemy would be included in the party?

Meribe was quite proud of her aunt. Other than a slight flaring of the nostrils, Aunt Phillipa gave no sign that she was not happy with the inclusion of the infamous Mr. Swinton.

"I suppose we shall have to include you also, Mr. Rudd, so that Hester will have a dinner partner," Aunt

Phillipa said with a grimace. "And now, if you will all excuse me, I feel a headache coming on." So saying, she rose to her feet and with her head held high sailed majestically out of the room.

Meribe breathed a sigh of relief that it had all gone so easily, but before she could comment on her aunt's capitulation, Hester also rose to her feet, mumbled something about being fatigued, and likewise left the room.

For a moment there was silence; then Lionell spoke. "Do you know," he said, eyeing Meribe and Demetrius with a smile that bordered on a leer, "I am beginning to feel quite *de trop* with the two of you smelling of April and May. I must leave you alone now in any case, for if I am to join your party, I must see about canceling my upcoming engagements. When do you wish to set out, my lord?"

"Would nine o'clock be too early for you ladies?" Demetrius asked Meribe.

She shook her head. "Quite the contrary, it would not be soon enough. My aunt firmly believes that making an early start on a trip shows great inner fortitude and strength of mind and vast moral superiority. Eight o'clock would set you up better in her esteem."

"Almost you persuade me to change my mind about going," Lionell said, "but I have never yet turned down an opportunity to visit one of the great country houses, and it would be a bad precedent to start now. Although"—he turned to Demetrius with a look of embarrassment—"now that I think on it, perhaps I should not have accepted without hearing the invitation from your own lips, my lord, since you are to be our host."

"No, no, of course you must come. Hester would be quite bored without you," Demetrius said.

At this point, it was obvious to Meribe that there was nothing else Demetrius could say if he did not wish to be appallingly rude. Which was unfortunate, since Lionell was not a person with whom she wished to become better acquainted. Catching Demetrius's eye, Meribe read his understanding of her feelings, and somehow that made it easier to be civil to the dandy when he finally, with great profusions of gratitude, took his leave.

As soon as they were alone, Demetrius stood up and moved to join her, but before he could sit down beside her, the door opened and Jane, her abigail, marched in and plopped herself down on the settee.

To be sure, it was disappointing to have such a determined chaperone, but Meribe was thankful that at least they'd had an hour or so of privacy in the garden.

Accepting the setback with good grace, Demetrius soon excused himself also, leaving Meribe to retire to her room and begin her packing. Her feet felt like dancing, and it was all she could do not to tell Jane her secret, but she remembered Demetrius's admonition to maintain the strictest secrecy regarding their betrothal.

While her agibail bustled about the room packing for the trip, Hester sat on a chair and gazed out the window. She did not see the little walled garden, however, because her mind was too engaged with her own problems.

No matter how she tried to come up with a solution, she found herself well and truly caught on the horns of a dilemma. On the one hand, if Lionell were doing something wicked, it was clearly her duty to warn Lord Thorverton. On the other hand, what proof had she? When all was said and done, she had nothing at all to go on except a feeling of uneasiness.

How his lordship would scoff if she told him that she suspected that Lionell Rudd, of all people, was behind the attack in Hanover Square. Lionell consort with such a ruffian as Black Jack Brannigan? It was too preposterous to be credible, and Lord Thorverton had already made it clear that he did not believe in fatal curses or any such nonsense. Doubtless he would likewise scoff at her and consider her a gullible fool if she tried to make him believe in her woman's intuition.

And what was worse, if she were to voice her suspicions, then she would have to admit that poor old Wimbwell had, all those years ago, betrayed her father's confidence and told her the terms of the trust. And destroying his reputation after he was gone would indeed be serving the poor old man an ill turn.

''Do you wish to take your new Egyptian brown cloak

with you?'' Jane interrupted her thoughts. ''I have heard
it can be quite windy on Dartmoor.''

Hester stared at the garment, but her mind was too
preoccupied with potential assassins to consider such
trivial matters as her wardrobe. ''You decide,'' she said
finally. ''I care not what I wear when I am off in the
wilds of the West Country.''

''Are you sickening with something?'' the abigail
asked. Crossing the room, she laid her hand on Hester's
forehead, then said, ''Well, at least you do not seem to
be feverish. More than likely you are just burnt to the
socket from all the parties and balls that you have been
attending this Season. It will do you and your sister good
to have a short repairing lease in the country.''

Hester forced a smile, which seemed to reassure the
abigail, since she returned to her task.

If only, Hester thought, someone could give me reassurance that we will find peace and quiet in Devon . . .
and not murder and mayhem.

Now she was being ridiculous—murder and mayhem
indeed! If he had any inkling of the preposterous thoughts
that were rattling around in her head, Lord Thorverton
would be quite justified in thinking her completely ad-
dlepated.

With firm resolution to keep her imagination under
control, Hester got up from her chair and began helping
Jane sort the clothing as to which needed to be packed
and which could be left behind.

Murder and mayhem—such nonsense! She had to smile
at where her fancies had taken her. More than likely she
had eaten something last night that did not agree with
her and that had caused her irrational thoughts.

Before they had even reached the River Colne, Meribe
realized she had made a terrible mistake. Not that there
had been another murderous attack on Demetrius or a
suspicious accident or anything like that. So far the journey was completely uneventful.

Mr. Hennessey had borrowed his father-in-law's coach
for the journey, and since it was more luxuriously ap-
pointed than Aunt Phillipa's, it was decided that the four

ladies would ride together in it, and the luggage and assorted servants would follow in Aunt Phillipa's coach. Demetrius, his uncle, and Mr. Hennessey were all three driving their phaetons, and with the addition of several burly grooms plus Lionell Rudd, there was truly no way Meribe could arrange to ride with Demetrius, who had explained to her the true role Malone and Mulrooney were playing.

It had required less than an hour after their departure for Meribe to become distinctly uncomfortable, despite the fact that the carriage was well-sprung and the velvet squabs were the softest she had ever been privileged to sit on. It was the company—or more precisely, the conversation—that was rapidly destroying what little peace of mind Meribe had regained after hearing that someone had tried to shoot Demetrius.

Hester was still being most strangely silent; Aunt Phillipa, as was her custom on long trips, was soon snoring softly in her corner, which left Meribe with no one to converse with except Mr. Hennessey's wife.

To be sure, there was nothing the least bit objectionable about Lady Delilah, who despite her name did not look at all like a sultry temptress. With carroty hair, green eyes, and a sprinkling of freckles across her nose, she seemed quite approachable, and indeed she did try her best to be friendly.

Unfortunately, their conversation languished, since Lady Delilah knew nothing about gardening, and had no interest in the latest gossip about the *ton,* but Meribe was too polite not to make some effort to put the other woman at ease.

In the end, all it took was a simple question—"How was the hunting this last season?"—and Lady Delilah began to describe in enthusiastic detail the famous runs they had had, the wily foxes they had chased, the horses she and others had ridden, the spectacular falls various members of the hunt had taken, and so forth.

It was soon obvious that although her range of interest was not broad, she knew everything there was to know about horses and horse breeding and pedigrees and hunting and training and racing and foxhounds, and all those things that Meribe was totally ignorant of.

In addition, the more Lady Delilah talked, the more depressingly obvious it became to Meribe that she herself was not at all the proper kind of wife for Demetrius. He needed someone like Lady Delilah—or at least someone who knew more about horses than that they were large beasts with four legs that habitually consumed a fortune in hay and oats.

Meribe was not even sure what a horse's hocks were, much less whether it was good for a horse to jump off them or not, and she would have been thoroughly bored listening to Lady Delilah rattle on in what was to Meribe a foreign language, had she not soon discovered that once Lady Delilah was well-launched, all she herself needed to do was smile, nod her head, and occasionally murmur such things as "Oh, really?" and "My gracious." Which left Meribe free to think about how well and truly Demetrius's life would be ruined if he married someone like herself, who was totally ignorant of everything he cared about in life.

After making her acquaintance, his friends would doubtless pity him from the bottom of their hearts, and it would not take him long to realize also that he should never have taken such a step as marriage when all he felt for her was compassion.

Remembering his kisses, she was forced to admit that there was a certain degree of passion between them also, but how long would that last when she could not share any of his interests? How long before he began to regret their marriage? If indeed things ever progressed that far.

A wedding was beginning to seem like quite a remote possibility, and not because of any would-be assassin. She simply was not the proper wife for Demetrius, and sooner or later he would realize it. Although being a gentleman, he would more than likely try to conceal his true feelings.

Which in turn meant that she was the one who would have to cry off. The only thing she found to be thankful for was that no one else knew about their clandestine betrothal, and consequently no one else would know when it was broken.

Meribe gradually became aware that Lady Delilah was waiting for her to say something. "Pardon me?"

"I asked if you have ever hunted with the Quorn?" Lady Delilah repeated.

Without thinking, Meribe said, "I do not ride," and Lady Delilah was so flabbergasted she could think of nothing more to say. They drove in silence until they stopped for lunch, which they shared with the gentlemen of their party at the King's Arms in Bagshot.

Afterward, when they once again climbed into their coach, the afternoon stretched before them like an eternity, and in desperation Meribe decided there was nothing for it but to reveal the full state of her ignorance. "What is a splint, and why does a horse throw it out?" she asked.

Obviously relieved to be able to talk about horses again, Lady Delilah smiled in the most friendly manner and proceeded without the slightest bit of condescension to answer that question and all the others Meribe could think of. Except, of course, the one that Meribe could never, ever ask anyone, namely, did Demetrius really want to marry her?

They had been at Thorverton Hall for three days, and Hester had managed to convince herself that there was nothing for her to be worried about. Looking around the dinner table, she acknowledged that although Lord Thorverton was a charming host, her sister showed no signs that she was planning to marry him before her birthday, which was now only a week away.

Despite occasional *sotto voce* grumblings from Aunt Phillipa—elicited whenever Mr. Swinton ventured too close to her—the party was most congenial. This evening they were also entertaining Lord Leatham and Lady Anne, who had driven over from the neighboring estate.

Sitting beside her, Lionell Rudd was his usual foppish self, but without a source of gossip for his acidic tongue, he was forced to fall back on fashion as a topic of conversation, and consequently he was pleasanter to have

around than usual. Hester could no longer believe that he
was a murderer, either in person or by proxy. Indeed,
she wondered that she could ever have suspected him of
having committed any deed more dastardly than giving
some encroaching mushroom the cut direct or ruthlessly
depressing a would-be dandy's pretensions to glory.

In short, all the worries that had plagued her in London seemed to have been caused by the overexertion and
fatigue of the Season, since they had quickly vanished
like popped soap bubbles in the more sane atmosphere
to be found in the country. It was almost enough to make
Hester decide that even after she inherited her father's
fortune, she would spend most of her time rusticating in
Norfolk rather than living a life of gay dissipation in London.

Well, perhaps that was a bit extreme. A few weeks in
London during the Season would not be unwelcome. To
be sure, she would need to replenish her wardrobe peri-
odically, and it was nice to visit the theater occasionally.

Rising to his feet, Lord Thorverton tapped on his goblet to get everyone's attention. Once he had it, he made
an announcement that caused complacency to fly out of
Hester's mind and consternation to replace it.

"My dear friends, it is with great pleasure that I wish
to inform you that Miss Meribe Prestwich has done me
the honor of accepting my hand in marriage. She has her
aunt's permission, and we have decided to be married
here tomorrow morning by special license."

Amid the general cries of congratulations, Hester heard
a low curse, and turning to her dinner partner, she saw
such coldness radiating from Lionell's glance, she felt
chilled to the marrow of her bones. Staring at his expression, she no longer had the slightest doubt but that
he was capable of personally committing cold-blooded
murder.

To her consternation, Hester felt as if she were seeing
the real Lionell for the first time, and she could read not
merely anger in his eyes but also a frightening madness.
She was so terrified of what he might do—indeed, if looks
could kill, Lord Thorverton would have been struck down
dead in his chair—that she could not utter a sound.

Then Lionell shifted his glance slightly and caught her in the act of staring at him, and the hideous anger vanished instantly behind a benign smile. With no apparent effort, his face assumed the fatuous expression of a London dandy. Lifting his goblet, he joined the other guests in toasting the forthcoming nuptials.

But having once seen beyond his polished facade, Hester could no longer make herself believe he was totally sane.

She wanted very much to tell someone else what she had seen. Even more, she wanted to spring up from her chair and dash screaming from the room—to get as far away as possible from the madman who was sitting so close to her.

But she was too petrified to move. What would he do to her if she cried out for help? Would he turn on her like a frenzied beast and strangle her? Would he pull a loaded pistol from his pocket and shoot her?

Or would he even need to do anything? If she accused him of heinous crimes, would anyone believe her? Or would everyone believe him when he denied everything? He had only to smile pityingly and murmur a few words about overheated imagination, and she would doubtless be sent to bed with a glass of warm milk laced with laudanum.

Even now, when he was again acting completely normal and rational, she herself was already beginning to wonder if she had actually seen what she thought she had seen. Lionell was her best friend in London—or at least, he had been her almost daily companion. Could she have known him these six years without really knowing him at all? Could he have been merely playing a role? Hiding behind a mask with which he had managed to deceive everyone in London?

But no matter how she tried to reassure herself, the image of the mad glitter in his eyes would not leave her, and she knew she was sitting only inches away from a very dangerous man, no matter how foolish and foppish he might appear to others.

14

The atmosphere in the drawing room was so strained, the tension was almost visible, and Meribe realized that the source of it was Hester, who was sitting on the edge of her chair as if poised to leap to her feet. Which she did as soon as they heard the men approaching in the hallway.

"If you will excuse me," Hester said, rubbing her forehead distractedly, "I seem to have a bit of a headache. I believe I shall retire early tonight."

So saying, she slipped out by way of the connecting door that led into the blue salon, rather than going out into the hallway, which would have been the normal thing to do.

Meribe wished there were some way to warn her sister not to make another attempt on Demetrius's life. With so little time remaining, who knew what desperate measure Hester might attempt? And with all the men on their guard, she was bound to fail, which meant she would be banished from England forever.

Do not try anything foolish, Meribe thought. Please, Hester, protect yourself—if you do nothing more, no one will have any proof that you ever did anything wrong.

No sooner had the one door shut behind Hester than the other door opened and the men entered, and with them the tension returned to the room. The only ones who seemed to be unaware of it were Lionell Rudd, who minced over and began talking to Aunt Phillipa as if everything were normal, and Lord Leatham, who went to sit beside his wife.

To Meribe's eyes, Mr. Hennessey and Mr. Swinton made it rather too obvious that they were protecting Demetrius, who made no attempt to join her, as might be expected of a bridegroom the evening before his wedding. He seated himself a little apart from her, and his uncle and his friend both hovered close to him and stared suspiciously around the room, as if expecting assassins to leap from behind the sofa.

Aunt Phillipa was the first to admit defeat. Apparently unable to withstand any more of Lionell's inane babble about his troubles procuring decent neckcloths and obviously unwilling to risk being thrown together with the despised Mr. Swinton, she excused herself and left the room.

When Lionell moved to sit beside Lady Delilah, she also bolted, claiming that she wished to be fresh for an early-morning ride.

From the significant look that passed between her and her husband, it was obvious to Meribe that Mr. Hennessey had explained everything to his wife. Meribe could only hope that others in the room did not notice how odd everyone was acting.

Demetrius would never have made a good spy, she decided. Conspicuously ignoring his duties as host, he invited Lord Leatham to play a game of billiards. Murmuring something to his wife, Leatham stood up and left the room with Demetrius, followed by Mr. Hennessey and Mr. Swinton, who stumbled over each other in their hurry to follow them through the door.

There was an element of humor in their attempts to appear casual, which would have made Meribe laugh, had she not known the seriousness of the earlier attempts on Demetrius's life.

"Since my husband has seen fit to abandon me, Miss Prestwich, would you be interested in taking a turn around the gardens? The moon is full, so we shall not need a lantern," Lady Anne said with a smile.

"That would be lovely," Meribe said, willing to fall in with any suggestion that would remove her from Lionell's presence.

Then for a moment she thought it was not going to work, because Lionell simpered and said, "I have always enjoyed strolling in the moonlight."

Lady Anne turned to him, and although Meribe could not see her face, apparently her expression made it clear to the dandy that the invitation had not been extended to him.

"But on the other hand, I fear the day's activities have quite exhausted me," Lionell said, "or perhaps it is the country air that is so fatiguing. In any case, I believe I shall also make an early night of it." Bowing deeply, he minced out of the room.

Meribe could not hold back a sigh of relief when he was gone. "I do not know why," she said, opening the French doors that led out onto the upper terrace, "but I have never learned to like that little man. Perhaps it is because he likes himself so well, he leaves nothing for anyone else to appreciate."

Lady Anne was quite the most knowledgeable person Meribe had ever encountered, and yet she was also the easiest person to talk with. Their conversation moved pleasantly from one topic to another, until Lady Anne casually asked, "Do you think you will like living here in Devon after you are married? I know some people fail to see the beauty of the moor, and note instead only the isolation."

"I have no great love of London," Meribe confided, "and I cannot fail to be happy here, since Demetrius has promised to give me free rein to improve the gardens as I see fit. So I am sure I shall be most content."

"The reason I asked," Lady Anne continued, "is that you do not seem as ecstatic as a bride should be the evening before her wedding."

There was such obvious sympathy in Lady Anne's comment that Meribe burst into tears. A short time later, seated on a bench beside Lady Anne, Meribe found herself pouring out all her worries and anxieties into her companion's ear. Without holding anything back, Meribe related the whole story of her father's trust, Mr. Wimbwell's murder, the two attempts on Demetrius's life, her fears for his safety, and last she admitted the pain caused by her sister's apparent involvement.

"She was such a good sister, I cannot believe the evidence that seems to damn her," Meribe said, wiping her

eyes with the man-sized linen handkerchief provided by
Lady Anne. "I know Hester can say the most cutting
things, but I am sure she does it only because she is
unhappy. But no matter how Demetrius explains it, I cannot accept that she has chosen to be so totally depraved—
so lost to all that is good and right."

"Then more than likely she has not," Lady Anne said
matter-of-factly.

Sitting up straighter, Meribe asked, "Why do you say
that? Do you think it really was a fatal curse? Demetrius
says that is ridiculous, but then, he is sure that Hester is
the one behind the murders and the attempted murders."

"He can say what he likes," Lady Anne replied, "but
it has been my experience that people do not change in
any fundamental way. The kindhearted remain compas-
sionate, the self-centered continue to be greedy and
grasping, and the busybodies never leave off meddling in
other people's lives. If your sister was kind to you when
you were growing up, then doubtless she is still basically
a good person, even if she has been led astray by London
society, which is full of incredibly shallow people, like
Mr. Rudd, who fail to understand that the world does not
particularly revolve around them. But as to your sister,
if she willingly shared her toys with you when you were
children, then I cannot accept that she is now conspiring
to cheat you out of your inheritance."

There was much truth in what Lady Anne was saying,
Meribe realized. Rack her brain though she might, she
could not think of a single person she knew who had
changed his or her personality in any significant way.
"Oh, how I wish my father had simply divided his estate
equally between us," she said crossly. "Because Demetrius says that the idiotic trust my father arranged gives
Hester the best motive—indeed the only motive—for
keeping me from marrying anyone before my birthday,
which is only a week away."

"Men do have a tendency to believe what is obvious,"
Lady Anne said calmly. "But so often when one looks
below the surface, the situation can become quite murky.
Demetrius is undoubtedly looking for a good logical motive, but as Bronson and I learned before we were mar-

ried, villains often have quite strange and irrational reasons for doing what they do.''

"But Demetrius says—''

Lady Anne's laugh interrupted Meribe. "My dear child, once you are married, you must not, under any circumstances, allow your husband to do all your thinking for you. As much as I admire Demetrius, God did not provide you with a perfectly good brain if he did not expect you to use it.''

At the mention of marriage, Meribe had to bite her lower lip to keep from bursting into tears once again. She knew she should not allow Demetrius to sacrifice his happiness for her, but on the other hand, she wanted so badly to be his wife.

Misunderstanding her silence, Lady Anne apologized. "My dear Miss Prestwich, I did not mean to cause offense by my remark. I am afraid my husband encourages me to speak my thoughts quite plainly, and I therefore sometimes forget that being too frank can cause unintentional offense.''

Meribe took a shuddering breath, then said, "I have taken no offense. It is only . . .'' The words caught in her throat. How could she explain to this woman, who knew everything, who could do anything, and whose husband clearly adored her, that she, Meribe, would not be an adequate wife for Demetrius? But on the other hand, how could she go on this way, with no one to share her misery, with no one to give her support and understanding? Oh, if only she could confide in Hester.

"Does it concern your wedding tomorrow?'' Lady Anne asked, and there was so much compassion in her voice, Meribe blurted out her greatest fear.

"I am persuaded that Demetrius is marrying me only because he promised to help me, and he is too much a gentleman to do anything else. But I am afraid that after the ceremony he will soon regret what he has so nobly done and wish he were free again. I am not at all the sort of wife he needs, since I am woefully ignorant of horses and can neither ride nor drive a team. He really needs a wife more like Lady Delilah . . . or like you,'' she concluded miserably.

Lady Anne laughed softly. "But, my dear Miss Prest-wich . . . may I call you Meribe, for I am sure we will become the best of friends . . . ?"

Meribe nodded, and Lady Anne continued, "As I was saying, my dear Meribe, if Demetrius needs someone who understands about horses, then he has to go no far-ther than his own stable, which is filled with trainers and grooms and stableboys who are most knowledgeable, and he also has his cousin, Lawrence Mallory, whom I be-lieve you have met, who is also quite capable where horses are concerned. So you see, he has no real need for his wife to be a noted horsewoman. In addition, might I point out that although you may think Demetrius would prefer a wife like me, in point of fact he actually met me before Bronson did, and although Demetrius was quick to ask my advice about equine matters, he at no time made the slightest effort to court me or even to flirt with me.

"Moreover, it has been my experience," Lady Anne went on, "that people can fall deeply in love with the most inappropriate people and at the most inopportune times and still be quite happy together."

"But you see," Meribe confessed, "he has never said he loves me. I am afraid his motives for wishing to marry me are strictly practical."

"Oh, I am sure he truly believes he wants to marry you for the most logical of reasons," Lady Anne said with a chuckle. "Men have a habit of finding the most implausibly logical reasons to allow them to do exactly what they wish to do."

"Demetrius said . . . he said that he needs someone here to take care of his gardens, which you will have to admit are sorely neglected."

"Indeed? And did he explain why, after managing suc-cessfully all his life to ignore his flowerbeds and lawns, he now feels such a strong compulsion to set them to rights that instead of hiring a gardener to work on them he must take himself a wife?"

"Logically, it would be much more economical to hire even a half-dozen gardeners," Meribe said, beginning to feel more cheerful.

"Men will come up with any number of reasons to justify marrying, but the only one I believe is valid is that two people wish to spend the rest of their lives together."

Meribe could only be glad the moon did not provide sufficient light for her companion to see her blush. "Do you know, now that I think back on what was said, that was the main reason Demetrius gave when he was trying to persuade me to accept his offer. He said he wished to spend the rest of his life with me."

"Amazing," Lady Anne said. "Apparently the boy has more sense than I have been giving him credit for."

Instantly riled up at the other woman's denigrating words, Meribe snapped out, "Of course he has sense. And he is not a boy either. He is quite the most mature, responsible, reliable man I have ever met."

"Peace, peace," Lady Anne said, holding up her hands in mock surrender. "I am sure Demetrius will be the best possible husband for you and that you will be the perfect wife for him."

To her own surprise, Meribe began to think that perhaps Lady Anne knew what she was talking about. Perhaps Demetrius did truly wish to marry her. Looking up at the mostly darkened house, she wondered if he was likewise thinking about her and wondering if she really wished to be his wife.

Unfortunately, she was not likely to have a chance to reassure him.

Demetrius finished explaining to Leatham the events in London which had led up to his unexpected announcement that he was getting married the next day.

"I would say the odds are better than even that Meribe's sister will make one last desperate attempt to prevent the marriage, but I believe we have the situation well in hand."

"Swinton and I will both spend the night hiding in Thorverton's room, so we will have no trouble overpowering any intruder," Hennessey explained, "and none of us will eat any food or drink any beverage that we did not bring with us, so there will be no opportunity to drug us or poison him.''

"If you wish," Leatham said, "I can return after I see Anne safely home."

"I appreciate your offer," Demetrius said, "but that would doubtless cause talk among the servants. Since we wish to prevent scandal, the fewer people who know of Hester's infamy, the better. I am sure we are prepared for whatever she may be plotting. If she has any sense of self-preservation, she must realize that if she tries anything, she will only be condemning herself. Yet from her expression at dinner when I announced that I was marrying her sister, I fear that despite the odds against her, she is desperate enough to make one last attempt."

"It is to our advantage that we have successfully isolated her here," Uncle Humphrey added. "We have, of course, told the servants to report to us immediately if they see a stranger lurking about, without telling them why we are especially interested."

Leatham did not look completely convinced. "What worries me is that on too many occasions I have seen the most foolproof plans fall apart."

Jane had helped her into her nightclothes, brushed out her hair, and at last had left her alone, but Hester was feeling too on edge for sleep. Sitting in a chair by the window looking out at the endless moonlit moor, she had never felt such desolation of spirit. It was as if she were trapped in a nightmare, unable to wake up. Except that this was no dream.

A slight movement of air on the back of her neck caused her to turn her head in time to see the door to the hallway closing. Before she could cry out, a black figure rushed at her and a gloved hand covered her mouth.

"Not a sound," Lionell's voice hissed in her ear, "else we are betrayed."

Easily breaking loose from him, for in truth, any muscles he appeared to have were nothing more than tailor's art, Hester whispered back, "How dare you enter my room this way! Be gone, before I scream the house down!"

"Ecod, surely you do not think I have any intention of compromising you? No, no, my dear, I want no scandal to attend our marriage. And do not forget that if you do not keep your voice down, we may attract some unwelcome attention. It would indeed be disastrous for our plans if I were caught in your room."

"Marriage? Plans?" Hester asked, feeling again the chill she had felt at the dinner table when she had seen the glitter of madness in Lionell's eyes. It had been bad enough when she had been in a well-lighted room, surrounded by family and friends, but now, isolated in her bedchamber with a madman, her terror knew no bounds.

Ignoring her questions, Lionell continued, and his whispers had the intensity of a religious fanatic she had once seen preaching damnation in St. James's Park. "I have come to warn you not to try to stop the wedding tomorrow. Thorverton knows too much."

Hester was grateful that she was sitting down, because her legs were trembling so much, she doubted they could hold her. "You may rest easy; I shall not try anything," she whispered back, hoping if she could just appease him, he would be reassured enough to leave her room, giving her an opportunity to find help.

"They are now plotting together in the billiard room," Lionell said with such a gloating tone in his voice, Hester was quite nauseated, "and from what I have heard, so far neither Thorverton nor any of those other fools has even begun to suspect me. That is why it is better if I do everything alone this night. All I require from you, my sweet, is that you stay out of the way in your room. I would hate to dispose of Thorverton only to discover that you have done something to make yourself a suspect."

With a heartfelt cry, Hester leapt out of her chair and made a dash toward the door, but Lionell was too quick for her. She felt a sudden jerk on her nightgown, lost her balance, and went down onto her hands and knees. Before she could scramble to her feet, Lionell was crouching beside her, and the moonlight coming in through the window was adequate for her to see that he had a silver-chased dueling pistol in his hand.

"Oh, no, my sweet, you shall not turn against me

now—not when I have expended so much time and money in helping you secure your father's fortune.''

''You are responsible for the fatal curse—for the accidents that happened to my sister's suitors!''

He did not make any effort to deny her accusations. Instead, the gun came closer. She tried to back away, but Lionell grabbed her arm. This time she was afraid that if she struggled to free herself, he might—accidentally or on purpose—pull the trigger.

''Do I detect a certain reluctance to fulfill your part of our bargain? Oh, no, my precious, you will not cheat me out of my due when we are so close to winning the prize. We have had an understanding lo these many years, and I shall not lose when it comes down to the wire.''

Without stopping to think about the possible consequences of angering the madman who was beside her, Hester blurted out, ''We have had no agreement.''

''But of course we have had an understanding, and we shall be married just as soon as you inherit your father's fortune. Do not think you can cheat me, either, for if you even try, I shall swear an oath on the Bible that you were with me every step of the way. In fact, by the time I finish, I shall have everyone convinced that I was but your unwitting pawn, cleverly manipulated by you. So keep in mind, my sweet, that if I am hanged for murder, I guarantee I will lay such evidence against you that you will find yourself swinging from the gibbet beside mine. Now that I have done your dirty work, it is too late for you to cast me aside for another bridegroom.''

''But I never even so much as suggested that you . . . that you should kill anyone. I never even hinted at such a thing.''

''Bah, even I cannot believe your protestations of innocence, and a jury would laugh in your face. After all, what motive could I have for involving myself in your affairs, other than that you had asked for my help and promised to share your fortune with me?''

''I shall turn all the money over to you—every penny of my father's fortune—if you will only give up your plans to try to kill Thorverton.''

''But you forget, my love, that if Thorverton lives, you

will have no fortune to give me. No, no, I am afraid I have no alternative but to have my assistants dispatch his lordship to his heavenly reward. Do you know, I had been regretting that I was forced to shoot Mr. Brannigan, but I believe the two new men I was able to hire in London will serve my purposes better. They seem much more capable of using finesse. The giant tended to rely on brute force rather than intelligent planning.''

Covering her face with her hands, Hester began to cry. Large sobs racked her body, but for all that she could not stop them, at least she managed to weep silently.

Pulling her hands away, Lionell slapped her across the face, cursing her and calling her the foulest of names.

It took her only a split second to realize that he had used both hands, and without stopping to think, she lunged for the shadow that must have been concealing the pistol.

So close—her fingertips actually touched the barrel of the gun—but Lionell was again quicker than she was. Before she could regain her balance, the pistol was once more pointed at her forehead.

''You begin to annoy me, my dear,'' he said coldly. ''I think the time has come to ensure that you do not interfere in this night's work.'' Reaching inside his jacket, he pulled out a silver flask and held it out to her. ''Drink this,'' he commanded, ''and do not try any other foolish tricks. We have already determined that you are not as fast as I am, so it will avail you naught to try to throw the wine in my face.''

She hesitated, and he rose to his feet and stood over her. Pushing the barrel of the gun against her temple, he again ordered, ''Drink it!'' and such was the menace in his voice that she could not doubt but that he was capable of shooting her dead on the spot.

With a shudder she unscrewed the cap and lifted the flask to her lips. The wine was nauseatingly sweet, but still she was able to taste the bitterness of the laudanum with which Lionell had apparently laced it. After several swallows she began to gag, but Lionell prodded her with the pistol and commanded, ''Drink every drop,'' and somehow she managed to comply.

He stayed beside her while the lassitude crept up her limbs, and with her last conscious thought she wondered if he had given her enough laudanum to put her to sleep for a few hours . . . or forever. But the question no longer seemed important.

Her wedding morning did not dawn any too soon for Meribe. The night had been overly long, and she had lain awake through most of it, her body tense, her ears straining to hear any sounds of a scuffle coming from Demetrius's room. Not that she could have heard anything through the thick walls and solid oaken doors of Thorverton Hall.

Lying there wondering how long she would need to wait before she could reasonably ring for Jane, Meribe heard a scratching at her door.

She hurriedly climbed out of bed, pulled on a robe, and opened the door a crack.

Lionell Rudd stood there, but it was a Lionell she had never seen before. His jacket looked as if he had slept in it, his cravat was askew, and most astonishing of all, he was wringing his hands and appeared to be crying.

Thrown into a panic, Meribe grabbed his arm and dragged him into her room, most improperly shutting the door behind them. "What has happened? Has Demetrius been hurt? Oh, tell me, for I cannot bear this suspense."

"No, no, he is all right," Lionell managed to gasp out. "But my poor Hester—how could she have done such a vile thing? I had no idea . . ."

Seizing him by the shoulders, Meribe shook the little man until he ceased his useless wailing. "Now, tell me what has happened," she said with a calmness she was far from feeling.

He hiccuped once, then blurted out, "She tried to enter Lord Thorverton's room—she had a dagger, and it was obvious what she intended to do. She was like a madwoman, but Hennessey and Swinton managed to subdue her, and they sent me . . ." He hiccuped again. "They sent me to fetch you. They are even now smuggling Hester out of the house, and we are to meet them just outside the gates."

Taking a deep breath, he continued, ''They told me to be sure none of the servants see us, else there will be a terrible scandal. Oh, dear, this is all so dreadful.''

''Yes, yes, I understand,'' Meribe said, opening the door and peering down the corridor. No one was in sight in either direction, so she pushed the dandy out of her room. Before she shut the door, she whispered, ''I shall meet you below in the library in ten minutes—no, in five minutes.''

The driveway leading up to Thorverton Hall was long, and Meribe was frequently forced to pause so that Lionell could catch up with her. Then, spotting a closed carriage ahead, she abandoned the dandy, held up her skirts, and ran toward the vehicle, her feet fairly flying across the gravel.

''Demetrius, are you all right?'' she cried, flinging open the door and peering into the shadowy interior.

The coach was empty—no Hester, no Demetrius, no one. Turning, she saw Lionell surprisingly near her, and the expression on his face made it immediately obvious that he had tricked her.

Instinctively she backed away from him, and to her dismay, she bumped into another person, who was so solidly built he did not even stagger. She gasped, but before she could cry for help, a large meaty hand covered her mouth and a harsh voice rasped in her ear.

''There's no cause to struggle, missy. It'll do you no good, and if'n you're not careful, you'll hurt yourself.''

She did struggle, but the man was right: her efforts were pointless.

A second ruffian joined the first, and as they were both armed with wicked-looking horse pistols, Meribe was soon seated in the coach beside Lionell, who was smiling in the most odious manner. On the opposite seat, the larger of the two ruffians was likewise grinning at her—and even worse, his gun was pointed directly at her chest.

15

Demetrius was bound to come after her, Meribe realized, and when he did, he would be facing three armed and dangerous men. If only there was something she could do to lessen the odds against him. But the man seated opposite her was no weakling like Lionell. A heavyset man, he was wearing a shabby gray-brown overcoat, and so fierce did he look, she could well believe he was in the habit of shooting one or two people before breakfast every day.

Despite her efforts to be optimistic, an image filled her mind—an image of Demetrius riding to her rescue . . . followed by a second image of him lying on the ground, a bullet hole through his chest. She should never have—

But such thoughts were useless now—worse than useless, in fact. She had no time to waste wallowing in self-recriminations. What she needed to do was devote all her energies to discovering a way to escape from Lionell's trap.

Knowledge was power, her governess had always told her, so perhaps if she learned more about what this madman had done, she might be able to figure out a way to outwit him. There was only the slightest chance of success, but she had to make every effort. Trying to keep her voice from trembling, she asked, "Do you mind explaining to me where we are going and why?"

Lionell smiled—no, she realized, it was actually more of a leer. "I found, my beloved, that when it came down to it, I could not allow you to marry another. I could not even bear the thought of another man holding your hand, much less—"

"What rubbish!" Meribe exclaimed. "If you expect

me to believe that you care one whit about me, then you are deluding yourself, for it is quite obvious you love only yourself—and perhaps your tailor.''

His laughter grated on her nerves, and she clenched her fists to keep from slapping him. ''I see we shall deal famously, my sweet. I also prefer dealing frankly, and indeed, you are quite correct—it is only your father's money I love, not your person, and that is why I have done my poor best to see that you did not squander his fortune on another man. My friends here have therefore arranged for a yacht to be waiting for us in Exmouth, and once we are at sea, the captain has agreed—for a fee, of course—to marry us.''

In a pig's eye, Meribe wanted to say. She had never been so angry in her life, but with two pistols pointed at her, she had to maintain a calm facade even while she was seething inside. ''So you are the one who hired Black Jack Brannigan to kill poor Collingwood and Thurwell and Arleton and Fellerman?'' So little emotion was in her voice, she might have been asking about the weather.

''In truth, it was not necessary for me to kill Collingwood. But his accident was most fortuitous for me. When you were left at the altar, so to speak, I realized that all I needed to do was hire Black Jack to kill off all your suitors, one by one, and then after Hester inherited your father's fortune, I could marry her and be a rich man. But Black Jack failed to kill Thorverton, and then, like a fool, he came looking for me and wanted fifty guineas from me despite his lack of success. When I refused to give him a farthing—and indeed, why should I pay for a job not completed to my satisfaction?—the man threatened me, and I was forced to shoot him.

''Looking back on it, I can see I acted a bit rashly. I should have tricked him into giving me the name of another assassin before I killed him. Do you know, it is not as easy as one might think to find a professional killer for hire. It took me far too long to find my two new associates.''

Clenching her hands in her lap, Meribe asked, ''And was it you yourself, then, who poisoned Mr. Wimbwell?''

Lionell smirked. "I did that very cleverly, you must admit. I acquired the poison several years ago, thinking it might come in handy, and so it did. He was such a stupid old man, coming to Hester and telling her his suspicions. If he had gone to the authorities and laid information against us, all would have been lost."

Hester—dear lord, was it true, had she indeed condoned the murders? "And what about my sister? Is she meeting us later?"

Now there was more than anger to be seen in Lionell's face; now Meribe could see the madness that had been festering away all these years in his soul.

"The devil take that sharp-tongued harpy! After all I have done for her, she has had the gall to try to cheat me out of my due. Last night she claimed she had never made a bargain with me . . . insisted she had not even known I was arranging all those murders . . . pretended she had said nothing to lead me to think that she would marry me if I helped her inherit a fortune."

"And did she ever say anything?" Meribe asked, praying that his answer would be what she wanted to hear. "Did she actually come right out and say, 'Yes, Lionell, I will marry you'? Did she ever ask you directly to kill anyone?"

He now looked as sulky as a spoiled child who has been crossed for the first time. "I don't remember if she ever used the word 'murder,' but what difference does it make? She kept whining to me about how you would inherit everything, and she told me repeatedly that she wished you were not going to marry and thereby gain possession of the fortune that should have gone to her as the elder child. To my way of thinking, that is the same thing as asking for me to arrange things so that they would fall out to her benefit."

To Meribe's way of thinking, it was nothing of the sort, and despite the dreadful situation she found herself in, she felt a vast relief that Hester had not been involved in the murders.

"But I have taken care of your sister. Last night she made the mistake of trying to escape me. She was even going to warn Thorverton of my intentions. But I am nothing if not well-prepared, and I simply held my pistol to her head and forced her to drink all the wine in my flask.'' He smiled to himself, and began to stroke the barrel of his gun.

Meribe had an ominous feeling that the wine might likewise have been poisoned. "Did you . . . did you put something in the wine?" she asked, trying to inject a note of admiration into her voice.

Turning to her, Lionell preened as if she had complimented him on a new waistcoat. "Just some laudanum so she will sleep."

Some of Meribe's relief must have shown on her face, because his smile became malicious and he added, "On the other hand, I *may* have put in too much of the powder that brings us dreams, who is to say? Perhaps she will sleep the sleep from which no one awakens. That would make six sent to their cold, dark graves—the first three I had my hireling kill, and the last three I have murdered myself. There is a certain symmetry in that, which I find most pleasing.''

By the time Demetrius woke up, the sun had already burned the mist off the moor, and the day promised to be fair. Standing at the window, it occurred to him that this was the last morning he would wake up alone in his bed. Excitement began to curl its tendrils through every muscle and sinew of his body, and he stretched his limbs until every joint popped. Much to his surprise, he had slept deeply, and he now felt well-rested and clear-headed.

The same could not be said for his two companions, Thomas Hennessey and Uncle Humphrey, who emerged from behind their curtains bleary-eyed with fatigue.

"The next time we do this," Hennessey said, coming up beside him, "I volunteer to be the one sleeping in the bed, and you can hide behind the curtains." Then, moving as stiffly and slowly as a very old man, he walked over to the bed and collapsed facedown upon it.

Demetrius turned away from the window and began to dress himself, his mind preoccupied with visions of undressing his own fair lady. Only a few more hours, and he would be leading her back into this room.

"If there is a next time," Humphrey said with a gigantic yawn, "I shall . . . I shall . . ." He yawned again. "I shall bring a deck of marked cards and then at least in the morning I shall have something to show for my efforts. Dash my wig, but I could almost think that wretched woman's niece has deliberately stayed in her own room just so we would have to suffer the whole night through."

There was a moment's silence, while Demetrius—and apparently the other two men as well—thought about the possible significance of the night's want of excitement. There must be some reason for the lack of action, some nefarious purpose, that they had not yet discovered.

"When is the parson coming?" Hennessey asked.

"Eleven," Demetrius replied, pulling on his boots.

Hennessey looked at the clock on the mantel. "That means she has only three hours in which to make her move. Frankly, I did not anticipate that she would wait until the last minute. Now that it is broad daylight, it will be that much more difficult for her to escape detection, since the servants will be up and about."

"You don't suppose she means to waylay the vicar, do you?" Uncle Humphrey asked. "Prevent him from performing the ceremony?"

"That would be pointless," Hennessey replied. "She'd have to keep him prisoner for days, and besides, what's to stop us from finding another parson able to perform the ceremony?"

Demetrius felt a chill envelop his body. There were only two people who were crucial to a wedding—the bridegroom *and the bride*. With an oath, he ran from the room, hurrying down the corridor to Meribe's room and throwing open her door without pausing to knock.

The room was empty, and her nightgown lay in a heap on the floor. There was nothing to be seen that was the least bit sinister, and yet he knew at once that he had made the most appalling miscalculation.

Coming up behind him, Hennessey glanced around, then said, "She might be having breakfast in the morning room. We do not yet know whether . . ." He did not end the sentence. He did not need to. They both knew that disaster had struck from an unexpected direction.

Uncle Humphrey came puffing up to join them. "Not a good idea to burst into a lady's room unannounced, don't you know. Might find yourself in a compromising position. Though I don't suppose it matters, since you are marrying the young lady today anyway." Gazing around the empty room, he also grew silent.

"Which room is her sister staying in?" Hennessey asked, but Demetrius was already striding down the corridor.

This time he knocked on the door, but there was no answer. When he tried to open it, he found it locked. He yelled Hester's name and pounded loudly enough to wake the dead, and several shocked servants began to collect a safe distance away. Turning to them, Demetrius bellowed, "Fetch Mrs. Berriball, and tell her to bring her set of keys."

One of the footmen scurried to do his bidding, and behind him another voice added to the general confusion. "Just what do you think you are doing pounding on my niece's door at this hour? And in your shirtsleeves to boot. Have you no decency at all? No sense of shame that you are roaming the halls half-dressed?"

"Get rid of that woman," Demetrius muttered under his breath.

With a wicked smile that was almost a leer, his uncle began walking purposefully toward Miss Phillipa Prestwich, who with a squeal of alarm backed up into her room, slammed the door in his face, and then turned the key in the lock.

Obviously pleased with his prowess at terrifying spinster ladies, Humphrey returned to where Demetrius was standing frustrated by the door to Miss Hester's room. "Why do you think she locked herself in?"

"I don't think she has," Demetrius replied. "I think . . ." He did not want to say the words, but he finally managed to force them out. "I think she has changed her tactics. Instead of preventing the wedding by killing the prospective groom, I believe she has . . ."

His mind tried not to accept the horrible visions his imagination insisted upon showing him. "I very much fear she has done something wicked to Meribe. I think we will find the room empty."

He was wrong. When Mrs. Berriball, the housekeeper, appeared with her keys and opened the door, they found Hester lying unconscious on the floor. Jane ran forward and knelt beside her mistress. "Oh, she is so cold! I fear she is dead!"

Joining her at Hester's side, Demetrius ascertained that the unconscious woman was still breathing, and her pulse was weak but regular. But she was indeed quite cold, and his attempts to wake her failed. "I suspect she has been drugged," he said, "and she is definitely suffering from exposure."

He picked her up and carried her to the bed and tucked her in under the covers. Behind him, Jane began ordering the servants around as if she were the mistress at Thorverton Hall and not merely a visiting abigail. "You, there," Jane commanded, "build up the fire, and be quick about it. And someone fetch some hot bricks. We need to warm up Miss Hester before she succumbs to the effects of the cold. And tell the cook we shall need a pot of hot tea with plenty of sugar in it for when Miss Hester wakes up."

But Demetrius was not about to reprove her for stepping out of line. He was more than willing to turn the task of taking care of Meribe's sister over to whoever was competent to handle it, so that he could organize a search for Meribe herself.

His mind already turning to other, more desperate matters, Demetrius went back out into the corridor, followed by his uncle, who was plaintively asking him to explain what was going on.

Before Demetrius could begin to organize his thoughts, Hennessey emerged from a room close by. "Rudd has flown the coop," he said. "It would appear that we have been thoroughly hoodwinked."

"Impossible," Humphrey said with a snort. "That little dandy is not strong enough to force Miss Meribe to go with him. If ever I met a puny weakling, he is one."

"He does not need muscles," Demetrius replied. "All he needs is the other silver-chased dueling pistol."

Hennessey and Humphrey were silent, and Demetrius knew their thoughts were going along the same path his were, especially when Hennessey said, "Well, at least we can be assured that he won't kill her. The only way he can successfully get his hands on Sir John's fortune is to marry Miss Meribe."

"And he cannot force her at gunpoint to marry him," Uncle Humphrey pointed out.

"Can he not?" Demetrius asked, unable to keep the anger out of his voice. "Perhaps not in this country, but I am sure in Scotland or on the Continent he can find someone to marry them who will look the other way and pretend not to notice that the bride is unwilling. And we are so close to the sea, he can have her on board a ship within two hours after leaving here. To make matters worse, we have no idea when he kidnapped her. They may have already sailed with the tide."

His friends could think of nothing to say in the way of encouragement, so without further delay Demetrius went to the stables and began to organize a search, praying the whole time that it was not already too late. With all his heart and soul, he wanted Meribe there safe beside him, but he had an ominous feeling that it would take more than wishing to get her back.

And suppose he did not succeed? Suppose she was lost to him forever?

Already he felt such loneliness as he had never before experienced—as if a part of himself had been cruelly ripped away—and the pain was more than he could deal with. Only by ruthlessly pushing all thoughts and memories of her into the darkest corner of his mind was he even able to saddle his horse and lead it out into the courtyard, where he was astonished to see a dusty black coach pull up and stop.

"What is this? Why are we stopping?" Lionell looked out the window, and quicker than Meribe would have expected such a large man to move, the stranger seated opposite them reached over and plucked the dueling pistol from Lionell's hand.

"What? Here, now, you can't have my gun. Give it back!" Lionell blustered, but to no avail.

Tucking the fancy pistol into his side pocket, the ruffian now pointed his much larger gun at the little dandy. "Lionell Rudd, I arrest you in the name of the crown."

Just then the door was flung open, and the driver of the coach reached in and grabbed Lionell by his lapels and dragged him bodily out of the coach. Astonished at this turn of events, Meribe scrambled out after them, and tumbled right into Demetrius's arms.

Ignoring the people around them, he kissed her quite thoroughly. Like a totally shameless hussy, she kissed him right back.

"I do not understand," she said when he finally allowed her to speak.

"Nor do I," he replied. Keeping his arms firmly around her—not that she wanted to be anywhere else but right there hugging him—he turned to the men who had assisted Lionell in abducting her. "You look familiar," he said to the larger one. "Are you not the Bow Street runner I hired to fetch back my brother?"

"Indeed I am, m'lord. Josiah Stevens, at your service." The man was grinning from ear to ear.

"Then . . ." Demetrius turned to the other, more lanky ruffian, who straightened his back, stripped a fake mustache off his face, pulled off his dirty cap, and stood revealed as . . .

"Collier! What the deuce?" Demetrius began to laugh.

His brother merely smiled. "You must accept some of the responsibility here, Demetrius. After all, if you had not sent Mr. Stevens after me, *as if I were a recalcitrant child to be dragged back home,* then he and I would not have had all the long ride from Reading to London in which to plot this course of action."

"And thanks to this young lady's persistent questioning," Stevens added, "we have all the evidence we need to convict this villain. In my presence Rudd freely and without coercion confessed to murdering two men and to arranging for the deaths of three others. There is no way he can escape the gallows.''

Remembering her sister, Meribe felt a sudden panic. "Hester—he told us he drugged her, perhaps even killed her. Is she all right?''

"It appears Rudd gave her only enough laudanum to ensure that she did not interfere with his plans," Demetrius reassured her. "And I have left Jane in charge of her.''

But Meribe could not rest easy until she saw with her own eyes that her sister was all right. Accompanied by Demetrius, she hurried into the house and up the stairs to Hester's room, where she found not only Jane but also Aunt Phillipa and Lady Delilah in attendance.

Hester was awake, but she still looked quite pale and wan. "You were right, Lord Thorverton," she said. "You told me that someday I would regret every mean-spirited comment I ever made. And I do—I regret each and every one of the nasty things I said." Her voice broke, and tears ran down her cheeks.

Meribe hurried over to embrace her.

"I am so ashamed of myself," Hester sobbed out. "I had no idea Lionell was . . . was . . .''

"Shhh, do not fret yourself," Meribe said. "Lionell has freely confessed everything before witnesses, and you have been completely exonerated.''

"Never completely," Hester insisted, "for it was my complaining about the terms of Father's will that gave him the idea in the first place.''

"Rudd was clever enough to fool each and every one of us," Demetrius said firmly, "so there is no reason to expect you to have seen through his act. In addition, no one can possibly hold you responsible for his madness, so let us hear no more of these self-recriminations.''

"But I should not have told him of my dissatisfaction," Hester said weakly.

"Well, as to that," Meribe said with a smile, "I defy you to find anyone in all of England who has not complained to someone about something.''

Before she could utter any more words of reassurance,

Thomas Hennessey entered the room to report that the vicar had arrived.

"Tell him the wedding has been postponed until the day after Meribe's birthday." Demetrius said, and Meribe could almost hear all the jaws dropping around the room.

"After her birthday? But that means—" Hennessey started to protest, but Demetrius cut him off.

"I am quite aware of the significance of a week's postponement, but I still wish the wedding to take place after Meribe's birthday." He looked so fierce when he said it that no one dared to raise an objection.

Meribe remembered his saying that he had enough money of his own that he did not need her father's, and she was grateful that he was willing to relinquish what could have been her inheritance. Legally, the money could easily be his; morally, however, she also felt that her sister had a greater claim to it, and she felt nothing but respect for Demetrius that he was willing to do what so few men would have done.

Which left Meribe with only one more task, and she dreaded it most of all. Now that the murderer was caught, she knew she was likewise honor-bound to release Demetrius from any obligation to marry her. And despite Lady Anne's assurances that he truly did want her to be his wife, Meribe thought it more likely that he would not hesitate to accept his freedom when it was offered him.

Meribe looked up at him with eyes that were so troubled, so sad, that Demetrius knew before she even spoke what she was going to tell him.

"I think we should discuss our plans in private," she said softly.

Discuss. A polite way of putting it. She obviously meant to cancel the wedding rather than merely postpone it. Offering her his arm, he said, "Shall we take a turn around the garden, then?"

Almost shyly she laid her hand on his arm and allowed him to lead her away from the other three women, who were staring at him with such morbid curiosity, he was tempted to pick Meribe up in his arms and carry her off to his own room for their little *discussion*.

But he was a gentleman, and she was a lady, and he was bound by the strictures of social custom, which insisted it was not proper for a gentleman to be alone in his bedroom with a young lady, even if she was betrothed to him.

Betrothed, yes, but for how long? Until she could jilt him in private?

Propriety be damned, he decided. His entire life was at stake here. Scooping Meribe up in his arms, he strode down the corridor toward his room, ignoring the gasps of dismay that followed him.

Meribe did not shriek, nor did she offer any protests. What she did do was wrap her arms around him and press her face most satisfactorily against his neck. She also trembled in the most delightful way, and looking down at her, he could see that the pulse in her neck was beating at an even faster rate than his own.

Entering his bedroom, he pushed the door shut behind them with his foot. Without putting down his sweet burden, he said, "Now, then, what was it you wished to discuss with me?"

She continued to hide her face in his neck. "I think . . . I think it would be easier to talk with you if you would set me down." Her breath warmed him and sent shivers down his back, all at the same time.

He laughed and hugged her tighter. "Do you know, I am not at all interested in making it easier for you to tell me you are not going to marry me."

"I gave you my word of honor that I would release you from any obligation to marry me," she protested softly.

He would have been more worried if he had heard any resolution in her voice, but all he could hear was reluctance to say what she felt obliged to say. It was not going to be at all difficult, he realized, to persuade her that she was being singularly foolish.

Resolutely ignoring the temptation offered by the bed, he crossed to the window and sat down in a comfortable chair, still holding his love on his lap. She made no effort to escape from his arms, which only confirmed his suspicions that she was merely attempting to be noble.

"If you will remember, you made that offer after my

brother put the phony announcement of our betrothal in the *Morning Post*. When my mother canceled *that* betrothal, she in effect also canceled your promise to release me from any obligation to marry you. But since that time, I have made you an offer in form, and you have promised of your own free will to marry me. Therefore I have no obligation to release you from your commitment to marry me."

She tilted her head back far enough that she could look into his eyes, and in her eyes he could see such anguish, such pain, that he began to doubt that he knew anything at all. Could he actually compel her to marry him if she truly did not wish to? Was he such a brute that he could force a woman into a distasteful marriage?

"Do you truly wish to marry me?" she asked, and he mentally cursed himself for having made such a botch of things that she did not even know how deeply he loved her.

"I cannot ride, and I know nothing about horses," she continued, "and my needlework is only adequate for hemming sheets, and I do not sing or play the pianoforte, and . . . and all I am really good at is growing plants—"

He stopped her with a kiss—a very long and deeply satisfying kiss. "I have been such a fool," he said. "Please forgive me. I should have told you long ago that I love you, but I was too witless to recognize what I was feeling. It was only when I thought you might be gone forever that I realized how deeply I love you."

She was beginning to look a bit more cheerful, but there was still anxiety to be seen in her eyes. Wanting more than anything in the world to reassure her of his eternal devotion, he said recklessly, "If I had to choose between you and my horses, I would give them all away without a moment's hesitation."

"Oh, I would *never* ask you to do a thing like that! You must not even think for a moment that I would entertain such a notion!"

Which was one only of the many reasons he loved her so much, and he was about to tell her that when there was a knocking at the door and Collier stuck his head into the room.

"I hate to interrupt," he said with a smile that revealed not the slightest trace of reluctance, "but I have been nominated to be the one to inform you that betrothed though you may be, still the proprieties must be observed. In short, you must leave off your cuddling for another week. The cook has laid out a splendid repast in the morning room, and the rest of our guests are already assembled there. But if you can postpone breaking your fast for a few more minutes, Demetrius, there are one or two things I wish to discuss with you."

After one last quick kiss, Meribe obediently went to join the others, and as soon as she was gone, Collier began to present his case.

"I know you have made it clear that you disapprove of my spending money I do not have, but I fear I must again ask you to advance some of my next quarter's allowance. Stevens and I did our best to persuade him, but Rudd adamantly refused to pay us a penny in advance. As things now stand, I am afraid he is not likely to reimburse us for the rent of the coach, nor does he show any sign of wishing to fork over the usual fee that Stevens charges per day."

Demetrius clapped his brother on the shoulder. "You know very well, nodcock, that I shall pay all the charges and count myself lucky that you showed such clever initiative."

Collier grinned. "Actually, I was counting on you to offer to do so. And now we come to my second proposition, which unfortunately I am not as sure you will approve of."

He paused, but Demetrius merely waited without saying anything, even though he was ninety-nine percent sure he knew exactly what his little brother was going to ask for.

"I still wish to be a soldier," Collier said bluntly. "I shall not make any idle threats about taking the king's shilling, but I do want you to know that if you still refuse to buy me my colors, I shall live here at Thorverton Hall like a monk and save every farthing of my allowance until I have the required sum.''

"That will not be necessary," Demetrius said. "On your birthday I shall purchase your commission for you. But,'' he added as his brother began to grin, ''I shall not intercede with our mother.''

"Are you saying that I must gain her permission before you give me the money?'' Collier asked dubiously.

"Not at all,'' Demetrius said, and this time he was the one grinning broadly. "All I am saying is that you must be the one to tell her what your intentions are.''

"Well, at least if—that is to say, *after*—I manage to face her tears and reproaches and recriminations, not even Napoleon himself will be able to frighten me.''

"I now pronounce you man and wife,'' the Reverend Mr. Goodman Thirsk intoned, and immediately such a vast sigh of relief went up from the crowd of friends and servants assembled in the chapel that Demetrius realized they had all, each and every one of them, been secretly afraid that a fatal curse might still strike him down at the last minute.

As he had always insisted, he himself was not a superstitious man, but looking down at the radiant face of his bride, he had to admit that he had done nothing to deserve such a marvelous wife, such a delightful companion, such a joy and treasure.

It was sheer good fortune that had brought them together, and he acknowledged himself to be the luckiest of men.

Epilogue

About to leave his room, Thomas Hennessey paused in the doorway and watched with lifted eyebrow as Humphrey Swinton tapped gently on the door of Miss Phillipa Prestwich's room.

It was none of his business what the older couple was up to, and he shouldn't—he really should *not*—meddle. But he knew he was going to. Closing the door until it was open only the merest crack, he deliberately minimized his chances of being seen.

Now that the murderer had been taken back to London to stand trial, Devon had become a rather boring place to be, and Thomas was resolved to take his amusement wherever he could find it.

"You!" Miss Phillipa barked out with loathing upon opening her door. "How dare you even approach me!"

"I want to talk with you privately," Swinton said with more resolution than Thomas had given him credit for having. "Now that your niece has married my nephew, it is time for us to bury the hatchet—or at least, if you are not willing to forgive and forget, which *I* am fully prepared to do for their sake, then we should be able to pretend that we have reached some measure of tolerance for each other."

"You are asking me to pretend to like you? You, the person I most loathe in all the world?"

"All I am asking is that you be a little more civil when we are in public," Swinton replied firmly. Then, much to Thomas's delight, voices were heard approaching along the corridor, and with a look of dismay, the older man pushed his way into Miss Phillipa Prestwich's bedroom, closing the door behind him.

The possibilities inherent in this situation were so delightful, Thomas waited only until the two chattering maids had gone by before he slipped along the corridor and pressed his ear against the panel of the door. Whatever Swinton and Miss Prestwich were saying, they were speaking too low for him to hear, but it mattered not. They were about to be "discovered in a compromising situation," and the ensuing scene was bound to be amusing, if not enlightening.

Boldly opening the door, Thomas so startled the older couple that they did not even think to ask what business he had bursting into a lady's room unannounced.

"Ecod," he cried, feigning total astonishment, "Swinton, what the deuce are you doing . . . but I beg your pardon, madam, you and . . . that is to say, are you? . . . is he? . . . oh, my . . . oh, dear . . . oh, this is dreadful!"

Quickly putting distance between himself and Miss Prestwich, Swinton tugged at his waistcoat, looking as miserable as if he were facing a firing squad. "Now, see here, Hennessey, it is not what you think. My intentions are strictly honorable." Turning to his longtime nemesis, he gulped, then blurted out, "Miss Prestwich, willyoudomethehonorofmarryingme?"

She looked at him with undiluted loathing. "Almost, you had persuaded me you had reformed, but now you are at it once more. Your persistence in forcing your suit does you no credit, I'll have you know. Do not ever, *ever* speak to me again." With a last glare for Thomas, she stalked out of the room.

" 'Once more'? Have you perhaps offered for her before?" Thomas asked with unfeigned interest.

"Of course," Swinton replied with a scowl, "and that is why that wretched woman—that contemptible *spinster*—has hated me all these years. Thirty years ago I laid my heart at her feet, and she . . . she did not even do me the courtesy of refusing politely. No, not that despicable female. From the way she acted on that fateful day, you would have thought I was offering her a slip on the shoulder, and ever since then she has acted as if *I* was the one who did something wrong."

"She's obviously touched in the upper works," Thomas commented cheerfully. "Otherwise she would have jumped at the chance to nab a fine fellow like you. And then where would you be?"

Straightening up, Swinton began to grin himself. "Married is where I would be—and doubtless living under the cat's paw." He strolled over to the door, then turned to wait for Thomas to catch up. "Do you know, Hennessey, as much as that woman hates all men, it's me she hates most of all. Now, what does that tell you?"

For what was surely the first time in his life, Thomas could not think of a single clever reply.

"Why, it tells you that I am more manly than other men," Swinton explained proudly.

"Just so," Thomas agreed. "I could not have put it better myself."

DILEMMAS OF THE HEART

☐   **THE AIM OF A LADY by Laura Matthews.** "Diana Savile has an interesting way of attracting a husband—she shoots him. Don't miss this one, it's a classic!"—Catherine Coulter   (170814—$3.99)

☐   **HEARTS BETRAYED by Gayle Buck.** The exquisite Michelle du Bois, who had broken so many hearts, risks having her own broken by a lord who shows no pity.   (168763—$3.95)

☐   **THE DUKE'S DAUGHTER by Melinda McRae.** Elizabeth Granford firmly resisted the Earl of Wentworth, and rejected his proposal of marriage. For she was someone who wanted nothing to do with wedlock, and even less with love. . . .   (169743—$3.99)

☐   **A CHRISTMAS COURTSHIP by Sandra Heath.** Beautiful Blanche Amberley knew she loved Antony Mortimer. She also knew she thoroughly disliked Sir Edmund Brandon. She was quite immune to the good looks and gallantry that made this arrogant blueblood the most eligible lord in the realm. But then Christmas approached and Cupid gave Blanche a gift that came as a most shocking surprise. . . .   (167929—$3.95)

☐   **THE DUKE'S DESIGN by Margaret Westhaven.** Miss Matilda Graham made it clear what she thought of the Duke of Arden's proposition. Yet how could she refuse this lord whose looks, wealth and charm won him any woman he wanted?   (169182—$3.99)
